HEARTS IN THE LOOKING GLASS

THE CURIOUS TALE OF WENDY DARLING

M.A. KERSH

Dedicated to my darling Mother.

Thank you for always believing in me. It is because of your teachings

and unwavering support that my dreams became possible.

CHAPTER ONE

WE MUST

On a rather depressed street, behind the tall golden trimmed windows of one of the most prestige houses in all of London, was the Darling's home at the corner of Bloomsbury road. It was the hour of sleep for most, but within the hidden bedroom of Number 14's household, the air was filled with the shrill cries of Wendy Darling's nightmares.

George and Mary Darling rushed quickly into the room, illuminating the darkness with the light from the flickering lamp that was held within her father's hand. Wendy's mother was the first to reach her bed with a small cloth ready in her hand to wipe away the sweat of fright from upon her head, and a dainty cup of calming tea for Wendy to drink. It may have seemed strange to approach such a sudden frantic scene prepared, but in truth, this had all become a rather torturous routine within the household.

Nothing had ever been the same for Wendy Darling ever since *he* had come into her life... ever since *Neverland.* But it wasn't just the constant night terrors that plagued her mind. It was everything. For it wasn't just every waking hour that was conflicted with battling memories of past encounters, it was the unbearable fact that she seemed completely unable to calm or steady any of her thoughts at all.

The truth was that she had absolutely no memory of how she got home that last evening beyond the second star to the right. The last thing she remembered was Hook's sparkling, golden ship flying out into the dark sky, but the entire adventure before and after was both a dark and sinister tale.

True, there were two extremely different versions of what truly happened in her head, but both were a most frightful and murderous experience. But as awful as that would already be to endure or witness, the real problem was the cause. She couldn't remember who the true hero of the story was... and who was the villain.

She thought and almost believed that it *was* Pan who had saved she and her brothers from Neverland, but something about the trip from the Lost Island back into her world hadn't been an easy one. In fact, it had been disturbing in almost every way.

Flashes of such pain and blood spilled upon the Jolly Roger that night. Pan should have been thrilled after such a victory and in part he was, but he had lost something of great value too. He had lost his precious Neverland and was now on the run from the Elders. Though he was careful not to take any anger out upon the Darlings, the shrill pleasure he took of disembodying the Lost Boys aboard was enough to send one's mind into all manner of terror. She wasn't sure if it was Pan's doing or if the horrific vision was too much, but it wasn't long after the carnage upon the ship that all went black in her mind.

When she and her brothers woke the following morning lost and confused in their beds, it was as if home is where they had been all along... like it was just a vivid bad dream. When her parents came in to wake them that terrible morning, they told her that she and her brothers had not been gone at all. They said that they went to their dinner party and when they returned, everything was as it should be. They assured all three of them that what they were considering to be real was not only utterly impossible, but absolute nonsense. After all, if it *were* true, then they would have been gone from this world for days.

John and little Michael were soon uncertain of their otherworldly encounter, but Wendy was not convinced.

To Wendy, such a notion was absolutely impossible. Sure, she was a bit of a dreamer, but never before in her past had she been so sure of something. This was not a dream. Neverland was real... she was certain of it. But *what* had actually happened on the island was anything but certain. She fought her case time and time again, but with so much difficulty coursing through her troubled mind, even her brothers had given up believing; not only in Neverland, but in her.

After such extreme fits that were deemed unladylike and of unnerving proportions, the Darlings found that Wendy wasn't well enough to go to school any longer. The boys, however, were only too keen to abide by their parent's logic and will; that such ridiculous notions of fairies and Peter Pan were nothing more than a story they had all dreamt up.

Whether the Darlings were truly capable of believing that all their children had indeed merely shared the same dream on the same night was never questioned, since the only other explanation wasn't an explanation at all. Most adults found magic to be an absurd idea, or worse... that it was of a wicked nature. Either way, it was never good or looked at lightly. Nevertheless, Wendy never ceased her efforts to tell her parents of her magical encounter... That she *had* been to one of the other worlds... that she *had* seen a flying boy fight the notorious Captain Hook, and that she *had* seen mermaids, Indians, and of course the small murderous pixie called Tinker Bell.

The fact that she had seen all of these things never wavered in her mind, but how things happened on the island, well, that was far more difficult. For the fact was that she had no idea what really did or didn't happen inside her head. Some of the memories happened one way and other times they were completely different. Soon, the conflicting images within her mind began to change by the day.

It was so incredibly frightening for her to both love and fear Peter Pan. His eyes once so gentle and kind would often appear dark and wicked in her mind. Not dark in color, for they were rather a golden brown, but the darkness in the soul behind them seemed to paralyze her inside in the dream world. Everything was so unbearably confusing. But Wendy wasn't the only one who found her predicament intolerable.

The sad truth was that the Darlings were tired, exhausted from their daughter's constant nightmares and tales of foolish fantasy. Wendy's terrors and misery had disrupted the household and had reached beyond her parent's grasp of control.

George Darling had dismissed the housemaid for fear that word may get out concerning Wendy's condition and though the boys had been sworn to secrecy, the endless paranoia of such shame seemed to eat away at him.

Meanwhile, all duties of the house fell to Mary Darling: tending to Wendy, the boys, the cleanliness of the house, and George's frustration... but against all her efforts, the house had become dark and dreary in every way. The Darlings had a terrible decision to make, and it was on this very night that one such decision would finally come to pass.

"It is time, Mary. The carriage is here," George whispered.

"Oh, George dear, I cannot bear it. Please," Mary tearfully replied, caressing her daughter's cheek.

"The medicine we put in her tea is working. She will sleep through the night and wake up in a place properly able to care for her. Though I love her too, there is nothing more we can do for her here. You know that it is the right thing. We *must* be logical. This screaming that she does every night is starting to raise questions in the neighborhood. It's only a matter of time before people start to talk. I'm sorry, but I will not allow everything we are and have worked for to be destroyed by this... this nonsense."

"You are right. I know you are right. But I do not think I can handle this. The loss is too great. She is our daughter, George. Our only daughter. What is there to gain from protecting our family name if we have to lose what makes us a family to do it? I can't, George. If you do this, you are on your own."

Her words twisted his stomach, but nothing was going to change his mind. "I will do what I have to, Mary. It is my job to protect this family... at *any* cost," he said with a cracking voice.

"But... I shall miss her too much," Mary said, wiping her tears from her swollen eyes. Wendy couldn't hear her parents battle of sadness and reason; for as her father had said, the tea had already taken her mind far into the darkness.

The tea... how she hated it. There was a time when she would throw the most violent of fits to avoid drinking its contents. It wasn't just the unpleasant taste she detested, it was the way it made her feel and where it would ultimately send her.

After such suffering throughout the many hours of the day, falling asleep at night with a quiet mind would feel like a miracle to most, but inside a tormented mind like hers, such a visionary would be in all manner a most frightening nightmare.

"Please don't cry, Mary. We must be sensible. We must send her away. It's for the good of the family. We must..."

His words were cut short as his precious wife suddenly fell to the ground weeping. George had never seen her so dismayed; so out of control with grief and sorrow. He hated seeing her so heartbroken. Her sobs slicked him like a hot knife through the soul; the heat of its blade intensifying with every glistening tear that fell beneath her crystal blue eyes.

With a choking breath and a quivering lip, he wrapped his arms under their beloved daughter and carried her bundled up in her favorite quilt down to the carriage alone. He kissed her cold forehead softly and felt his heart cringe as he closed the door between them.

Finally, the tears he had tried so hard to keep suppressed, fell in long streams down his cheeks as he turned to see Mary through Wendy's bedroom window. With her dainty hand wearing the very wedding band that tied her to him on the window, she sobbed painfully as she watched the black carriage drive away with her one and only daughter.

"We must."

CHAPTER TWO

I PROMISE

When Wendy woke the following morning in her usual burst of absolute panic, she was shocked to find a doctor and two nurses rapidly approaching her instead of her parents.

"Do not worry, miss. You are safe," they said.

"Where am I? Where is my mother?" Wendy asked, frantically looking around at all the unfamiliar faces hovering above her.

"Your family is not here, child. They have put you in our care, but we assure you that all will be done for the best," the doctor said.

"Yes, dear. You are safe, I promise," one of the nurses said in a dreadfully dull tone; void of any real compassion.

'I promise.' Such strong words; possibly the strongest to a child. But in the case of Wendy, she didn't put much trust into such trifles anymore. She had enough trouble wondering what to believe within her own head, the mere promises of a stranger meant absolutely nothing to her now... let alone offer her any

sort of comfort. Tears began to fall from her troubled hazel eyes as she realized that she wasn't just in a strange place, but what being here meant. She knew now what her parents had done.

They had sent her away to a madhouse in the middle of the night to protect their precious name. No one; not her parents nor own her brothers who had once treasured her love, had even said goodbye. Her entire family had thrown her away, to save only themselves from the tarnish she would surely have brought to their respectable family name. In all honesty, she had felt separated from them for so long now that missing them or rather mourning what her family once was... had haunted her soul for quite some time. Still, she was not prepared for the harsh fate that had been wrought upon her.

"If only you would stop this. Just say it was a dream. Just say it was a story." Is what her brother John would say. *But how do you smile when you see things in the room with you? How do you lie and say you are fine when you wake up screaming in a panicked sweat every single night? How can you say it was all just a story when the story has two sides constantly flashing in your mind? Was Pan the hero, or was he an evil villain that could come back to my window at any time and take me away?* These are the kind of thoughts that made it hard to breathe, and the torturous pain that came with them was impossible to hide.

She wanted answers. She wanted help. *But who could help her now?* Surely, if her own family wouldn't believe her, then a staff of doctors and nurses would certainly judge her case harshly. Because of Neverland... because of Peter Pan, she had lost her home, her parents, her brothers, and possibly her very own sanity.

Wendy hadn't realized how large the hospital was until later when she was escorted to her new room. This building didn't look at all like the terrible tales she had heard of; the places for the mentally insane. She had heard many scattered whispers about *where* they should put her. Not to mention that the horrific scream her mother had made after the mere mention of Bedlam. It was a sound Wendy wouldn't likely forget.

The truth was that as she looked around at the beautiful new hospital, she could see her father's last gesture of gracious love he had to offer. How fitting that she be sent somewhere that her father would deem proper for a young lady of her standing.

Money. Money. Money. It was what makes her father's world go-round. For him, it meant prestige, honor, title, respect, and even love. Yes, for the Darling children, love from their father came in forms of gifts or luxury. Wendy knew that she no doubt had the best doctor in the hospital assigned to her. But in this place, far away from everyone she loved, such luxury didn't seem to help mend her shattered heart. She had been abandoned to face the world utterly alone. Magic had torn her whole life apart.

She laid her head upon the small pillow that lay on top of her bed. As the crashing facts of her reality hit her, she began to cry. Only now, she realized that she was to face the worst nightmare yet, and this time, her mother would not be there to dry her tears.

CHAPTER THREE

A KNOCK AT THE DOOR

It had been several weeks since Wendy had been sent away, but the dreary sadness seemed to linger on through the Darling household like a chilling ghost. The most haunting room of all was the nursery. The sound of Wendy's screaming still woke Mary Darling every night, but what was genuinely heartbreaking was how much she truly hoped to find Wendy on the bed each time she entered the room.

George, on the other hand, managed to bury his grief by putting all his efforts into putting his family back in proper order. And on the surface, that's precisely what they were: *proper.*

The house was once again clean, and George no longer felt paranoid about the boys going to school or having a maid in the house for fear of word about Wendy's mental condition spreading. Yes, for George Darling, the damage his daughter and her troubles had caused him had all but vanished in his mind. He had successfully restored his household to absolute prestige.

On this night, after a long day's work; full of praise and respect, George eagerly sat upon his favorite chair by the fireplace. There was another chair across from his, Mary's chair. It was the chair she had done her knitting and reading in so often before. Oh, how he used to adore watching her read her books; her face beautifully glowing by the light of the fire. Both of the chairs had been made in France, upholstered in vibrant green cloth with gold trim, and covered in Victorian pattern design. The Darlings had always treasured them. But now, Mary's chair was empty, just as it had been since the night Wendy had been carried away in the dark carriage.

The real truth of the family lay hidden in the room where Mary sobbed; for behind closed doors, was the pain and suffering of a mother who had lost her child. The house was divided in feeling, but it was everyone in the house that felt the silence of the night broken by a sudden knock on the front door.

George was the first to walk towards the front door with the same hesitance one has when they aren't expecting company. Mary wiped her face and collected her breath before making her way down the spiraled staircase to stand behind him. Both John and Michael quietly cracked open their bedroom doors; each curious to see who it could be at such a late hour. But nobody was ready for what awaited them on the other side of that door. George pulled the knob and opened it hesitantly.

"Good evening, sir," said a deep, profound voice, hidden in a dark shadow beyond the entrance.

"Yes, good evening. Can I help you?"

"I hope so. Though it be strange, I am here to inquire about your children, Mr. Darling."

A pretentious scoff huffed through the doorway, "Pardon me, pirate! You..."

George's tempered scolding was cut short as Mary intercepted. "The children? Please tell me, sir: who are you?" She asked in a weak voice, raising a lantern with her hand. But as the man's face emerged from the darkness, it was John and Michael that gasped.

"Hook," John whispered. The sight of him sent chills up the young boy's spine. His very breath felt as if it had been ripped out through his stomach. Fear had struck little Michael frozen upon the steps below him. John quickly grabbed him by his tiny hand and ran, dragging him back to his room. As soon as he closed the door, his breath returned at a pace that seemed to race against his heart.

He closed his eyes, trying to collect himself, but no matter how he controlled the breathing of his body, he couldn't deny the guilt and fear that suffused his every being. He waited with burning impatience, unknowing of what might happen next. It was then that the frightening sound of their father's booming voice called out their names. With all the bravery he could muster, John stood up straight and opened the door.

Michael crouched fearfully behind him as they walked down the large staircase towards the doorway. He gazed through his round glasses at the tall pirate standing before him as if he were looking into the eyes of a ghost. *How was he alive? How could this be happening?* His thoughts stirred wildly in his head with each step he forced forward. Pressure built up in his chest as he reached his eager parents.

"John, Michael, do you know this man?" Their father asked in a most angry tone.

Michael buried his face into John's formal nightshirt, trembling. It was up to John to answer, yet, he could not say a word.

His eyes fell to the floor as his father asked again, "John! Do you know this man?"

John looked down at Michael, whose eyes seemed to mirror Wendy's so precisely that it pained him. He shook his head ever so slowly that one might have missed it had they not been looking at him directly. John wanted to say yes, but if he did, what would happen. He didn't know what Hook was doing here or if it was truly him at all.

John didn't remember exactly what happened on the island either, but he did know what happened to his sister afterward. It made things so much easier to just deny it all, but now the story he had deemed to be just a dream was now standing in his doorway; the truth staring him in the face. He had just wanted everything to be normal; not to mixed up in such things as magic and other worlds. *Didn't he?* "No, sir. I do not know him."

His father inhaled a deep breath of relief and turned his harsh gaze back upon the man before him. "Well, there you have it. My children do not know you, nor will they ever. Do not come knocking at my door again, pirate... or I will have to alert the proper authorities. I bid you a farewell and goodnight," he said, feeling mildly fearful of the tall figure that stood hovering his doorway. Nevertheless, George was in front of his wife and children. So, unwise as it was to spout off to a man that could clearly harm him brutally with great ease, he wasn't going to permit any further shame upon his person, especially the kind that came from a coward. He had fought too hard to protect his honorable name to let a pirate take it from him now.

Hook looked down at John with understanding. He had known that Peter had changed their perception of what truly happened on the Lost Island. Still, the truth was clear... the boy *did* know who he was. But it was no matter, for Hook merely wanted to be sure of their safe return home, which brought to light a much darker realization. *Where was Wendy?* Their father had not called her name as he had for theirs.

Nevertheless, Hook nodded politely in return to their father's farewell. At that, George Darling closed the door.

Tears welled up in John's eyes as his mother took both he and Michael back up the stairs to their rooms. She picked up little Michael and laid him down in his bed as John made his way back into his dark bedroom and closed the door. The moonlight shined a silver glow through the window that seemed to call him forward. With a deep gulp of his throat, he walked towards its view. Upon the stone street of Bloomsbury below, he saw Captain Hook starting to walk away.

John's tears fell down his cheeks as a sudden guilt of obligation overwhelmed him. Only one word could escape his lips at that moment, "Wendy." Without another thought, he rapidly opened the window. It was something none of the Darling children had been able to do since that night, but now, in this instant, something much stronger willed him to do so. "Captain!" He screamed. Luckily, though Hook was already farther down the street, his ability to hear a raindrop as clear as a bell had not changed.

He turned and looked towards him. John urgently waved him over. Hook walked back towards the house and stood just below the window.

John's voice cracked as Hook waited for him to speak. "I am so sorry that I lied. I... I am afraid."

"Afraid of what, lad? Where is Wendy?"

"Well, see... that's why I am afraid. Wendy-she... was sent away."

"Away? Why?"

"She wouldn't stop," he cried. "She wouldn't stop telling our parents what happened. They did everything they could to handle her, but she just wasn't getting any better. Our parents thought her mad."

"Mad? You mean to say that she was sent to a madhouse?"

John nodded, sobbing harder than before. "We... She wanted us to... but we couldn't- We just left her all alone. My poor sister, I'm so sorry," John said sadly.

Hook exhaled in understanding. "I know. It is not your fault, lad. The fault lies with me. I promised I would return you to your home safely. Had I not failed, then Pan would not have had the chance to toy with her fragile mind."

John gasped with every crying breath, "I abandoned her. She was trying to tell everyone the truth, and no one believed. Even I convinced myself it was just a dream. But she was right all along. She fought so hard, and I just left her to deal with her demons alone. I abandoned her. I abandoned my sister."

"No. You did what was needed for yourself and Michael too. I fear the memories of the otherworlds burden your sister far more than you and your brother. Peter twisted her mind in a most torturous way, and after surviving such suffering, she is sent away to an asylum by her own family. I cannot imagine something more terrible; that poor child."

"But you can help her, right?" John asked with utmost desperation in his plea.

"On my very soul, I shall try." Hook assured him.

John finally took a deep breath as a weak smile appeared on his face.

Hook smiled in return, seeing the hope he had restored in the frightened boy. But there was still one very important question left to ask: "Where is she... Where- is Wendy?"

CHAPTER FOUR

IN MY WORLD

Though Wendy had spent many weeks speaking with a large staff of the best nurses and doctors that money could buy, she had found no one who could truly help her. Though it was not without their many extreme efforts. She had been given a large assortment of medication, yet all they did was make her feel the way she had when she had been given the old tea she loathed. But as terrible as the medicine was, nothing was as horrible as the '*treatments*' they did on her.

She had fought such experiments at first; for they were painful and uncomfortable to endure, let alone feeling like some part of you had been stripped away afterwards. But after so many mental and physical defeats, she had lost her power of will. After relentless pleading, she had still not found anyone to believe her story. The odd thing, however, was that just like her brothers, the doctors and nurses may not have believed what she had to say, but everyone loved listening to her tell a story. There was just something special about how she could make a story come to life. So as bad as it was that no one around could see or hear her as anything but crazy, they did at least ask to hear her 'version' of what happened over and over. The problem with that though was that her story continued change; a fact that didn't help her cause at all. But it was still true. And though she knew her words should have been just a simple answer; the truth was that every answer she had to offer sounded like complete nonsense. The memories were all so diffcrent, and the more she said things like mermaids, fairies, pixie dust, Captain Hook, magic smoke, and a flying pirate ship that saved her, the more she started to doubt herself. *Maybe they were right. Maybe she was going mad.*

So much of her had given up. The days and long hours had drifted together into an amorphous cloud of confusion and fear. Food and sleep had so often gone forgotten as if everything- maybe even life itself no longer mattered at all. A childhood turned into a mere dotage. Lost and beaten, she had given way for them to use her as they pleased in every possible way but one. Despite her many lengthy conversations she had had with all of those around her, it was as if no one remembered knew who truly she was.

The staff never addressed her by name, but instead merely called her '*Patient 1217.*' Her nurse said it was more for the sake of not shaming her family. *But what did they mean? Was she not a Darling anymore?* Wendy wondered as she gazed at the label upon her door. Patient 1217 is what it said... plain and simple. That is who she was now. *So, what happened to*

Wendy? Was the silly adventurous girl she once was still inside of her somewhere?

If she was, then she must be lost in the darkness that was consuming her every being. She didn't feel like Wendy at all anymore. Her parents hadn't come to visit her once since she had arrived, though after so many written letters to her mother about her loneliness and grief, her mother had sent her but one conciliation for her sadness... a beautiful tabby kitten.

Though it did not absolve her unhappiness, the small creature had somehow become her one and only friend left in the world. She had large jade eyes, two white paws, and had a beautiful pink gift ribbon that was tied around her neck.

"What an adorable little cat," said a passing nurse.

"Thank you," Wendy replied, petting her purring friend that was laying upon her lap.

"Is the kitten going to stay here with you then?" The nurse asked.

"Well, of course she is," Wendy said in a definite tone.

"I must say, I am not too sure about such matters, but I do not think the doctor will permit a patient to have an animal within the hospital."

Animal! I might be labeled as just a patient, but how dare they do this to my kitten! "She has a name!" Wendy shouted feeling provoked.

"Oh, and just what *name* have you given your little creature?"

Wendy thought for a second, but as she gazed into her friend's large eyes of jade, it came to her as if the kitten herself had told her. It wasn't the first time she had believed that such a thing could happen. After all, it was she who had named the family dog Nana, but she wasn't wrong. A Nana was exactly what she was. The big dog took care of the Darling children each and every day. She was precisely the gentle soul care giver that the family needed, living up to her given name in every way. This was however something that Wendy dared not say to the nurse. For even she could see how crazy it may seem to believe that animals were talking to them. So instead, she answered carefully: "Dinah. Her name is Dinah, and I am keeping her." When the nurse gave her a disapproving gaze, she pressed the matter in the only way she knew how. "I should hate to write to my father with such a trifling matter. Such news could cause quite a nasty stir," she said in a bratty tone. Wendy may have just been a patient to the hospital but bringing up her father and the possible discontinuation of coming money was not only her only card left to play... it was the right one.

"I see. Well, maybe we shouldn't make a fuss about it. Your cat... I mean- Dinah, seems to be a quiet little thing. I suppose if she remains well behaved then she may stay here with you. Just be sure to take good care of her, for it is up to you to do so... and you alone.

"Yes, ma'am," Wendy replied, needing no reminder of such a cruel fact.

"Good. Then let us make our way to the gardens for your reading lesson."

"May I take Dinah with me?"

The nurse smiled, "Yes, you may."

Going to the gardens was the only thing Wendy didn't hate about this wretched place. For it seemed the land of exquisite trees and such elaborate gardens were in a world of its own. For Wendy, it was the only time she felt as if she could leave her sad world behind. Once the doors had closed her, and she could walk towards the vast gardens of vibrant flowers with the sunshine on her face, she felt as if the light could pierce the darkness within her. And it was in that moment that she could almost feel like herself again.

There was only one part of the garden that was shaded at this time of day, and Wendy knew that was precisely where her nurse would be taking her. But instead of sitting on the ground as she was expected to, she climbed up to one of the high branches of a tree, sitting Dinah down beside her.

The nurse sat down on a bench that stood on the soft green grass below her. She looked rather annoyed by Wendy's adventurous behavior, but merely sighed with frustration before opening her book. She collected herself and began to read.

Wendy had always loved books: fantasy, love stories, mysteries, and of course fairy tales. But the book that the nurse was reading was none of those things. It was a book of etiquette and other such things that bored her.

"Ugh, I hate these books. They do nothing for the soul," Wendy whined.

The nurse scoffed just as she was nearly hit in the face by one of the girl's dangling feet. "These books are how things are done in the world, and a young lady like yourself should try to learn all that she could to be proper."

There was that word was again- *'Proper.'* It was the very mark her father had so desperately wanted her to achieve. Wendy rolled her eyes and with no hope of interest from the book being read to her, she simply settled for the joy that came with playing with Dinah.

Soon she was lost in her own little games, and before she knew it, she found herself talking to Dinah as if the kitten understood her every word. It was silly, but somehow to Wendy, it felt real. "The nurse speaks to me of the world, of proper etiquette and the poised manner of a lady, but I came from such a *world*, so I do not need anyone or any book to teach me of it. Worlds... how curious they are to me. I fear what I do not know, yet I fear more what I myself have come to discover. And it has all brought me here- with you... talking to a cat." Wendy chuckled softly to herself.

She expected a harsh scolding by the nurse for interrupting her again, but as Wendy looked down, she found that her stern nurse had fallen asleep.

"See, madam, I told you that story was a bore," Wendy said giggling to herself again. She jumped down off the tall branch and then reached up to help her tiny kitten get down to the ground. With a few tiptoes away, Wendy was able to venture farther into the gardens then she had ever been allowed to in the past.

Beyond the vast field of flowers was a gorgeous set of ancient trees. To see them was like gazing into a time before the destruction of man. All of the leaves were so full of vibrant life and colorful shades, and the bark below them appeared both aged and strong. Unknowing as to how far away from the hospital she was, Wendy suddenly came upon a small pond of beautiful fish. Each were different in both size and color, yet each was equally mesmerizing to watch.

Something about the tranquil way the fish and water moved made her suddenly feel hypnotized. As its overwhelming power slowly came over her, she started to hum a soft melody. Something inside her told her to turn around but as she did, she noticed something strange- the flowers- they looked as if they were dancing to her song. She giggled to herself, once more turning back to the pond. "Now that's silly. Flowers do not dance." But such a logical notion was rapidly diminished as a vision appeared in the water. Not a fish, but the astonishing reflection of a White Rabbit dressed in formal attire, running across the garden.

Wendy quickly looked up to find him. Overwhelmed with unbearable curiosity, she chased after him without a single thought of logic or reason to stop her. The White Rabbit sped into the wooded area beyond the gardens and far away from the hospital. Suddenly, a faint little meow from Dinah standing below the dashing Wendy was enough for her to stop for a moment. *This is nonsense.* Yes, that was all. Likely due to the medicine they had given her earlier.

Yes, that is... Suddenly, her thoughts were struck down as she heard a small urgent voice.

"I'm late. I'm late. For a very important date."

"Dinah, did you hear that? That was the rabbit. He spoke. How curious. And what could a rabbit possibly be late for?" Wendy asked feeling her excitement turning into anxiety. "Oh, Dinah, he is

28

getting away. I must know where he is going. I don't know why, but I must."

She ran as quickly as her legs could carry her as Dinah dashed behind her. Finally, to Wendy's instant relief, she spotted him just as he climbed in a rabbit hole at the bottom of what appeared to be the largest tree in the small forest. Wendy crouched down on her knees, inching forward to look inside, but she couldn't see a thing. It was just a black hole of nothing but darkness. Still, if she was going to find out where he was off to in such a dreadful hurry, then she was going to have to climb in.

"Don't worry, Dinah. After all, it is only a rabbit hole. What is the worse that could happen? Though maybe I shouldn't be doing this. After all, it is not as if I had been invited," she joked making herself laugh again. "And besides, curiosity always leads to trou-bl-e." Her voice trailed off as she suddenly fell, tumbling down the rabbit hole. The small kitten almost fell in after her, but like most cats, she was very quick with her footing. After seeing that her sweet companion had successfully caught herself, Wendy waved a farewell to her friend. "Goodbye, Dinah! Goodbye"

As she fell downward, she quickly realized that she had completely lost sight of the White Rabbit, but her eyes had plenty more strange things to see. The walls of the rabbit hole were covered in the most random colors and design. Furniture and other objects like lamps, portraits, and clocks were floating upon the air of upward gravity. Random things were going up and yet somehow, she was going down.

It was then, after what felt like several minutes, that she noticed the air had suddenly changed. She was no longer falling at a normal pace, but rather floating down slowly like the lightest of clouds. "Just a rabbit hole, indeed!" How am I to get out of here?"

Just as Wendy was growing fearful that she may never reach the bottom, she was elated to see a solid ground deep below her.

The hole grew bigger towards the bottom. Vibrant colors of books and other things surrounded her as she was suddenly turning upside down. A rising tall, crooked mirror appeared before her, but as she gazed upon her refection, she saw that it was not *her* reflection at all. Her curly auburn hair now appeared long, straight, and blonde! Her hospital gown had vanished and had been somehow replaced with an adorable blue dress. She looked down to also find that she was wearing white stockings and shiny black shoes around her feet.

But it wasn't just her clothing and hair that had changed, but her face as well. It seemed the only remaining feature left upon her that she recognized was her bright hazel eyes. "What is this nonsense?! I look nothing like myself!" As the mirror finally rose above her, she looked all around. Strangely, the portraits and objects around her were also upside down as if meant to be seen from that point of view. It was all so... *Boom!*

She had hit her head on a grand piano that was oddly attached to the floor, unlike everything else. As she bent down to put her feet on the ground, her eyes quickly caught the fleeting shadow of her unquenchable curiosity- the White Rabbit.

CHAPTER FIVE

THE DOORKNOB

To her utter amazement and awe, she was in what appeared to be a fancy little house. With each step, however, she noticed something tall and dark moving about the black-and-white checkered floor. A chill crawled up her spine as another shadowed figure moved out of the corner of her eye, but as she rapidly turned to face it, it stopped. A mere moment was all it took for her to doubt her eyes; to doubt herself. A nervous giggle echoed through the narrowing hallway as she took another step forward.

Suddenly, a loud thump came down right behind her! "Yelp!" She screamed, jumping around in absolute fright. When she opened her eyes, horror overtook her as a tall, black chess piece towered above her head. All of the sudden, a long line of pawns moved in and stood alongside it. Hot panic burned throughout her body as each piece scurried around her like predators eyeing their prey.

I am on a chess board! She tried to run, but with every step of her shiny black shoes, another towering piece blocked her path, entrapping her until there was but only one direction left to take. In a most deadly game of cat and mouse, she raced through every opening until she finally reached the end. Using every ounce of strength that she still possessed, she quickly jumped off the board.

Once her feet touched the ground, she turned around to find all of the pieces had already slipped back into the darkness from whence they came.

Such immense relief from her escape brought both a giggle to her breath and tears to her eyes. But before she could collect a single thought of rationality, she heard a familiar voice.

"I'm late! I'm late! For a very important date! No time to say Hello- Goodbye! I'm late! I'm late! I'm late!"

Excitement rapidly replaced her recent fear. "The White Rabbit!" She exclaimed as his speedy shadow scurried down the narrow hallway into a darkly lit room. It was filled with walls of all different types of hue and design.

The White Rabbit's feet seemed to fly through the air, barely touching the ground as he rapidly raced through the unusual room. He urgently tapped on an extremely large pocket watch. He had to carry it in his hand, as it was ironically far too large for any pocket.

He ran through a small door on the farthest wall, and it closed rapidly behind him. And even though she had come up to it a mere second after it closed, when she opened the door, she was stunned to find another right behind it. It was smaller in shape and different in color.

"Hmmm, why have a door that leads to nothing more than another door? For it seems that anyone who is trying to get somewhere would only find frustration in such nonsense. Oh well..." She sighed, but as she turned the doorknob and pulled the second door open, she found yet another smaller door.

Scrunching her face, she angrily opened door after door until finally there was but a tiny velvet curtain that hung upon a crooked rod. Her head craned with a wonderous interest as she excitedly opened the way to find... "Another door!"

Within that moment, such immense frustration swelled up inside her that she could not decide whether she should be furious or sad. Heavy tears welled up in her eyes as she stomped her feet in a temper.

Suddenly, the entire room began to rumble and quake around her, causing even the rows of lit lanterns that hung from the ceiling to sway and the flickering flames to bounce inside.

"Miss! Miss! You must calm down," said a small, masculine voice from below. Her tears were instantly silenced as she curiously crawled down to put her ear to the last of the tiny doors, thinking someone must be speaking to her from the other side.

"Hello? Who is out there?" She asked.

"How should I know the answer to that when I too, am in here?"

"Huh?" Wendy said as she slowly backed her face away from the door to find that what had formally appeared to be no more than the normal screws above a doorknob, had suddenly changed into small beady eyes. They were not human-like, with colors around circles of black and white, but instead shined with as much gold as the rest of its shiny face.

How could she have never seen a doorknob in such a way before now... with golden screws for eyes, a nose made up of the knob and a keyhole for a mouth? Strange as it was, she couldn't help but reflect upon all her past visions of a door. Quickly realizing how silly such a thought was, she shook her head and rubbed her eyes with both hands. "No, doors do not have faces! Impossible!"

"You mean *impassible*," the golden knob said rather snobbishly.

"Impassi-what?" She replied as if her distaste of correction had caused her to completely forget her doubt that she was now, in fact, engaged in conversation with a doorknob.

"I said impassible! For nothing here is impossible," the Doorknob replied mockingly.

"*Here*, you say!" She said as if struck by the word.

"Yes, my dear... here."

A moment of pause filled the colorful room as a frightful realization coursed its way through her clouded mind. "Here. Then it is true. I *am* in another world."

Flashes of memories, be they true or otherwise, began to stir wildly in her head. It was her most hated feeling in the world, but there was no doctor, no mother, and no tea that could calm her fear of manic proportions... not *here.*

Rapid breath and pain filled her chest as she spoke her next words: "Then I shall like to leave this place! Leave here! But how do I... I couldn't possibly climb back up the rabbit hole."

The Doorknob laughed mockingly at her again. "Yes, I fear the only way out of this room is through-"

"-You," Wendy replied, finishing his sentence.

The Doorknob smiled. If it was even possible, a crooked smile, before opening his mouth so widely that light came shining through. But it was not just any kind of light; it was sunlight. Wendy stooped down and crawled forward, squinting one eye and widening the other. She peered through the gaping keyhole to find a beautiful garden covered in a bed of vibrant flowers on the other side of the tiny door.

"The garden! That leads to the hospital! That's it! Oh, thank heavens! Then I shall just... Wait! How am I to get through? For surely, I could fit no more than my head through such a small doorway and what good would I be without my head?"

"It is not always a bad thing."

"What isn't?" She asked.

"Losing one's head," he replied.

"Well, I do not plan to lose mine, and in any case..." She giggled, "I should much rather like to close up like a telescope."

"A what?" He asked, looking mildly intrigued by such an odd concept.

"A tele..." Her answer was cut short as a flash of past times suddenly overtook her. A spiral of pictures stirred around inside her mind until she finally found herself in a room that was both familiar and strangely not. She was talking to Captain Hook. His face, though once intimidating, now seemed to have softened and was full of far more compassion than what she thought she remembered. But it wasn't just Hook she saw in the room, but herself- her true self. She looked calm and serene, unafraid in his presence. He stood next to a large golden telescope on a stand before the tallest window. The image rapidly faded, sending her back to the present a little wiser. "I was there," she whispered.

"You were where?" The Doorknob asked inquisitively.

"The Jolly Roger. I was there. I remember it with such clarity! Oh! You wouldn't believe the relief I feel in this moment," she said clapping her hands and spinning around. For a brief moment, her panic was dormant, and a tiny ember of bravery was lit within her. "Tell me, Doorknob, what must I do now? For I must get through your door and back to the hospital."

"Why?"

"Because I remembered something! Something important!" She screamed.

"How rather boring. What unimportant things do you remember?" He asked rudely.

"I'll have you know that I know a great many unimportant things. For instance, I know that four times six is twelve! No, wait... that is not right. Okay, five times three is seventeen." As the words left her mouth, she knew they were wrong.

The Doorknob scoffed and had somehow managed to appear as if he was looking down at her, which was odd as he was so small and low to the ground. But such matters, in all manner, did not seem to matter now.

"Alright, so I have forgotten multiplication, but I am sure I know Geography. Let me see- yes, I know London is the capital of Paris, and Paris, you know, is the capital of Rome!" No, wait! That is all so wrong! How could I have forgotten things today that I knew just yesterday? How puzzling it all is," she said feeling quite low-spirited consequently.

The Doorknob rolled his golden eyes at her ignorance but remained silent as her thoughts of knowledge continued to trail off.

"It is not as if I was changed overnight, for I know I was myself this morning. So, when did I start to become someone different? And if I am, in fact, a different person, then who then am I?" As she spoke, she noticed her voice sounded unusual and hoarse. "If I am not me, then tell me how to make the me that I am now, small enough to pass through your door."

The Doorknob smiled slyly, "You mean that you do not know?" He laughed. "Try the bottle on the table."

"What table?" She asked, suspiciously turning to gaze at what had previously been an empty room. Yet, to her utter astonishment, a round glass table came twirling in from the darkness, landing perfectly in the center of the room followed by a tiny glass bottle that landed ever so gently on top of the table's glass surface.

With great hesitation, she walked towards the glass table and picked up the small bottle. A single piece of a papered label hung from the its neck. Inside was a bright rose-colored liquid. Never, in all of her life, had she ever seen a drink that was such a glowing shade. Upon the label was two simple words that were written in beautiful handwriting...

Drink Me

"Drink me? Hmmm, I'd better look first. For if one drinks too much from a bottle marked poison..." She went on talking, reminding herself of all the wise advice she had come to learn in her young life, but while she was rambling on, the Doorknob began watching her with a most sinister glare. For though there was, in fact, no man-made poison within the contents of the bottle, the dark truth of its purpose was something far worse.

Despite her own words of wisdom and warning, she brought the bottle to her lips and sipped the bubbling drink. Her first taste was incredible, the second was sweet, the third was savory, and before she knew it, she had shrunk down to only ten inches high.

The Doorknob chuckled at the sight of her. "Wow, one more sip of that and you might have gone out like a candle."

The very idea was horrific to her, and understandably made her very nervous. She stood perfectly still, hoping and praying that she wouldn't shrink any smaller. After a few minutes of not moving at all, she decided it was finally time to head towards the door. She eagerly ran towards it, ready to leave. She reached for the Doorknob and turned it forcibly.

"Ouch!" He screamed glaring up at her most disgruntled.

Wendy gasp, "Oh! I am terribly sorry."

"I'm locked!" He bellowed back at her.

"Locked?" She replied dismayed.

"But of course, you have the key so..."

"What key?" She asked, now feeling desperately worried that she had forgotten something dreadful.

It was a feeling only more amplified by the look on the Doorknob's face as he spoke his next words. "Surely, you did not leave it all the way up there," he said with his golden eyes looking straight at the top of the table.

Wendy's breath failed her as she walked back towards the table with slow discouraged steps. As she reached the very bottom of the table and looked straight up, a long brass key suddenly appeared completely out of thin air.

She looked around, hoping that some chair or latter would magically appear to help her, but alas, nothing came. Her frantic heart began to race as she tried to climb up the table, but each time she got close to the edge- she would always fall. The Doorknob's menacing laughter felt as if it was reverberating through throughout the room, as if her suffering was making him more powerful somehow.

After her last discouraging fall, she pitifully sat on the ground with her legs kicked out and her hands on her hips. "Oh, I suppose I should already know the answer to this, but I don't! And I fear I am running out of breath. Please tell me, Doorknob! What should I do?"

A not-so-hidden smirk came upon his face as he answered, "You should try the box, naturally."

Naturally. "It would seem this doorknob takes great pleasure in making me sound as if I do not have a brain at all," she whispered to herself as she looked around for a box, but no matter how hard she looked, she just didn't see it. Her frustration mounted as she turned to face the Doorknob once more. "What box?!"

With a calm, belittling tone, he replied, "Why, it is right there in front of you, of course, do you not see?

"I think if there were a box right in front of me, I would see it, but I have looked all over, and there is not a box anywhere..." Her voice trailed off as a fancy little trinket box poofed before her feet. Without any further hesitation, she opened the box to find four different dainty French treats inside; each were marked:

Eat Me

in brightly colored icing. "Alright... If I take a bite and I grow bigger, then I will have the key, and if the bite makes me shrink shorter, then I will be small enough to walk right under the crack of the door. So, I must not fuss. I must be brave. Be brave and take a bite."

With her eyes closed, she put one of the inviting little cakes to her lips, but it didn't take more than a single bite for her entire body to shoot straight up to the ceiling. Standing at over nine feet tall, she reached down to grab the key off the glass table, but as she crouched back down to look through the keyhole again, she felt even more hopeless than ever before. She was to be stuck in this place... this room, forever.

Tears welled up in her eyes; not tears of just sadness, but also those of pure anger. Her thoughts, every single one of them, started to pour from her eyes. Gallons of tears fell down her face and splashed onto the floor until nearly half of the entire room was flooded.

Then suddenly, she could hear the voice of the White Rabbit again. He came running into the room with two white gloves and a fan, till muttering, "Oh, the Duchess! The Duchess!" He was in such a state of urgency that his entire body shook from his fret. It was because of this that the White Rabbit accidentally dropped his fan and gloves. Before Wendy could utter a single breath, the curious creature quickly scurried back off into the darkness once again.

Watching the White Rabbit get away this time was more than Wendy could take. The constant game of him being just barely beyond her reach had become quite tortuous for such a little girl. She had come in this world to follow him, and yet she couldn't escape the hopelessness that was crashing over in this very moment. Watching the rabbit disappear again had brought the volume of her tears of sobbing showers to an all-out raging storm that was beyond even her control.

The Doorknob below, however, could scarcely breathe a word before a crashing wave of water thrashed over his mouth, nearly choking him. He pleaded for her to stop, but she just couldn't. Despite her confusion and her uncontrollable shedding of tears, she suddenly remembered the gloves and fan.

She picked up them up and began to fan her face. To her utter amazement, she was starting to shrink at a rapid rate! She quickly turned it away from her before it shrank her out of existence, but within a mere moment, she was falling through the air and landing right into the same little bottle that started it all.

Looking at the massive depth of the salty sea around her, she felt so ashamed of her previous hysterics. "Oh, dear, I do wish I hadn't cried so much." But as she continued to float along the moving water, she was ecstatic to see she was heading right towards the keyhole; only this time... she was finally just the right size.

CHAPTER SIX

WHERE IS WENDY

Being a Captain without a ship would for most pirates be the hardest fall. But for Hook, he had but to merely step inside a single tavern before pirates were welcoming him aboard their ships. For everyone knew that he would eventually be back on top, and no pirate wanted to be his enemy when it happened.

Though he did not like it, Hook accepted one of the many offers. The chambers he had been given were well enough, though he did miss his own upon the Jolly Roger a great deal. As he entered his quarters, he was surprised to find that Ainsel had still not returned from her fairy gathering.

Normally, she would avoid such a thing, but after the escape of Pan and Tinkerbell, the gathering in the woodlands was mandatory by all. To not attend would be seen as an accomplice to the traitors and would then be hunted down as well. Though Hook had still not mastered the time of the other worlds, Ainsel had assured him of her return on this night. It was a fact that made him nervous.

He had so wished to be there with her... to protect her, but they both knew such an idea would cause utter chaos! Nevertheless, he hated sending her off on her own to a kind, still unable to see them as anything other than cruel and untrustworthy. Yes, the only thing he could do at this moment was worry... worry about his beloved, Ainsel, and worry about Wendy.

The best thing for a worried heart is a busy mind, so that is just what he did- stay busy. While Mr. Smee was out walking Catcher, he stayed busy by collecting all that he would need to travel again. He would set aboard a new ship; For as things were now, he wasn't the kind of pirate who wanted his whereabouts known. His constant moving around from ship to ship seemed to be working. It seemed by the time people had learned what ship he was on; he had already boarded another. And tonight, it was no different. It was time to go.

He took out all the chest, books, and clothes that his father had sent him and started to pack them away when suddenly, a blue glow appeared behind him.

A smile spread across his face as he turned around to embrace his Blue Fairy properly. "I am so glad you are safe, my own darling," he whispered softly in her ear. As he pulled away to look upon her, his eyes sparkled in awe of her beauty. Her long, wavy azure hair waved slowly in the air as if she was underwater, and her eyes were like two crystals that could shame any

47

jewel, but it wasn't just her astonishing beauty that he loved beyond measure; it was her kind heart. She was the bright light in his dark world. It seemed like she had always been there when he needed her most. Throughout adventures and battles, whether by sword or by soul, she had been there for him.

He leaned in to kiss her, but something on her face seemed off. "Where are you going?" She asked.

"Oh, I need to find another ship. I spoke to the Darlings tonight and though the boys are okay; Wendy I fear was sent *away*. I will be leaving tonight to find her."

Suddenly, a tear welled up in Ainsel's eyes. "You need not bother."

"What? Why?" He asked completely confused by her words.

"Because... I know where she is."

Shock suffused him as he asked his next question: "Ainsel, I do not understand. You were at a fairy gathering. How could you possibly? Wait!" He stopped as a thought of realization entered his racing mind.

"Wendy is *far* away from here."

"I know that! She is in a hospital. I am going to go get her!" He declared.

"That's what I am trying to tell you, my love. Wendy is *not* in a hospital. She was, but she was lured away."

"Lured away? By what?" He said with tone that could have frightened the very air around them.

Ainsel wiped her eyes and took a deep breath before she answered: "The White Rabbit."

Hook felt even more confused and agitated than before. "Please... explain," he said trying with all his might to express patience.

"When Pan and the Green Fairy escaped the island, they had but one place to go. They each traveled to the Third Realm, but only one of them was allowed to stay. The Snow Queen couldn't risk the fairy who had made so many mistakes to have any power within her realm. Tinker Bell was just too much of a risk. She would have sent away the boy as well, but when she discovered who he was, she found that he was the only one who had delivered her the justice she so desperately wanted.

By killing you, Pan has earned Her Majesty's favor, and a place next to her very throne. Dismayed with the loss of Tiger Lily, Pan decided to stay in the realm of stolen souls with the ambition to take them unto himself; an act that only one fairy has dared to do before- The Snow Queen herself. It is the most unforgivable act against the laws of magic. But for the first time in his immortal life, Pan isn't doing it for thrill of breaking rules like he always has."

"Then why is he doing it?" Hook asked.

"He does so in hopes that with enough power, he may find Tiger Lily again."

"Ah, that makes sense," Hook said smiling. "You know, I believed that the cruelty of dividing him from his love would bring me immense satisfaction forever... I was right," he chuckled. But after a scolding gaze of Ainsel's instant disapproval of such behavior, he collected himself and regained his thought process. "But Peter seemed so fond of the little green one. How is possible that he would dismiss her from his life so easily?"

"His violent grief of such a loss was enough to cloud his judgement. With you dead, he still needed someone to blame, and unfortunately for the Green Fairy, his hatred would turn him against her due to her bargain with you. Tinker Bell begged for forgiveness and reminded him of the bomb she had taken to save him, but no matter what she said, she couldn't change the fact that it was she who had cost him his love, and in doing so... she had lost his."

"Wow, I always knew he was a cold-hearted bastard, but I must admit... that surprised me. So then, where is the Green Fairy now?"

"Well, having lost everything, and nowhere to go, the traitorous pixie was forced to return to face the Elder's wrath. She expected the eternal death, but her punishment as it turned out was to be far worse."

"Where?" Hook asked overwhelmed with intrigue.

"They announced it tonight. As part of her punishment, her new life was to be announced tonight in front of everyone; bringing such shame. So, it was tonight that I heard the Green Fairy was sent somewhere else, and given a charge deemed by the fae, to be the worst of punishments. She had been sent to a far-off land, stripped of her ability to bargaining for souls, she was given the charge of collecting madness. It is a fate most terrible and beyond anything she had imagined. She has lost everything, even her best friend. So..." Ainsel stopped as if afraid to finish the rest.

"So... what, Ainsel? Tell me!" Hook shouted.

"So now she seeks revenge upon the one that she blames for all her sorrow."

Finally understanding it all, he started seething through his teeth, "Tinker Bell." Her very name spilled from his lips with agonizing distain.

"Yes. It is her job to collect the sanity of others, so when she found that Wendy was in a..."

"Madhouse."

"Yes... She immediately sent the guardian for her."

"You're saying that the White Rabbit is a guardian?"

"Yes, and the veil is the rabbit hole," she replied.

"But I thought guardians tried to keep people away from the veil."

"Not this one, for much like the realm itself, nothing is what it should be."

With a sigh of great stress, Hook rubbed his temples in frustration. "My heart aches for that poor child. For I fear that all her suffering surpasses even my own by now. And now... I find out that she is to be put through more torment within another world because of that blasted creature! Agh! Fairies!" His hurtful words seemed to cut at Ainsel like a hot blade. The pain he had caused was quickly written upon her sweet face.

Seeing this, his eyes instantly fell, and he reached his only hand out to her. "Forgive me, love. I only spoke in anger, and though I know it does not excuse my heinous offense towards you, I humbly beg for your pardon."

Ainsel smiled, nodding in understanding. "Remember, it is only your temper that will weaken you and cloud your mind; a fact that is of most importance since you are going into the one realm that will use it to bring about your downfall."

At this, Hook kissed her hand. "How did you know I was going? I know you cannot read my mind. No fairy can."

She smiled slyly, "I don't have to resort to such magic when it comes to what you might do next. I knew you going to venture to the realm where the girl was taken. I know this because you are a hero."

"And just what is the name of this unfortunate realm?"

"Wonderland. It is called Wonderland," Ainsel replied, seeing the guilt that burned him.

"And the veil... the rabbit hole; where can I find it?"

"You cannot go there, my love."

Hook turned his head in surprise, "Why not?"

"Because the quick rabbit would surely alert the Red Queen of the realm and Wendy would, I fear, be killed before you could reach her."

"But I cannot!... I will not just leave her there!" He screamed.

Ainsel quickly rushed to him, "I know... I know. And I will help you," she said, reassuring him as she caressed his face.

Hook collected himself. The sight of her loving gaze was enough to calm his heavy breaths of fury.

"There is another way in..." she said.

Hook's piercing eyes widened with fierce intent. "What it is it? Tell me."

She took a deep breath and looked into his eyes, but something within her couldn't bring forth the bravery she needed to say it, for she knew that the instant she did, he would venture off into danger once again. And maybe, just maybe... he would not be able to come back to her this time. She just needed one moment; the kind of moment that someone can hold onto forever. And it was in that special moment that she took the time to memorize his face. But after that moment, all that was left was the sparkling tear that fell down her pale face as three little words left her quivering lip: "The Looking Glass."

CHAPTER SEVEN

THE LOOKING GLASS

Many portals could be found around the earth's plane. So many, in fact, that tales of warnings could be heard all over the world, but only one as the legends go, is so dangerous that the entire town around it behaved in such a way that most wouldn't dare venture to its eerie old domain. The town, as humanity would call it, was Dreary Hollow.

The town's dark and grim population was full of people that had been born there and like all small towns, no one ever left. It was as if they simply belonged there, and any unlucky stranger that came to pass was unlikely to leave at all. At least, you wouldn't leave the same person.

It wasn't that the town of Dreary Hollow was inviting, for it was anything but. In fact, it was the very opposite of welcoming. Rude gazes and snarling scoffs of breath were all you would receive from those that lived there. There would be no gleeful wave of hello nor would there be any of the kind of small talk you would expect from a neighbor. And yet, it was their harsh greeting that may very well be your saving grace as it is their unnerving behavior and the eerie fogged streets of the town that makes you feel as though you ought to turn away and never come back.

There was but one inn within the small village. In fact, it was right in the center of the town square. I know this again makes the town appear like an inviting one. Why else would the town surround an inn for unwelcome strangers, but if you knew anything about the town of Dreary Hollow, it was that everything within it was more ancient than any living person today could remember.

The stones within each building, home, and road was so withered and worn that it was soft to any gentle touch. One might have found some beauty in its age, but the cracks crawled up every piece like a poisonous mark of time spreading across the walls. Much like everything else in the area, it was old and decrepit. It was as if every piece within its musky depth was its own version of death. The stones and glass were broken. Paint peeled off of every wall, and no amount of greenery or life could be found no matter how hard you looked. A fact that was most noticeable as you pass beyond the dreaded town's sign.

Though Ainsel had given clear direction of where to go and what to do, Hook couldn't help noticing the chill that inched up his spine as he and Catcher crossed the town border. The vision of the town appeared like that of an ancient graveyard. The sorrow was so thick in the air that you could almost taste the death.

Catcher's ears perked high in the air with more alert than Hook had ever seen them. The dog's eyes and snout whipped back and forth rapidly as if expecting something to jump out at him in any second. He stayed right at Hook's side with an overwhelming sense of protection for his master coursing through his every panting breath.

"It's okay, boy. It's okay," Hook said, hoping his calm tone would help his loyal companion. The buildings were unusually close to one another and stood right along the edge of a thick forest that surrounded the area. The trees closest to the town hadn't a single leaf of life upon their branches and the night was filled with an eerie silence. It was the silence that Hook hated. It just wasn't right... nothing about this town was right.

Finally, the sound of footsteps came around the narrow corner of one of the houses. A horribly thin man and a crooked looking woman pushed a small brown baby carriage upon the cobblestone road. They looked over to him with a suspicious glare, but it wasn't their cruel gaze that made Hook's blood run cold, but rather the disturbing silence of the carriage. The ominous couple dressed in unfashionable old drags didn't take their eyes off of him as they stepped forward.

Catcher growled at them with a warning, yet it didn't shake their stare. Hook gulped subtly as they finally crossed paths and gave a relieving breath once the strange couple was behind him. Trying to make light of the sinister situation at present, Hook quietly spoke in humor to his nervous pet, "It is a good thing we did not bring our Mr. Smee, ay Catcher?" Hook chuckled. "Why I can hear the squeal of terror now."

To his great surprise, Catcher looked up at him as if unamused at such a snide joke against their friend. Catcher had never done this before, but somehow in this town and in this instant, Hook was sure that Catcher had understood every word he had spoken. Hook's face scrunched up, feeling both scolded by his pet and confused by the unnatural connection.

Finally, they reached the Unwelcome Inn. An ominous glow from the full moon above shined down upon its grey cracking walls. The door, brown with broken, rotted edges, was open. Swaying back and forth, it creaked in a way that seemed to make Hook's nerves cringe. Catcher froze, looking into the darkness beyond with a blank stare that concerned him. "Come on, boy. We are almost there." His voice, to his relief, broke Catcher's trance and they both walked inside.

A tiny man with a scruffy appearance looked up at him. His face turned up as if he were suddenly in the presence of something so wretched that he may be ill. For though it was not completely unheard of, you could tell it had been some time since a stranger had approached the decrepit place. It was uncomfortable, to say the least. Nevertheless, Hook proceeded with as much normalcy as he could being stared at in such a way. "I need a room, sir," Hook stated.

The man's expression didn't move an inch as he responded through his darkly stained teeth: "Which room?" It was a question that would only be asked in such a place- in this place. Much like a password to a place of secrecy, given the wrong answer could end in a most dreadful fate. But for Hook, one such secret had been already been shared by his love, Ainsel.

"Room number 4," Hook responded coldly.

The innkeeper nodded before slowly turning to a small silver chamber behind him. He opened it and grabbed a long brass skeleton key. Without another word, Hook took the key from the pale man's tight grip and looked around for the sacred door.

Catcher guided him down a narrow hallway, though as it turned out, Hook did not need Catcher to find the hidden veil. For with each step closer, Hook found himself becoming surrounded by an odd feeling. With six doors on either side, the path itself was very dull and grey as if the building had been made in a world without color.

Hook squinted his eyes to the first door, but there was no number upon it. He quickly glanced upon the others to find that they too were blank. Suddenly, as if the innkeeper had heard his frustration, he spoke: "The room you seek is on the second floor."

"Second floor?" Hook said in a confused tone.

The man did not speak again but instead just raised his long thin hand to point grimly at the shaded darkness around the corner. He hesitantly stepped onward. As he descended into the black, a large metal staircase that hung by rusty chains, swayed before his very eyes. He looked down at Catcher, and it was within that instant that he saw the fear in his companion's eyes. Like most dogs, climbing up was a fun pastime, but this staircase looked like a death trap. Hook bent down and carried him onto the first step.

Though he kept a firm hand over Catcher's eyes in an attempt to keep him from absolute panic, the anxious dog whined as his master carefully made his way up the jangling metal staircase. With each step sounding as if it were about to collapse to the floor, Hook didn't dare look down.

After a trip well beyond anyone's comfort, Hook stepped off the staircase onto the second floor. He took a second to look around before putting Catcher down. There was nothing, not a picture on the walls, nor a potted plant on the floor. Yes, there was absolutely nothing but a terribly strange feeling that came radiating from the one door that stood down the long narrow hallway. Hook took a deep breath before making his way towards the barrier between him and a room hiding enchantment.

After he reached the doorknob and unlocked the door with the key, it felt as if an awful chill were coming from the other side of the hole. A sudden moment of hesitation overcame him. "Don't be a cowardly bastard. Wendy needs you! Open the door!"

And that is exactly what he did. With a turn of the knob, he pushed open the door of hard splintered wood and walked bravely into the old room. Inside, it was damp and cold. It looked as if no one had been there in many years. To his shock, there was however a small bed within the room. A blanket of dead leaves covered its surface, and a simple wooden nightstand with a small lamp sat beside it.

Hook stepped across a tattered oval rug that lay in the center of the floor, to pull upon the lamp string. To his amazement, the light came flickering on. "Well look at that, boy." But as he looked over at Catcher, he found the dog staring straight at a thin closet door in the corner. "What is it, boy? What do you see?" He whispered, but Catcher did not move. Suddenly understanding, Hook stepped towards him, but before he opened the closet, something under the door caught his eye. Squinting, he reached down to find what he thought at first was a piece of paper, but as he turned it around, he saw that it was not paper at all, but a dusty old playing card.

Before he could muster another thought, the closet door creaked open. Hook stood as a magnificent tall mirror suddenly appeared before his eyes. The frame was in all manner a work of art; such craftsmanship was beyond all he had ever seen before. It looked impossibly old and covered in dust, but it was in every way remarkable.

Feeling overwhelmed by the curiosity that laid hidden behind the blanket of age, he reached into his pocket for a small cloth. As he carefully swiped a single stroke of dust away, a shadowed figure moved on the other side. Such a sight would have frightened anyone else, but as the shade of magic moved beyond the glimmering looking glass, it was Hook's sinister smile that could be seen upon the mirror's warping reflection.

"Alright then, Wonderland, here I come."

CHAPTER EIGHT

THE OTHER SIDE

Traveling by mirror was merely one of many for the fae, but it was this particular looking glass that not even the most daring of fairies cared to venture through, for what lay on the other side was in every way a world of strange horrors. Nevertheless, the brave pirate stepped through the reflective portal, and a most unnerving chill reverberated through him.

The sound of a crisp dead leaf that had followed, crunched under his large boot. Hook looked down to see its broken pieces. One couldn't help but notice its displacement upon such a pristine floor. Then he looked around at what appeared to be the exact same room, and yet it differed in every possible way.

The walls of this room were covered in the most vibrant of wallpaper, with dozens of animal portraits in various sized frames of silver and gold hung randomly upon each of them. Every animal had been painted with the sharpest of colors. All were dressed eloquently and with as much poise and posture as any figure of royalty. A magnificent rug that was perfect in both size and design lay crooked and beautiful below his feet, and two exquisite wing-back chairs sat opposite in the room's front corners. One was emerald green, and the other was the most violet of purples.

In the center of the room was a large wooden canopy bed; the impossibly carved pillars were twisted beautifully with four different colored curtains of silk and soft velvet. The headboard and footboard, however, had the most curious carvings. The most visible features were that of the flowers, keys, eyes, and at the very center of it all- a heart. The dark cherry wood shined as if it had been stained on this very night. The tinge of red upon the wood was complimented in every way by the thickest of crimson-red bedding. Two shining, golden lanterns shined a charming glow of candlelight upon the room. A dark wooden nightstand sat beside the bed, just as it did upon the other side of the mirror, only instead of a dingy lamp on top of the surface, there was but a single small jar.

Hook walked towards it, as it was the most suspicious part of the room. *Why was there a jar on the nightstand?* He wondered as he picked it up off of the table. Once he held it up, he could see a beautifully designed label upon the glass.

Printed in a curvy shimmer read the words:

Orange Marmalade

The mysterious jar was unopened with a bit of fabric and a piece of string tied around its neck. There was something quite undeniably inviting about it, but it wasn't as if there was any... his thoughts were interrupted as a fancy little saucer with two perfectly toasted pieces of bread suddenly appeared on the table. Placed ever so precisely upon the plate's side was a tiny silver knife.

Hook smirked at the magical temptation. "Well, this realm certainly doesn't waste any time."

Catcher looked up at him with concerned eyes as he spoke.

Hook smiled at him, taking a moment to adore how smart his companion was to such things. "Do not worry, boy. I have no intention of eating anything while I am here. But I didn't forget about you. I brought a little bag of treats for you from home."

Hook reached in a little pouch tied onto his leather belt. It was then as Catcher ate the small savory treat that his master had pulled out of his right pocket, that he remembered the other very important matter within his left pocket. He reached in and pulled out a sack of fairy dust- Ainsel's fairy dust.

He walked back towards the looking glass. It was as he gazed at his lie of a reflection that he remembered all that Ainsel had said to him before he ventured into Dreary Hollow.

His dark waving locks of hair that reached halfway down his back now appeared straight and with the length barely past his shoulders, and it was in the absurd shade of bright blue. His nose was now more defined, and his face was now smooth; completely without his normal facial hair.

He wasn't without a hat in this form, but by the look of it, he wished he was. It was misshapen and covered in feathers and ribbon. It was awfully strange, and within a moment, he snatched it right off his head. Then there was the matter of the dispensing of the mismatched long purple coat that was full of colored buttons, crooked mix matched stitching, and too many pockets. The shirt and pants he wore beneath were brightly colored but well enough and his belt and boots seemed to have only changed in vibrancy. But just like Ainsel had assured him, his ocean blue eyes remained his own.

True, his refection *was* meant to make him lose his sense of self, but for Hook, this massive change of appearance was going to be a rather significant advantage. For with such a guise as this, no one- not even Tinker Bell would recognize him. But there was one set of eyes that would see his true appearance. Ainsel had set upon him a particular spell for Wendy's sight, and in doing so- he too would see the real her. As important as that little spell of hers would prove to be, the magic dust he was about to use was for something even more important.

CHAPTER NINE

A TERRIBLE DAY FOR A MOUSE

As Hook left the enchanting room of unusual things, he was admittingly pleased to find the staircase was also changed. A wide wooden spiral with a dark blue rug carried him down to the first floor, but as he reached the bottom, he was shocked to find that the blue rug that wavered like water was actually turning into water.

With great displeasure, he stepped into the salty water below. Within minutes, he was out of the Unwelcome Inn and swimming in what looked like a dark and nasty swamp. It wasn't like Hook or any pirate for that matter to be so unhappy around water, but this swamp was different. It was thick, smelt, and didn't even move the way water should. It was exactly what one would expect outside of such a place. Nevertheless, it was clear that if one should want to get somewhere... they were going to have to do so by water, and such ways of travel were not lost on someone like Hook.

He had just made his way into the deep parts of the swamp when a sudden splashing noise came rapidly around him. Hook turned around in alarm, but then shook his head in annoyance as the sight of Catcher happily swimming, passed him.

They had swam a far distance with nothing but the stench in the air, and silence to keep them company, but Hook's tired arms and legs were quickly stunned as a sudden shrill scream came out of the distance. As Catcher was so far ahead of him, Hook hastened his pace for fear that Catcher may be in some sort of danger. But as he drew closer, he saw that it was Catcher himself that had cornered some other creature.

Hook's eyes widened as the vision of an impossibly large mouse cowered upon a small bit of floating debris. Catcher growled, aggressively swimming towards it. Hook felt a sense of pity as he looked into the creature's fearful eyes. "Catcher, come!" It wasn't that he doubted his friend's keen sense of detecting evil, for he knew it to be true and well beyond his own, but something about *this* attack seemed far more like a typical animal thing.

Nevertheless, Catcher did as he was told, though his stare upon the animal never wavered an inch nor did his growling ever cease. As Hook closed in on the trembling mouse, he was pleasantly surprised to find that his footing was touching solid ground. He was coming up upon land. Eager to now be upon land, he decided it best to begin his search for Wendy and leave the creature alone, for surely the farther away Catcher went, the mouse would go about its own merry way.

Such a notion however was shattered as Hook heard a voice coming from behind him.

"A dog! A dog! What a terrible day I am having!"

Hook turned in shock as the very large mouse crawled out upon the muddy ground. Ainsel had told him of such unusual things, though to see a talking animal himself was a whole other matter. Hesitantly, he decided to say something back to the creature: "Um, excuse me... were you- *talking* to me?"

The large wet mouse looked up in a temper, "No! I was not, in fact, talking to you!"

Hook's brow raised, for it had been some time since he had been talked to in such a rude manner. Still, he had not come here to quarrel with a disgruntled mouse. So, with a slight exhale, he decided to respond cordially: "I see. Well then, I bid you a good day."

The mouse scoffed at such an idea. "Good day indeed! First, that little girl speaks to me of cats! And now, after I'm rid of her, I get attacked and cornered by a dog! Good day! Ha!" The mouse huffed in anger as he was nearly shrouded in a large bush.

Hook gasped rushing the creature in urgent haste. The mouse turned and squealed in alert! "The girl you spoke of... where did she go?" Hook asked harshly.

The big mouse trembled in reply, "How should I know?"

An intensity swelled inside Hook, shaking the mouse in frustration. "You must know something! When did you see her? What direction did she go? Think!"

The mouse quivered in fear under the pirate's red stare, "All I know is that she said she was following the White Rabbit! That's all I know! Please, sir, let me go!"

As Hook looked into the terrified gaze of the panicked mouse, he remembered the promise he had made to Ainsel about his anger.

He loosened his grip, and the large creature quickly wiggled away into the brush uttering, "What a terrible day I'm having!"

CHAPTER TEN

CABBAGES AND KINGS

The unnerved mouse, little help that he was, turned out be right. He said the girl was chasing after the rabbit and following the White Rabbit she was indeed. But it seemed that for all her efforts, she was constantly being stopped by random creatures and overwhelming distractions.

While Hook and Catcher were talking to a mouse, she had only just escaped a most ridiculous caucus race. "That dance! What nonsense! Though something about the thimble I gave them... oh, I don't know. It was all too chaotic to think about anything," she said walking into the Dark Wood, hoping to find the elusive White Rabbit again. *He couldn't have gotten too far.*

After all, he *had* passed by the same set of trees only a moment before. Once she entered the silent brush, she tiptoed, listening carefully for any movement. But there was none. It was all just quiet- too quiet. She looked down in the odd pink grass, hoping to spot some of the rabbit's tracks, and to her sheer delight, she found them! But as she crawled, inching her way down the trail, she had somehow failed to notice that something *else* was tracking *her*.

Suddenly, two sets of eyeballs peered at her from behind the nearest brush. Then to Wendy's great surprise, two strange men that were dressed as boys, were moving in perfect unison towards her. They were the first actual *people* she had seen in this place. It was a fact that should have made her feel at ease, but there was something about them... something not quite human.

Their features more than a little out of the ordinary. With bright blue propellered hats, and red overalls that were way too small for their disproportioned body, the two men appeared as odd as anything she had ever seen before.

As Wendy stood up from the ground, she noticed that there were two written words on each of the men's collars. "Tweedle Dee and Tweedle Dum," she read in a whisper. They didn't sound like names at all, but rather titles of what they had become. Their bodies were unusually round, while their limbs were strangely thin. Their faces were like two fishbowls with large white eyes that held only a spec of black inside them. They each had a thin nose and even thinner lips. They were dressed the same, like a set of twins. But these round men were more than just twins. For beyond the chilling aspects of their appearance, to Wendy, it was their gleeful benevolent smiles that forced her skin to crawl on end. They appeared like two curious figures that would dance within your most bizarre of nightmares.

To hear them speak, one would have to wonder if their two minds had been molded into one. It was not only annoying to hear them talk, but the fact that nothing could stop them. At first, Wendy tried to escape their incessant ramblings that went on in both song and rhyme, but just before she had successfully snuck away into the darkness beyond the trees, the two strange twins began to tell a most enticing tale.

It seemed to be her weak spot. After all, Wendy loved a good story and surely, a story from this place ought to very interesting. "Oh no, please. I want to hear your story," Wendy said sweetly.

"No! They replied harshly; the one does when they are already feeling offended. "Unclearly, you are in far too much of a hurry," they said in unison.

Wendy pleaded further. "No, I have plenty of time."

A mad spark went off on their eerie faces as if she had suddenly said the magic words they needed to hear. "You do! Well..." They screamed happily. All of the sudden, they grabbed her by each of her arms and began to drag her until they reached a large broken log that laid upon the ground.

They sat her down and proceeded to jump up and down, clapping their hands in an alarming glee. Finally, after the twins had a good hard bump into each other, they began to announce their most troubling tale in song...

"That fatal morning when our father woke us
The sun was warm and bright
He bid farewell, kissed our heads,
And hugged us hard and tight

No more would we go so long
Without any food to eat
For he would build a restaurant
Right upon the beach

We'll live like royals he said,
Like cabbages and Kings
But such promises had been made before
So, we didn't believe such things

The small carpenter, however,
Took him at his word
And on the sand
He built his plan
Amongst the crabs and birds

With a promise of pay

At the end of the day
They decided to sit and dine
They had a table full of oysters
And a belly full of wine

To this day we still don't know
Who asked for butter and bread?
But when the carpenter found
That father hadn't a pound
The sun set with our father dead

When the moon rose
We covered our toes
And set out to look for him
But all that we found
Was blood on the ground
A vision so horrid and grim

And there amongst the clutter
Of wood, oysters, and butter
We curled up most sadly
To sleep with his slaughter."

Wendy gasp in utter horror, "Oh my!"

But they shook their heads and fingers and smiled eerily wide.

"No, do not worry,
that's not the end of our story.

You see...

The very next morning
Something came out the water
And to our delight
It was our own father!
We jumped in glee
He'd come back for us
But here's the funny part you see,
He'd come back a walrus!

We danced away to laugh and play
And talked of many things
Of shoes and ships and sealing wax
And of course, cabbages and Kings!"

Wendy's words failed her as her jaw seemed to have fallen frozen. It was only as the two strange men bowed at the finish that she realized the surreal performance was finally over.

"That was such a- sad story," she replied. It was the only words she could muster. Quite honestly though, she hadn't a clue as to how she should properly respond. Feeling overwhelmed with such a mental quandary, it felt the only thing to do at this moment was smile as her sense of wording stumbled away from her mind. How puzzling it was to hear such a tale, and all the while, the two odd men never ceased their grinning throughout their entire performance.

Luckily though, it was of little matter as the twins began to bounce and dance again amongst themselves. A part of her, a rather large part of her, had what felt like a million questions for them. *Like where was their father now? Was he still a walrus? And what became of the murderous carpenter?* But not even her most powerful of curiosities could overcome her desire to get as far away from the twins as possible.

It was an opening she didn't have to wait long for, as the two brothers had already begun to sing and dance, lost within their own warped world.

CHAPTER ELEVEN

MARY ANN

After escaping the strange twins, Wendy found herself in a very dark part of the woods. So dark in fact, that she couldn't even see her body. Her hands, her feet, everything was pitch black! There wasn't a sound; not a bug, not a bird, nothing. She was starting to worry.

"I sure hope I have not stumbled into some sort of void; a black hole that could suck me right out of existence. But I am moving, right? Yes! I can feel my legs and arms though I do not see them. Oh, and my voice. Surely, I must still exist if I can hear my voice. How dreadful it would be not to see anything. Wait! My aunt? That is strange. I know her name, yet I cannot seem to remember it. Well, in any case, she seems not to mind being blind, or maybe it is just not something one talks about. Still, her name, how curious that I have forgotten it. I wonder what other names I have forgotten."

Her thoughts were suddenly silenced as an opening of trees shined six rays of sunlight into the darkness. She quickly ran towards them. Then as she stood just beyond the trees, she was thrilled to find a small charming house.

She couldn't help but stop and admire its darling appearance. There was a sweet little picket fence that surrounded the entire house. Suddenly, she was overwhelmed with delight as the White Rabbit came running out the front door. "Oh, it's the rabbit's hou...."

Her words were cut short as he interrupted her harshly: "Mary Ann! What are you doing out here?" He asked in a scolding manner.

"Mary Ann?" Her moment of confusion seemed to infuriate him. He pulled out his loud trumpet and blew it hard right in front of her face.

"Make haste, Mary Ann! I need my fan and gloves!" He screamed shoving her towards the door, and before she could say another word, she was inside his little pink house.

"Oh, my goodness! I guess I shall be taking orders from Dinah next." Immediately, Wendy's face turned up with guilt for saying such a thing about her beloved pet kitten. "No, that would never happen, for Dinah is far too sweet to behave like that. My sweet Dinah, how I miss her now. I miss her pretty little bow, and the way she purrs whenever I pet the top of her head." It was in that moment that a small chuckle came into her throat as she remembered the way the kitten slept with her face buried down. But oddly, though Wendy knew this was how her precious kitten slept, she could not exactly picture it in her mind the way one does after a reminiscing a memory. "That is strange. Oh, well, it must just be the excitement of my hurry that I cannot remember properly. In any case, I hope she is okay," she said to herself, looking around the neat house of porcelain, exquisite furniture, and painted portraits of rabbits.

She suddenly realized that it wasn't just the pictures... everything was in the shape of a rabbit. But as she quickly glanced around with curious admiration, a certain anxiety rose within her as the pressure of her search grew more desperate. She could not find the white gloves and fan anywhere. Then, as if out of nowhere, she saw a white twirling staircase.

Without another thought, she quickly ran to the top step, but to her utter frustration, she found only a wall. She stomped in anger, and to her great surprise, the wall in front of her cracked open. "Oh, how wonderful! It's a hidden door!"

She opened the passageway to find a bedroom; the Rabbit's bedroom. It was covered in various clocks: wall clocks, mantel clocks, cuckoo clocks, hanging clocks, and an absurd variety of watches. The constant ticking seemed to echo throughout the room unbearably loud. *Goodness! How could anyone possibly sleep with such noise?*

There was a white wooden bed with a precious pink quilt and one fluffy pillow on top. Little books sat upon a tiny table, and next to them was another silver trinket box; much like the one from that horrible room with the Doorknob.

She opened it to find many more treats with the tempting words written in icing. "Eat me," she read. "Hmmm, don't mind if I do. I am a little hungry, and I would certainly like to grow back to my normal size again."

Her train of thought was lost amongst the incessant ticking. With each tick, and every tock- she felt as if they were twitching at her nerve endings. Finally, as she covered her ears and gained back a moment of focus, she spotted the White Rabbit's gloves and fan upon a nearby end table.

She urgently picked them up, but as the ticking of the clocks crawled back into her head, she put the alluring cookie to her mouth and took a bite.

Suddenly, she was shooting straight up to the ceiling. "Oh no!" She screamed as she realized she was still growing. She quickly tried to move and stoop down in order to remain fitting within the room. But against all her efforts, she was ultimately forced to shove her arms through the house's windows. It still wasn't enough. She was still growing. It was then, as she put one her legs down the staircase, breaking it entirely, that she heard the White Rabbit scream her name again, or at least, what *he* said her name was.

Suddenly, his shouting was followed by that blasted horn again. She knew right then that she had quite literally kicked him out of his own house. He wasn't outside long before she could hear another voice out there too; which considering how much screaming for assistance the panicked rabbit had done, it wasn't all that surprising.

Curious to see who the White Rabbit was talking to about the matter, she wrapped her gigantic arms around to the front of the house. She quickly opened the shutters, allowing her to see the outside of the house.

The creature he was speaking to was not a stranger at all. He was the Dodo that had led the absurd dancing earlier by the water. Something about his appearance struck her as more intriguing than some of the others; for there was something so human in his presence. It wasn't just his military clothing or that he always seemed to have an old smoking pipe in his mouth. No, it was something much more profound than that. It wasn't to suggest he wasn't unstable, for he was very much indeed; a fact that he was about to make undeniably clear.

First, he sends a lizard with a latter to come collect her from the chimney. *What an idea! Even if he could climb down the chimney and even if he could reach her, what was he to do then?* Alas, it did not matter for after the Dodo forcibly carried the fearful lizard up the latter and practically shoved him down the chimney, a massive dark cloud filled the house with ash.

Though she tried to fight it with all her might, an enormous sneeze blew through the house and shot the poor lizard out like a rocket.

"Well, there goes Bill," The Dodo said casually. Something about his non-shalant attitude towards the possible death of a friend felt oddly familiar and unnerving for her. Now if she had thought the Dodo cruel or simply unstable before, her opinion of him was about to drastically change for the worse as she heard him announce to the White Rabbit that he was just going to have to burn the house down.

A powerful anger boiled inside her very blood when she heard this. "Don't you dare or I'll... I'll sick Dinah on you!" She threatened loudly, though the Dodo seemed to pay her words no attention at all. But it wasn't just her he was ignoring, but the full-blown panicked White Rabbit that was pleading next to him.

The Rabbit sobbed harder and harder as the Dodo quickly collected as many of his personal belongings that he could from the first floor and smashed them into a large pile of splintered wood. In no time at all, he had grabbed a grandfather clock, a table chair, and anything else he thought would smash. Now all there was left to do was set the fire.

"Oh no, this is getting serious," Wendy uttered to herself. Whether it was a good thing or a bad thing, she wasn't sure, but even though the house was still full of smoky ash, she was able to look outside of the house.

Suddenly, her eyes caught the vision of a planted garden. It was then in her frantic state that she got an idea. *Surely, if I ate something, it would make me grow smaller. And even if it didn't, then at least I could sprout right out of this house and be done with all this burning business.*

Feeling confident, she reached urgently for a planted vegetable, but in a mere second, the White Rabbit pounced upon her hand in an effort to save all that he had left. Wendy tried to explain, but he was beyond listening. He was now in a full scale of bursting panic.

She pitied him, truly, but she had to do something, and it had to be now. She plucked up a tiny carrot and brought her hand up towards her mouth, carrying the screaming rabbit along for the ride.

His cries of protest did not cease until... *Chomp!* She took a bite of the carrot and immediately felt as if she was collapsing in on herself. *Down-down-down* she went until she was a mere three inches tall. The frantic rabbit believed at first that he himself had been bitten. The poor thing hadn't even had a breath of relief before his pocket watch began to ring so loudly that it vibrated him violently. His eyes instantly filled with fear.

Before Wendy could collect herself or even have a chance to get off some of the awful soot that was all over her, the White Rabbit had already begun to race away into the Dark Wood, screaming: "The Duchess! The Duchess! I'm late!"

CHAPTER TWELVE

SMOKE

Duchess or no Duchess, Wendy was furious! "Oh, Mr. Rabbit! Wait!" She screamed trying to make her way down the front steps. The Dodo was still so caught up trying to set fire to the house, that he failed to see her tiny body pass him by. She tried to chase after the Rabbit, following his echoing cries, but now she was so small that she could barely see anything beyond the gardens of flower beds before her. By the time she reached them, she found that the flowers towered her.

Though most feel rather fearful being the only thing so small, but for Wendy, her anger was so that there was very little room for any other emotion. Pushing through every stem that stood in her path, she found herself scolding the White Rabbit out loud to herself, "Try to burn me alive, will he!? Why, if I was only a little bigger! Agh! When I get past these flowers, I am going to find him. And when I do, I'll teach him a thing or two about manners! One can't just go around blowing up houses! It just isn't done!" She said uttering under her breath, stomping her feet as she spoke. Little did she know that while she made her way into the vibrant garden of flowers, Hook and Catcher were not too far behind her.

Though Hook had hoped Catcher would be able to focus primarily on tracking the girl's scent, it would appear that every creature, sound, and of course smell, would instead keep him wildly scattered and on edge.

When Hook finally made his way into the Black Wood, a familiar uneasiness set upon him. As the darkness covered both him and his furry companion, an ominous silence surrounded them. Up till now, the odd realm had been nothing short of vibrant chaos.

Stepping into the silent Black Wood was in all manner unnerving for both of them. How he hated the quiet of the woods. It was as if he had literally stepped into a nightmare. But somehow the forest in this place was worse, for it was practically impossible to detect any sort of direction. Not even Catcher knew where to go. Nevertheless, Hook never stopped moving, for the idea of standing still, here in this place, made him feel like prey in the midst of predators. He had learned a long time ago, that silence should never suggest that you are alone.

Just when Hook felt as if they may, in fact, be disappearing, an alarming smell touched his senses. It was smoke, and not just any kind of smoke, but the overwhelming scent of wood burning. A mounting fear suffused every fiber of his being at the idea that a forest fire may soon engulf them both.

The thickening smoke quickly filled the air, making it extremely difficult to breathe. Unwilling to give in to such a horrid death, Hook picked up Catcher and began to run away from the smoke.

It was an idea that as it turned out, didn't end with just Hook. A sudden burst of shrill screaming rapidly entered the woods; its wailing cry was coming closer and closer. He turned around to discover there was a burning figure running right towards him. He hadn't a moment to react before the torrid creature crashed right into him.

Despite the flames, Hook could see that it was large and covered in burning feathers. Hook rose from the ground and made every effort to help the panicked animal, but it was no use, for in a mere second, the screaming bird ran away. Sadly, the creature was so frantic that it seemed completely unaware that it was heading straight back into the smoke.

"Come back!" He screamed, but it was no use. The burning bird was too far gone and screaming too loud to hear the pirate's voice of reason. "Damn it!" Hook shouted as he chased after the animal with an overwhelming sense of obligation. But as he followed the sound of the wailing animal, he suddenly saw an opening between the trees.

Though the smoke was thick, and his breath was failing, Hook forced his way through the edge of the Black Wood and into what appeared to be the view of a house completely enthralled by a blazing fire.

The shocking sight illuminated upon the creature before him.

It was the Dodo. His clothes and feathers were almost completely burned off. Hook quickly took off his own shirt and smothered the flames before they singed the poor creature's skin.

The Dodo breathed rapidly, still submerged in manic fear. Catching his own breath, Hook tried to calm him. "It is alright... You're alright now. Shhhhh. Do you hear me? I said that you are alright now," Hook said as steadily as he could. Catcher stood beside him, unable to look at anything other than the blazing flames rising before them. Hook too, looked back towards the burning house. "*What* happened here?" Hook asked out loud.

The Dodo collected his breath and tried to speak through his dry beak. "The monster! Can't have monsters about. We had to burn the house down," the Dodo said in a dry raspy voice.

"Monster? What monster?" Hook asked looking around in sudden alert.

"She's gone now! Yes, she is gone!" The Dodo said as if somehow relieved.

"She?"

"Yes! That is what I said! She!"

Hook could see that the creature was frazzled, and though he knew he should offer every compassion, it was still so off-putting to be talking to an animal.

"Well, I am sorry you had to burn down your house."

The Dodo looked up at him, confused. "What?! This is not *my* house!" He scoffed. "The very idea!"

Hook was taken aback. "What! Then who's house is this?"

The self- important Dodo glared back at him harshly. "I do not permit anyone to speak to me in that tone."

Hook stepped towards him sternly, making the Dodo instantly squirm under his oppression.

"The White Rabbit! It was the White Rabbit's house!" The Dodo yelped.

The name struck Hook like lightning. "And now? Where is the rabbit now?" He asked. But the Dodo was no longer paying any attention. He was now scuttering around on the ground looking for something. Hook shook his head in boiling anger as he saw the Dodo reach for a smoking pipe he found amongst the ashes and debris. But before the Dodo could bring the pipe to his beak, Hook slapped it right out of his hand.

"Well!" Shouted the Dodo in shock.

"I said, sir... The White Rabbit! Where- is- he- now?" Hook demanded.

The Dodo cowered under Hook's towering presence. "I believe he uttered something about a meeting with the Duchess," he replied timidly.

Hook nodded, relieved to be finally getting somewhere. "Ah, and just where can I find this Duchess?"

The Dodo struggled to remember, fearing what might happen to him should he fail to answer in time. "Uh... Uh... I believe that she resides through the Black Wood and beyond the Garden Choir."

Hook turned around to look upon the forest again with dread. A stressed huff of breath left him as he picked up a long piece of wood from the ground. Torching the tip of it with the flames that still roared upon the rabbit's house, he turned and set his first step upon the path that would lead him and Catcher back into the darkness. But before his shadow left the light behind him, he asked the Dodo bird one final question: "The monster you spoke of... was she killed in the fire?" The very question made it hurt to swallow.

"No... I fear she escaped the fire somehow," the Dodo replied, picking up his pipe back up from the ashes and placing it into his quivering mouth.

Hook said not another word but instead descended with Catcher back into the Black Wood with a nod and a smile upon his face.

CHAPTER THIRTEEN

CHANGES

"This way, miss," said the kind Four Leaf Clover, guiding Wendy out of the garden. She didn't think she could take much more of this. *Had she really been chased out of a garden by a bunch of flowers?* She wondered. But it wasn't just that they had thrown her out of the Garden Choir; it was their reason *why* that had upset her so.

Yet somehow, the flower's rude manner that had just exploded upon her felt so oddly familiar. The way their phony polite words covered the not so hidden whispers of hateful judgment; much like the fancy parties she and her brothers had so often had to endure for their parents. The women there; each dressed so lavish, wearing the most extravagant of jewelry and furs as if each were trying to exploit just how much money they had. They were always so polite, but never were they kind. It seemed that in a room full of grown-ups, children are often unnoticed or even forgotten. Forgetting, for example, who might be hearing or seeing your true colors. Sure, all the women were nice to their mother's face, complimenting her dress or rather taking the opportunity to brag about themselves, but when their mother turned her back, their eyes gazed upon her cruelly, and their words suddenly turned sour.

Wendy had never understood it. For it was all so unnecessary; so mean. And now she had experienced it for herself.

How odd it all was, and yet perfectly symmetrical to the real world; a garden of beautiful flowers, each so cruel and vain, while the rare and kind four-leaf clover was to remain hidden. She supposed it shouldn't matter that she had always been so kind to flowers, just as it never seemed to matter that her mother was always kind to others.

But why did women have to be that way? So conniving and hateful. Why? But just as her sore feelings began to settle, did her anger start to swell inside her as she remembered the flower's harsh words. All of them, pointing and shoving her away, calling her a 'weed'! "Rude flowers! Why, if I were my right size, I would go back and pluck every single one of them!" She scoffed, ringing out the water that they had dumped upon her new blonde hair.

But as she looked ahead, towards the opening in the grass, the strangest sight caught her eye. Floating high into the air were colored smoky letters. An '*E*' followed by an '*M*' and so on.

Wendy eagerly pressed forward, squeezing in between every piece of the tall standing grass, into the thick brush to follow the letters that continued to float by her. As she drew closer, she could suddenly hear something. It was a voice; a man's voice. He was singing. It was then that she realized that his song was his letters. Each and every one of them had been composed into the air.

How very curious.

The smoky letters now appeared bigger above her, letting her know that she was getting close; closer to whatever or whomever was singing the song of letters. Finally, she made her way into a small clearing. That's when she saw the most bizarre vision of everything she had seen here. Standing before her was a very large blue caterpillar.

He was sitting on top of a big mushroom. He had the strangest pipe that she had ever seen in all her life, yet as she drew closer, something about the purple smoke coming out of it felt familiar. *How can a world that is so odd be so familiar to me?* Strange as it all was, she couldn't help but notice that a certain calmness came over her as she stepped into the clearing of mushrooms.

The Blue Caterpillar hadn't even seen her; as he was on the tallest of the mushrooms and her being so very small. She felt mesmerized by it all. Her awkward stare quickly unnerved the singing creature. His eyes had barely set upon her before he spoke to her.

"Who are you?" He asked in the same monotone singing voice, with smoky letters expelling from his lips with every single word. In all honesty, it was a question she couldn't seem to answer.

"I hardly know, sir. I have changed so many times, you see?"

"I do not see," he interrupted, opening his smoky eyes wider to get a better glance upon her. Suddenly his entire demeanor changed drastically. For it had been some time since he had set his eyes upon a human. But it wasn't just the surprise that one could see in his eyes, but concern. "You must think, girl. Reach deep within yourself: Who- are- you?"

But she didn't know. She was sure she knew such an answer before, for it was but merely a name... her name. But she had all but forgotten it.

"I've changed so much since I've come here. I just don't know the things that I used to, yet there are somethings... other smaller things that I somehow do remember.

"Explain," he said plainly.

"Well, I'm afraid I cannot explain myself, for I am not myself. I try to remember, I truly do, but then it is as if my memories are disappearing."

"Recite," he demanded in what sounded like a professor's tone.

Rude as it may have been, she was only too eager to oblige:

"Oh, how does the little busy bee..."

"Stop! That is not spoken correctly." He rose higher as if preparing for a performance. He took a deep inhale and sang his next words:

> *"How doth the little crocodile*
> *Improve his shining tail*
> *And pour the waters of the Nile*
> *On every golden scale*
> *How cheerfully he seems to grin*
> *How neatly spreads his claws*
> *And welcomes little fishes in*
> *With gently smiling jaws."*

"The Crocodile. The purple vision of the creature sent Wendy's mind far away. Back to the Jolly Roger; back to what truly happened. Somehow, in a place where nothing seems to make sense, the odd

98

realm was causing the things that didn't make sense before to now make sense here. "Curiouser and curiouser," she said a little baffled.

Concerned she may be getting lost in thought; something the caterpillar knew full well to be especially dangerous, he spoke again: "Who- are- you?" He asked, blowing his letters of smoke into her face, causing her to cough. It was so much smoke, in fact, that when she opened her mouth to answer, a little puff of smoke came out.

"Well, I'm afraid I still do not know. Maybe it would help if you told me who *you* are first."

"Why?" He asked in a deep tone as a big letter, 'Y' came right towards her again. To be honest, he was right. She did not know at all how that might be helpful. Discouraged, she plopped herself down on a mushroom. Seeing her so dismayed, he spoke plainly, "I too, do not know my own name, my dear. Nor will you find any creature here who does. In this land, we are what we are. It is as simple as that. We all have lost all our once true identity. But as I look upon your human form, completely without any... how shall I say? Changes..."

"Changes? What do mean changes?" She asked, more intrigued than alarmed.

"Everything will change, my dear girl. It started the second you entered this land. It will be small things at first, of course. It is a sure way of making you doubt there is any cause of real harm, but with every step you take, and every food or drink that you consume, you will bring that the changes of this world are upon you- and they will not stop until *you* are not *you* at all anymore."

Now, Wendy was a little frightened. She quickly looked herself up and down, remembering how her appearance had changed when she fell down the rabbit hole. *Had more changed?* "But I do not want to change! What can I do to stop it? Please help me, sir?"

The Blue Caterpillar took pity on the poor girl; for while he may help her slow down the process as he had always done for himself, if she should fail to get out of this world... she would inevitably become a part of it. "It helps to recite, as I have already shown you. Speak of things you know, however little they may be. Remind yourself who you truly are, and maybe you can hold onto that person. But I fear you will find that you have many against you."

"Who?" She asked fearfully.

"Everything you see, everyone you will meet wants you to... *stay.* You see, to bring about the transformation, one must lose themselves in extreme emotion. The creatures that live here, the lights, the smells, the very ground you walk on, they will all try to get the better of you. And if they do..."

"But wait! What about you? How are you so..."

"Sane?"

"Well... to put it bluntly- yes."

"As you can see, despite my many extreme efforts of patience and separation from the *others*, I have significantly changed a great deal from who I once was. I used to sadly reflect upon my true appearance, but the mortal man as I so long ago appeared as- is now a mere void in my mind; a memory that I no longer have to endure when I sadly look upon my form now. There is but one difference between me and every other creature you will find here, young lady. Though I know not how, I have my own bit of magic that I brought into this world with me. I feel as though I must have been a traveler of such worlds before, though I could be completely wrong. All I do know is that as long as I have my magic, my thoughts will be clearer than those unfortunate souls around me."

"Could your magic help me?" She asked.

He looked back at her with a striking appearance, "You! Who-are-you?" He asked, blowing massive amounts of the colorful smoke in her face.

She coughed and coughed, gasping for air, but it felt as if it were suffocating her. Finally, she dropped down from the mushroom, escaping the smoky cloud and stormed off back through the tall grass, furious as his rude offense.

But she didn't get far before she heard him screaming out for her. "Wait! Girl! Come back! I have something important to say!" He shouted in a most urgent tone. She turned to see his blue head popping out above the grass, looking around for her. His eyes looked worried as they raced around, searching for her tiny body.

"Oh, dear. Though I think I should not return, for such terrible rudeness should not be excused, no matter what one has to say. Still, he did say it was important," she said, turning back. She began to walk back towards the clearing of mushrooms. "But I dare him to blow smoke into my face like that again."

When she reached the tallest mushroom, the caterpillar was still stretched as high as he could go, looking for her. She went to tap on one of his feet when she suddenly realized that he had tiny shoes upon each of them. She thought it silly at first, but then she remembered what he had told her, and she felt ashamed for giggling at his last shred of humanity.

"Hello, Mr. Caterpillar. I am down here," she said, anxious to hear what he was going to say next. As he looked down at her, there was an intensity in his eyes that made her nervous. "What did you want to say to me?"

He calmly sat back down, closed his eyes, and took another puff off of his giant hookah pipe. "Keep your temper," he said plainly with the smallest puff of smoke circling like a perfect design in the open air.

Though she was relieved that he didn't blow the

smoke in her face, she found his words agitating.

"Is that all?" Her voice couldn't hide her annoyance.

He smiled and opened his eyes again. "I apologize for my behavior just then, but you see... the magic I have, it is my smoke. Each puff gives my mind a fighting chance. Each puff helps my thoughts. Each puff helps me not get angry. So, you see, I was blowing my magic in your direction to help you think, though now I realize that I must not have made my good intentions clear."

But Wendy was now suddenly very quiet. *The magic smoke. The smoke that helped to calm the mind.* It was another small thing that now made sense in her head, and the memory was more important now to savor it than ever. "Yes, I have heard of your magic smoke. I have seen it used before by a tribe of Indians that were trapped in another world."

Now it was the caterpillar that was puzzled, "Indians, you say?"

"Yes." Wendy said feeling a little excited.

"Do you think that *I* may have been an Indian? Do you think that is how I came to have such magic of theirs?"

She could instantly see the hope she had sparked in him. "I fear I do not know. You may have, or maybe you just came upon the Indians during your travels as you said before." Her words were of little comfort as they lacked any of the certainty that he so desperately desired. She could see the anxiety building up in his eyes; so many emotions painted across them: sadness, loss, anger, confusion, regret, and more. She felt so sad for him. "Mr. Caterpillar, when I do get home, I promise that I will do all I can to find out who you really are and help you back to your one true self. There must be a way. I know it is hard, but we have to keep fighting. Don't let this place defeat you."

The saddened Blue Caterpillar gave her a crooked smile. "Poor child, you are kind to say such things to me, but I know much more about this place than you do. The truth is, there is only one way to leave this place." He let out a hopeless sigh that stole Wendy's breath.

"How?"

A chill crawled up his body as he said the dreaded words: "Tulgey Wood."

"Where is that?" She asked timidly.

"You do not want to go there, child. What this place does to the mind... well, let's just say there comes a time that one might lose the ability or will to keep fighting. Tulgey Wood is for those who need to make one more transition into the darkness; into the end."

Wendy suddenly felt like running away. *But how? The best thing to do was to find the White Rabbit again and follow him back to his rabbit hole.* She didn't know how she was to climb back out of it, but the rabbit could talk, so maybe since he almost burnt her alive, he would be willing to tell her how to get out of here. But she needed to hurry, and it would be impossible for her to find him at her current size.

She sighed sadly. "Well, I *am* going to get out of here. I escaped Neverland, and I *am* going to escape this curious place. I need to find the White Rabbit, but I cannot do so this way. How wretched it is to be just three inches high. It is just too small."

It was at this precise moment that the Caterpillar charged at her. "After everything I have told you, to say something so insensitive; so utterly heartless! I have been turned into a caterpillar that is exactly three inches high! Or did my height somehow escape your pretentious sight!" His anger seemed to swell inside him. He looked as if he were about to explode. All his thoughts of what he once was and his great loss had been followed up with such a harsh and insulting attack on his altered form, and it was just too much to bear.

He desperately reached down for his pipe and huffed upon it, rapidly breathing it in harder and harder. But it was no use; for as the smoke settled, you could see the angry caterpillar was there no longer. All that remained was his shoes upon the giant mushroom. The very last bit of his humanity had shed away. Wendy gasped in shock as shame and guilt crashed over her heart. *Where had he gone? Did he just disappear?*

"You there, girl, I am up here!" He shouted from high above. Wendy looked up in absolute relief to find that the Blue Caterpillar hadn't disappeared, but merely transformed into a very beautiful butterfly.

"Oh, thank goodness. I am so- so sorry, Mr. Caterpillar."

"I care not to hear your apologies! I just want to convey to you one more helpful hint. One side will help you grow smaller."

"The one side of what?" She urgently shouted, since it appeared as if he might just fly away at any second.

"While the other side will help you grow shorter!" He sounded so odd. His words were short and no longer carried the dignified tone of a man.

"The other side of what?" She shouted again, utterly confused.

But her confusion soon turned to fear as he began to charge at her angrily. He got right up in her face and hollered with his breath of hot fury. "The mushroom, of course!" His face was red with bloody rage. He seemed so different; so frightening.

She didn't know what to say next, but luckily, she didn't have to; for in the next moment, the newly transformed butterfly fluttered away into the sky, leaving her and his shoes behind. Sadly, his final words would likely be the only help she would have to get out of this place... out of this *Wonderland.*

CHAPTER FOURTEEN

WRITTEN ON THE TREES

In a world where a single step can take you from night into day, Wendy had found herself standing before a very defined line of one such division in the sky above her. She looked up to see the sun and a full moon perfectly mirrored on either side. Something about the sun scared her, but a tiny smile appeared on her face as the memory of all the stories she had told her brothers of the man on the moon flashed in her mind.

But no sooner had the thought entered her mind, did it start to fade away. She rubbed her temples in frustration. "Recite," she whispered to herself. But as she spoke the words of the Blue Caterpillar, the words of the Butterfly also returned to her.

One side will make you grow taller, and the other side will make you grow smaller.

"The mushroom," she said, quickly looking around at a plethora of them around her. Being so small, she climbed up on top of one the fresher ones. She took in a breath of courage as she scooped up two pieces of the mushroom from either side of her.

One side will make me grow taller, but which is which? For I fear if I were to shrink any smaller, I might just cease to exist altogether. "No!" She shouted to herself. "I mustn't think like that. For as the Caterpillar told me... there are already so many who are against me, so it stands to reason that if I am to get out of this place on my own, then I alone must try to outwit this bizarre world. And why not?! For I am clever, am I not? I have escaped another world before, have I not?" She spoke as if scolding the very air around her.

Nevertheless, her boost of self-confidence was enough to diminish the fear that had all but consumed her only moments ago. "I shall not take a bite at all, but rather just a lick. Yes! A lick should do well enough."

She closed her eyes and brought the piece of mushroom from her left hand to her mouth. She winced in unavoidable anxiety as she stuck out her tongue and took a lick.

Just as she had hoped, she sprouted up into the air at what she believed to be her normal height. She now stood above the grass and the gathering of mushrooms that she had been far beneath just a mere moment ago, now looked no bigger than her hand. With a delighted spring in her step, and courage in her spirited heart, she took the step that would take her from the sun shining day into the darkness of night; back to search for the White Rabbit that could help her get back home.

As she made her way into the strange forest, she noticed that though it was very dark like the other woods, there was something far more curious in these. The trees were all different colors; each one of the most vibrant shades of yellow, purple, blues, and greens surrounded her. But it wasn't just the trees themselves that were curiously odd in nature, but what the trees were covered with. The very sight of it sent cold chills up Wendy's spine. Signs, carvings and even small pieces of old fabric hung upon them.

The evidence of such desperate efforts of the former people that had come here had been left on the trees. More than most of the signs were merely broken pieces of wood with words of direction painted across them. Each had been nailed to the trees.

But every word that was painted was all total nonsense. Such chaos could never offer anyone any sort of course.

Wendy felt dizzy just looking at them. She looked on the ground, hoping to see some footprints other than her own, but there were none. She looked back up at the trees. *How old are these markings here?* She thought as she dragged her finger softly down upon some strange lines that were carved into the bark.

Then suddenly, something caught her eye. Along the scratches that were etched into the wood, she found a broken bloody fingernail. Wendy held it up between her fingers for a mere second before dropping it on the ground.

It was then that she saw the woods for what they were; a place where the poor souls of Wonderland had come, hoping to find a way out, only to find that they were completely and hopelessly lost. The idea of how many people had been here, lost and afraid, made her tremble. And if what the Blue Caterpillar had said was true, then *none* of these sad creatures ever made their way home.

They were all still here; creatures roaming this strange world utterly unaware of who they once were.

How absolutely tragic.

Suddenly, even the air filled Wendy with dread. It wasn't the darkness that bothered her; for she had never really been scared of the dark. In fact, try as she did to look back, she couldn't remember truly being afraid of anything. That is- until *he* came to her window.

But even now, as the memories of Peter Pan had become so vivid and clear, it was not fear that suffused her when she thought of him, but rather anger.

Why, if she could only see him now, she would happily slap that smug smile right off his face. With all her thoughts of spiteful rage coursing through her, she had somehow failed to notice that the once dark forest she was walking in- was *changing*.

But her thoughts were quickly raptured as an ominous song began to echo off the trees. *There is someone or something singing out here. But what? I see nothing.* No sooner had she thought it, did the trees around her start to light up. Not all at the same time, and not for very long at all. It became almost instantly apparent that it was the song itself that was lighting up the forest.

The voice that was singing was deep, yet it didn't seem to be alone. There was a burst of humming laughter that echoed through the air as a bell-like ringing brought about the most colorful of flashing lights upon the trees. One might have thought there were hundreds of children laughing throughout the shadows hidden by the trees. They were coming from every direction. Yet somehow, Wendy could tell that this was only one creature.

She tried to make out what the words to the gleeful creature's song were, but the deafening laughter buzzed inside her head. It just repeated, its volume growing louder and louder. She knew it was getting closer, and that in no time at all, it will have reached her. She wanted to run, but, where could she? She couldn't even manage to pinpoint where this *thing* was coming from.

Suddenly, she spotted tiny tracks on the ground, coming right towards her. She fearfully backed up to a massive tree that stood behind her. Her eyes widened as she realized that the moving tracks of pawed feet were coming from an invisible figure. Now she was alarmed. She was corned. Whatever this thing was, it would reach her in three steps... two steps... one step.

She closed her eyes, waiting for what tragic end that would inevitably fall upon her, but when the moment came, all she felt was the breeze of something flying right in front of her. It was the kind of feeling you get when someone throws something really close to your face. It didn't touch you, but you felt it.

She looked up in absolute awe to discover the invisible creature had reached one of the large branches above her. Then the creature emerged as the figure began to sing its song again:

> *"Twas brillig*
> *And the slithy toves*
> *Did gyre and gimble in the wabe*
> *All mimsy were the borogroves*
> *And the mome raths outgrabe."*

Two large round eyes, each brightly glowing yellow above an impossibly stretched grin of the whitest teeth she had ever seen in her entire life, appeared before her. "Lose something?" He asked. Something about the way it stared at her, felt both mesmerizing and unnerving, to say the least.

Finally, more pieces of its strange body emerged from the darkness; each one more slowly than the last. It was the shock that struck her sight first. "Oh, you are a cat!" She said, pointing up to it.

"Yes, a Cheshire Cat!" He replied, lifting his ears off of his head with his tail as if his ears were a hat. The act was enough to make her wonder who this creature once was; to have such a proper manner of introducing one's self.

"Second course...
'Twas brillig
And the slithy toves
Did gyre and gimble in the wabe
All mimsy were the borogroves
And the mome raths outgrabe."

She could see that something was off about him. Maybe it was his sinister laugh. Maybe it was his bright wicked smile. Perhaps it was his song or his body of vibrant magenta fur... No, it was something else about him- something *mad.*

CHAPTER FIFTEEN

A MAD FAIRY

After the manic cat sent Wendy off in a most dreadful direction, he lingered within the forest, waiting for the one who had been hidden to come into the light.

In spite of Tinker Bell's subtle spurts of interference in Wendy's journey, the Caterpillar's advice was most unfortunate to her cause. Her all too brilliant collaboration with the Cheshire Cat proved to be most frustrating indeed. For while Wonderland was full of mad creatures, it seemed that not even the fae are immune to its influence. Her hatred for Wendy had grown obsessive.

"Are you sure she will succumb?" Tinker Bell asked the vibrant cat.

He laughed at the little Green Fairy. "As I told the girl, it does not matter which way she goes... We're all mad here. The Mad Hatter and the March Hare will no doubt drive her mind into insanity. Even I dare not visit their parties; for I believe if I did, then I would disappear completely," he said chuckling wildly with his tongue hanging out of his mouth of glowing teeth.

Tinker Bell's face contorted with absolute revulsion. This was this kind of tit for tat that she found infuriating. Sure, Pan had his moments of questionable sanity, but he was also clever and brilliant. She missed him. It was a feeling that only stirred more hatred towards the girl responsible for everything she had lost.

It was all her fault! We would still be ruling Neverland stealing souls from the human world if it wasn't for her.

The Cheshire laughed harder as if he could hear her thoughts. "A mad fairy... how horrifying indeed."

Tinker Bell chimed harshly in reply to such a notion. She stuck out her finger to scold him, but he was already disappearing into the darkness— his echoing laughter surrounding her, making her writhe in anger.

When his mocking chuckles finally faded away, the only thing left in the air was her huffing breath of fury. She stomped her feet, but before she took off to check on the mental status of her foe, a sudden movement behind the trees alarmed her.

Her big green eyes widened as she flew over to investigate the suspicious sound, but as she gazed into the darkness between the trees, she saw that there was nothing there.

She shook her head. *I'm just on edge.*

She didn't waste another moment and flew away-to look in on the mad tea party of the Hatter and March Hare.

But the Green Fairy's all too eager flight would prove to be an unfortunate mistake as Hook and Catcher emerged out of the hidden darkness unseen.

"The Mad Hatter and March Hare, huh?... Well, boy, I fear the next path we take will be the hardest yet.

CHAPTER SIXTEEN

A CUP OF MADNESS

As Wendy came into the clearing, she heard a delightful tune of music coming from behind a funny looking house. Feeling both nervous and excited, she walked around the house to discover a path of large glowing stones leading towards a beautifully crafted gate that surrounded a wall of tall bushes. Clouds of steam filled the air, burning her eyes as she opened the small latch.

"Oh my," she said as she entered, now hearing two cheerful voices singing. Something about it all brought a smile to her face. Through the cloud of hot steam, she found an absurdly long wooden table that was painted in blotches of various pastel colors.

Wendy's eyes suddenly filled with wonder as she looked at what appeared to be at least fifty different chairs sitting around the table. They were each so elegant, colorful, and refined.

She couldn't decide which was her favorite. Then she spotted the perfect one. It was a very large, red velvet wing-back chair. Unable to resist its inviting appearance, she sat down. Sitting in it made her feel incredibly small and cozy. The moment of relaxation unfortunately wasn't going to last. The singing came to an end, and the steam cleared just enough for her to see who sat at the head of such a table.

She excitedly clapped her hands in applause to their song, though she hadn't really heard exactly what words they were singing. Suddenly, a tall brown rabbit and a man came running towards her, demanding that she get up.

"But I thought there was plenty of room," she said, feeling attacked and confused.

"Ah, but it is very rude to sit down when you haven't been invited," the formally dressed March Hare said.

"Very, very rude indeed," said the Hatter, though he hadn't yet shot her a single glance. Wendy couldn't help admiring the Hatter's odd clothes. They looked quite fun actually. He wore a hat that was far too big for his head and was covered in magnificent feathers, pins, bows, and buttons. His clothes were also quite striking, to say the least; with a long velvet jacket that was dark violet and unevenly stitched in bright green thread, and shiny golden buttons that were lined on the front and the very long sleeves. His face was lined from smiling, yet his eyes held a hidden sadness. He must have felt uneasy under her gawking stare since he awkwardly turned to look at her.

But no sooner had his eyes looked upon her, did his gaze elevate in astonishment. "Oh, my stars... Alice!" He shouted, grabbing her by the shoulders. "I cannot believe it. I found you... I mean, you found me."

Wendy was shocked. She didn't know what to say to him. Something in his eyes as he looked at her felt so endearing. "I am sorry, sir, but I am not Alice."

"Oh, yes, yes you are! I would know that precious face anywhere. Why, I believe you were wearing this exact dress the last time I laid my eyes on you. Oh.... My sweet daughter, how I've missed you."

"I am sorry again, sir, but I fear that you *are* mistaken. I am not your daughter, Alice."

"That ridiculous! Who are you then?" Said the March Hare. "If you look like an Alice, and you sound like an Alice, then what else could you be but an Alice?"

The Mad Hatter was gleaming with joy. "Oh, what a swell day this is!"

"Come, my dear, have a cup of tea." The Hare said. As she thought of how to answer, the March Hare was prancing about the table deciding which of the many designed teapots he was going to use.

Wendy looked at all of them. It was all so odd to have so many. Suddenly, she realized something. *The teapots! That's where the music is coming from.* The steam expelled from their spouts like a lovely inviting song- the birthday song — each bouncing in the air like an odd little dance.

"They're alive!" She exclaimed.

The Mad Hatter looked at the singing pots across the table as if her words had sparked his memory of them. "Oh, that's right! They are!" He shouted in realization.

Wendy thought it was odd to forget such a thing, but her confusion quickly turned to alarm as the March Hare began to laugh like a raving lunatic. "Well of course... They all had a seat at this very table before they changed."

Wendy looked around at all the empty chairs, and suddenly she wanted nothing more than to get up out of hers. "Well, you must excuse me; I didn't mean to interrupt your birthday party."

But before she could move an inch, the March Hare shoved a cup of hot tea right in front of her face. But in the span of a second, he quickly snatched it away. "My dear child! This is not a birthday party!" Snapped the tall rabbit.

Displeased with how the creature was speaking to his beloved daughter, the Hatter spoke to her kindly. "My sweet, this is an Unbirthday party."

"Unbirthday?"

The March Hare laughed wildly at her idiotic response. "She doesn't know what an Unbirthday is!" He announced, causing all of the teapots to spout huffing whistling laughter.

The Mad Hatter then shot the March Hare a scolding stare that silenced the rabbit instantly. "Then why don't you explain it to her, my friend," the Hatter said harshly.

The erratic rabbit smirked before taking a sip from the cup he had offered to Wendy only a moment before. "If you so insist," he chuckled smugly.

"I do!" The Mad Hatter replied.

Wendy eyed the both of them feeling awkward. The March Hare took another sip of tea before going on a very theatrical explanation. In the end, it was all very simple... Nonsense! But very simple. Every other day around your actual birthday is your Unbirthday. Wendy had to admit that it had a certain ring of fun to it.

"Well, then today is my Unbirthday too!" She shouted excitedly.

"It is?!" Screamed the March Hare. "Let us celebrate by drinking tea!" He poured her another hot cup while singing an Unbirthday song.

But again, the Hatter quickly took the cup away. "What a small world this is," The Hatter spoke quickly as if trying to distract his wild partner. Something about the scene seemed to weigh on her. The steam was so hot, and the scale of excitement from everything around her felt exhausting. She reached down for a cup to take a drink, but this time, it wasn't snatched from her hand. Instead, *she* was ripped from her chair.

"Move down! Move down. Move up the cup. Move down." They both sang as the Hatter escorted her urgently around the table to get away from the March Hare. But against his efforts, the rabbit simply followed, prancing about wildly.

Halfway around the table, they each sat in a new chair. The March Hare quickly poured yet another cup. His drinking now seemed obsessive, like his thirst couldn't be quenched. But it wasn't just him; for though she could see now that the Hatter tried to resist, he too couldn't stop drinking.

"Would you like more tea?" The Hare asked.

"Well, I haven't had any, so I cannot really have more," she replied, taking the cup that he offered. But before she could reach the hot tea to her mouth, the Hatter quickly filled the cup with a mountain of sugar that mounted all the way to her nose.

"One can always have more than nothing," he said happily as he dipped a tiny saucer into a cup like a biscuit and took a bite. His mouth quickly filled with blood. The warm crimson madness spilled from his lips completely unnoticed. Wendy's eyes filled with horror as he spoke: "Now tell me, sweet Alice... How ever did you find me?"

Wendy looked up at the giddy man with pity, unsure of what to say. "Well... I guess it all started when I was sitting in the gardens with my cat."

"Cat!" Screamed a tiny mouse that suddenly popped out of one of the teapots, in absolute fright.

"Oh, my goodness!" Wendy said, shocked.

"Stupid girl! Get the jam! The jam! Now!" Screamed the March Hare.

Wendy didn't have a moment to think. She jumped up and quickly raced through the dishes. When she finally spotted the purple jam, the Hatter screamed, "On his nose, Alice! Put it on his nose, quickly!"

Wendy obeyed without a single thought, wiping the jam on the small mouse's nose. To her great surprise and relief, the frantic creature calmed. In fact, the tiny animal relaxed a little too much. Its round eyes rolled back into his head, and its body that was covered in a tiny pink shirt, collapsed back into another teapot. The whole thing was very off-putting to her. "I wonder if that is how I looked when my parents gave me the *tea*."

"Tea!" Shouted the March Hare. Wendy gasped, realizing that she had spoken out loud. The Hare pulled out a large knife from what appeared to be out of nowhere and cut through a teacup like it was butter. "Just half a cup if you don't mind.

The Hatter was very eager to oblige, pouring the hot liquid into the broken cup. The tea managed to stay impossibly inside the cup until the rabbit brought it to his lips and drink it all away. Wendy could no longer hide how uncomfortable she was. Once the Hare had downed the broken cup, the Hatter once again sought his opportunity to speak with her privately.

"Now, my dear, as you were saying..." His voice was so kind and endearing that it somehow calmed her.

125

"Well, I was saying..." She paused, seeing the Hatter and Hare down another cup.

"Yes... Yes, my dear. Go on," the Hatter said, now sounding rather inebriated.

"Uh... I-- I was saying that I was sitting in the gardens with my..." She leaned over to whisper in the Hatter's ear, "my C- A- T."

"Tea!" Shouted the March Hare, this time cracking open a teapot and pouring its spilling contents into yet another cup for her. This time, Wendy just waited for the Hatter to take it away, but instead, he grabbed her by the hand and danced her around the table again.

"Move down. Move down. Move up the cup. Move down." The Hatter and Hare sang in perfect unison.

Wendy was getting more exhausted by the minute. By the next chair, she was ready to curl up and fall asleep. Her eyes had nearly closed, when she heard the Hatter suddenly scream into her ear, "Wait a minute! My Alice didn't have a..."

"Ut- ut- ut! The March Hare interrupted. "You know you can't say *what* you were about to say! Are you mad, Hatter?! The Hare slapped his forehead, "What am I saying... of course you are!" He shouted before laughing so hysterically that it was frightening.

Wendy's heart began to race as the rabbit fell off his chair with manic laughter.

"Alice?" The Hatter spoke with shiny bubbles spraying out of his mouth into the air with the odd scent of what smelled like perfume."

"Why do you think I am Alice?"

The Hatter chuckled, "Why do I think you are who you are? Is this some sort of riddle?"

The March Hare jumped back into his chair and grabbed another cup. After a very slow and calm sip, he reached under the table and grabbed a huge mallet. Wendy froze in terror as he looked at her with a murdering gaze. "I have an idea!" He smiled, raising the mallet above his head, ready to swing. "Let's change the subject!"

He took a deep breath, jumped on top of the table, and prepared to slam the mallet upon her tiny head. Wendy closed her eyes and screamed in horror. But the Hatter managed to jump in front of her just in time. The mallet came crashing down with enough power to bash his brains in.

Tears welled up in Wendy's eyes, believing he was dead. The March Hare laughed uncontrollably as she jumped up to run away, but the Mad Hatter's sudden voice made her stop dead in her tracks.

"Why is a raven like a writing desk?"

Wendy turned to see that the old man's massive hat had simply covered his head. "A riddle?" She said, her voice shallow with fear.

"Answer him!" The March Hare demanded.

Fearing what the psychotic rabbit might do next, she tried to think... "Why-- is a raven like a writing desk?"

"What?!" Screamed the Mad Hatter.

"Why is a raven like a writing desk?" She repeated.

At that, the March Hare jumped on top of the Hatter's back and ripped off his hat to reveal the man's fractured bleeding skull. Wendy screamed at the gory vision in absolute terror.

The shrill sound seemed to push the Hare over the edge. "Do you hear that, Hatter? She's stark raving mad!"

"But you just said..." Wendy pressed on.

"Here, girl, just have a nice cup of tea!" The March hare said, reaching a small cup out to her. All of the sudden, a flash of green light came out of the distance.

"Have a nice cup of tea, indeed!" She shouted, starting to feel her blood boiling within her. "Well I'm sorry, but I just haven't the time!"

Something about her sudden rage brought the Hatter out of his painful hysteria.

"The time! The time! Who has got the time!" The March Hare shouted into the air. All of the sudden, to Wendy's utter amazement, a small figure came running through the gate.

"I'm late! I'm late! For a very important date!"

It was in that moment that everyone at the tea party gasped, including the teapots themselves.

"The White Rabbit!"

CHAPTER SEVENTEEN

KILLING TIME

Memory might have been a fleeting luxury to those in
Wonderland, but all who lived there never forgot the
one who brought them to it. The White Rabbit worked
directly for the queen of the realm, and the fact that he
had made an appearance at the tea party was of no little
matter indeed.

The mere sight of him was enough to strike
Wendy with overwhelming delight, and all the
consuming curiosities of a child came crashing like a
wave over her again. Once the frantic White Rabbit
knew he had been spotted by his victim, he began to
run past the table, luring her out into the woods
beyond.

But it was not just any woods... he was taking her
to the Tulgey Wood. Tinker Bell watched anxiously
from the tallest tree that overlooked the tea party.

This was it... She needed Wendy to follow him.
Her anger had swelled beyond that of what she could

handle at this point. She felt as if she was about to explode.

This is all I need. As soon as I am rid of her... I will be rid of all this hatred- all this anger. Once she is destroyed, I can feel sane again. I will. I truly will.

Her thoughts stirred so violently within her that she immediately began to change color. Her once beautiful glow of emerald green was now as crimson as fresh blood.

Yes! Take her into the Wood! Take her! Take her now!

Suddenly, the White Rabbit was whipped backward by his large, golden pocket watch. The choking 'Yelp' of the rabbit was enough to break Wendy's all-consuming trance.

The Hatter forcefully yanked the creature close to his face and whispered harshly into his long ears, "I know why you are here, guardian, minion to the Red Queen, but heed my words... You have come for the wrong girl. Now hop away while still can; for you will not be taking *my daughter* with you."

The White Rabbit's eyes widened in complete shock. "How dare you! Unhand me, Hatter!" He demanded. "I have a very important audience with Her Majesty, and I am running very late! So, if you please..."

But against all efforts of the White Rabbit, the Hatter did not let go. Instead, he snatched the pocket watch clean out of the rabbit's grip and slammed it on the table before them. "Please, sir, desist. I'm late. I'm late! For a very important date!"

The Mad Hatter and the March Hare then exchanged a sinister smile. Their eyes lit up with psychotic mayhem, alarming both Wendy and the White Rabbit. The Hatter opened the watch and began to inspect it in the most absurd ways. "Well, of course, you are running late! Why, this watch is two days slow!"

"It is?" The White Rabbit asked with immediate concern.

"Yes, but worry not, for we will fix it right up!" Said the Hatter.

"Yes- Yes! The March Hare chuckled. "Fix it right up." His tone was bone chilling. Then it was nothing short of an all-out attack on the White Rabbit's golden watch. The March Hare jumped, clapping rapidly for such thrilling chaos. All Wendy could do was watch as the Hare raced around the long table, grabbing everything the Hatter called for or requested. But through it all... food, salt, and tea still proved to not be enough for him. So next, jelly, jam, and butter were added, but it *still* wasn't enough.

The manic laughter of the March Hare now felt like thunder in their ears as the destruction of the watch had turned into a murderous frenzy. Soon the innard pieces from the watch were flying into the air as the Mad Hatter ripped them out with a massive fork from the table. Tiny bits of metal, silver, springs, and screws went flying over their heads.

The White Rabbit watched in absolute horror as his most prized possession as well as his last, was destroyed by two madmen. Tears fell down his soft furry face as the March Hare called out for the last ingredient: "Mustard!"

Completely caught up in the madness, the Hatter almost obliged his friend's insane suggestion, but then suddenly he stopped... "Mustard! No! For that is just too silly! Don't you agree, guardian?" At that, the Hatter threw the porcelain jar of mustard right at the White Rabbit, splashing its ugly yellow contents all over his royal garments. And just when the White Rabbit thought the madness was over, the Hatter took up a giant lemon and squeezed all of its sour juice upon what little was left of the poor clock.

Then it was done.

The Hatter closed the watch and cut off all the trimmings. The White Rabbit and Wendy both let out a breath of relief.

Even Tinker Bell, who was off in distance watching, was happy that the mayhem was over. The anticipation of Wendy's doom had almost made her lose control. Every part of her wanted to fly down there and drag the girl out by her pretty blonde hair.

But in Wonderland, there were *rules.*

How dare the Mad Hatter interfere with my plans! Agh! Why, I would love to go down and fillet the wretched brat right there in front him. He believes that she is his daughter. How delightfully curious. Belief really is a most dangerous thing. Well, let him dare to test me like this again, and he will witness his beloved daughter die by a true fairy's wrath. As her fiery rage spilled out with such disdain, it was as if she had poisoned the very air around her.

The broken clock suddenly began to fly about the table, wildly ringing and snapping angrily.

"Bad watch! Bad watch! Bad watch!" The March Hare shouted frantically. The Hatter, Wendy, and the poor White Rabbit all clasped their hands over their mouths in utter shock. But the March Hare was quick on his feet, "There is only one way to deal with a bad watch!" The Hare reached back for his massive mallet and smashed the clock to smithereens.

A small sniffle and whimper could be heard from the White Rabbit in that moment.

"Two days slow... that's what it is," the Mad Hatter said, smugly sliding his art of destruction towards the White Rabbit.

"Oh, my poor watch," The White Rabbit sobbed over his loss, meanwhile the Hatter was looking around the table, keeping a watchful eye on both the Hare and Alice. The March Hare was still consumed with the excitement of chaos.

Chaos! What was chaos if not the perfect distraction. This was the Hatter's chance; his only chance to save his beloved Alice from the mad tea party. It didn't matter what magical influence there was about; for all of Wonderland knew of the White Rabbit's great love for his pocket watch.

In this moment, nothing else mattered to the small creature. "And it was an Unbirthday present too," the White Rabbit sniffled.

"It is!" Screamed the Hatter and Hare. "Well, in that case!" The March Hare and the Mad Hatter scooped up the White Rabbit and threw him far away into the darkness, singing all the while, "A very merry Unbirthday toooo you!"

Though the White Rabbit was now gone, the Hatter could still sense that something else was nearby.

And whatever it was, he was sure that it was who had brought the White Rabbit here.

The White Rabbit may be the guardian of the veil, and under the command of the Queen of Hearts, but until now, the White Rabbit had never interfered with another's domain. It was one of the unspoken rules of the land. And while the White Rabbit may be a frantic animal, he would never willingly break the rules of Wonderland.

Influence. That was the rule.

So, what was powerful enough to influence the guardian? And why was it after my dear Alice? The Hatter looked around, but he didn't see anything. Maybe the creature had gone after the White Rabbit, or maybe it was still here. His heart fell as he realized what he had to do. *I have to send her away. For such power could easily influence me or the Hare to do something terrible to her.*

No sooner had the thought entered his crazed mind, did the March Hare pick up a long blade from the table. Something in his eyes looked different. It wasn't just that they were murderous; they were focused. He slowly walked around the table, moving towards her, singing the words slowly.

"Move down. Move down." Slicing everything around him as he moved. "Move up the cup. Move down!" Reaching the end of the table, the March Hare stuck the blade into the table with full force.

The knife was stuck.

"Alice! Run to the left path beyond the gate! Only the left! Remember now! Go!" The Hatter's voice suddenly snapped her out of her state of panic, and without another word, she ran towards the pink gate beyond the tall bush.

But just as her hand touched the latch, she turned once more to find that the Mad Hatter and the March Hare had already returned to their song amongst the lively teapots; each singing the song of the dreaded Unbirthday.

CHAPTER EIGHTEEN

TULGEY WOOD

As Wendy reached the division of the seven winding roads, a sudden familiar chime rang in her ears, stopping her footing instantly. The sound made her heart race, and her mind panic. In yet another instance of fear and strange clarity, she knew exactly what and who that sound was, and it was one that she had hoped never to hear again... *Tinker Bell.* In a state of crippling fear, she turned and ran away down the road; the *wrong* road.

The chiming fury of the Mad Fairy was struck silent as the sudden laughter of the Cheshire Cat began to echo throughout the trees. Emerging from the darkness, revealed the glowing smile of the creature known as *the spying eyes of Wonderland.*

"Well that was entertaining, I must say," the Cheshire said, barely able to contain his malevolent laughter.

"How does she keep getting away? I cannot bear this any longer!" Tinker Bell said in desperate frustration.

"Come now, Mad Fairy, you mustn't lose your head!" He bellowed, twirling his own head like a ball in the air.

Her head... The Queen!

"I've got it! I no longer wish to take away her sanity; for I realize now that in my hatred for her, she is robbing me of my own. There is only one thing that can be done now... Wendy must die."

Her words surprised the glowing cat. "You forget, fairy, there is only one in this land that can take the life of another. The..."

"...Queen," she finished. "Exactly! Enough of this nonsense. Find the girl and get her to the Crimson Palace now!"

But the Cheshire Cat just laughed at such a demand. "I don't take orders from you!" He replied, unable to contain his manic laughter.

It was in that moment that something changed inside Tinker Bell. Maybe he had pushed her too far, maybe it was the idea of Wendy getting away again, or maybe it was the stirring thoughts of all the things she had lost had finally caused her to lose the most important thing of all... her mind.

Visions of all her adventures, all of her mistakes, and even Pan had become difficult to remember, but in this one moment... she not only remembered who she really was, she *embraced* the madness that had been itching to consume her.

She whipped out the very wand that she had stolen from the Blue Fairy on her last night in Neverland. The sight of such power immediately stunned the ever-vanishing creature.

The Cheshire Cat lifted his paws in defense. "Stop, fairy! You cannot do this. Even the charms of influence here have rules! We all must follow the rules!"

Tinker Bell bent her head back chiming with sinister laughter, "Haven't you heard... *I* don't follow the rules."

Zap!

But Wendy wasn't so easy to find. Not even for a pirate as skilled as Hook. He had looked throughout the darkness of the seven roads, but it soon became apparent that she hadn't gone down the right one. And every bizarre sight, sound, and the variety of tempting smells were all too enticing for Catcher to focus properly. Hook didn't blame him, but his frustration only grew with each lost step he took within the dark colorful woods.

But far beyond the longest road of brightly glowing trees, did Wendy see the one sign that would that made her weak in the knees. She had come to Tulgey Wood. The place that was in all manner '*the end of the road*' was marked by a yellow tree with vibrant leaves that hung sadly from its bright branches.

Wendy knew what it meant if she took the last step off the road, but as her sad eyes gazed about the darkness around her, she realized that she had nowhere else to go. She thought back to the Mad Hatter, and where he had told her to go. He had been so clear... "How could I have gotten it so wrong again? How did I get here? If I had just not left my window open... If I never put my brothers in any danger, lost my parents, traveled to worlds beyond all imagination- If I hadn't lost everything over the magical charms of one little boy... But I did. And every wrong turn I have made had led me here to this horrible place. Maybe it's no mistake that I stand here before this sign- *maybe* this is exactly where I deserve to be."

At that, Wendy took the first step off the road, and with each step forward, a glowing pink path appeared on the ground. Suddenly she could see other creatures wandering around the woods. They all looked so strange; each body part was odder and more vibrant than the last. But there was something about them; something different than the other bizarre creatures of this world... parts of them were *missing*.

Wendy's eyes circled around the wood in terror. To be in the midst of such intense suffering- such pain... it was all so overwhelming. Some were missing eyes, others their limbs. The ones that wanted to scream were the ones that couldn't make a sound.

Suddenly, the sound of a small horn stirred around her footing. She tried to watch her step but still managed to step on the tail of what appeared to be a tiny armless platypus that honked in a burst of anger and pain.

"Oh, I am sorry. Please forgive me." But it was no use. The creature continued to cry out in wailing honks until it ultimately trailed off, wandering into the distance of pitch black. Wendy tried to run after it, to make amends if she could, but once she entered the darkness, she saw no sight of the injured creature. But what made it worse somehow was the fact that she didn't hear the creature anymore either.

"Where did you go? Please come back and let me help you... Please," she said in a tone most desperate, but there was no answer, and suddenly the dark shade of silence had begun to crawl towards her. Frightened, she ran back towards the glowing path within the vibrant trees.

As she entered the center of everything so bright in the woods, she should have felt relief, but she didn't. All she could feel in that terrible moment was guilt. Not just for causing the creature to run away in pain, but also because she left the poor creature to the darkness out of fear.

A tear of great sorrow fell from her eye, but when she went to wipe it away, she found that a tiny creature of what appeared to be merely a pair of orange eyeglasses and two blue feet had sat upon her nose. She heard a nearby creature giggle at the silliness, but Wendy was in no playful mood. Unable to even crack the smallest of smiles, she took off the funny creature and put him down on the pink path. "No, I'm sorry. No more nonsense," she said glumly. The creature looked sad that she had denied him such joy, and somehow, the disappoint of the two round eyes that laid beyond the glasses had made her feel even more guilty. The guilt; it was getting heavier.

As she watched the other suffering beast of the Tulgey Woods, memories began to race through her mind. But they were all awful, and the images were all coming in too fast: every time her brothers had looked the other way, every time they denied her truth of what happened, the look on her parents faces as they restrained her on the bed as the doctor forced the foul tea down her throat...

"Stop it! Stop it!" Wendy shouted, squeezing her skull with her hands. And for a brief moment, the images in her head slowed to just one. At first, she couldn't make out what it was she was seeing. There was something whishing around her. Caressing her cheek with the scent of her formal home was sheer white curtains that floated into the air. And then there it was... the open window from the nursey where it all began. She screamed in terror. It was the one thing she swore she would never see again, but that's the trouble with memories. They can burn themselves into the mind to be never truly forgotten.

Wendy's heart raced wildly inside her chest. She tried to move, think, and scream, but nothing removed the image of the nursery window from her mind. And the longer she faced it, the closer to the window she became; ever closer to the stars. "No! No! He is coming to get me! He is coming to get me! Close the window! Close it! Lock it! Lock it forever!"

After so panic, her fear began to drain her. Her voice began to trail off whispering, "Lock it. Lock it. Please just lock it." Engulfed by her fear and sadness, a certain absence overtook her. The guilt, the fear, the loss, the loneliness... it had all become so heavy. Then as Wendy looked around at the other pathetic creatures of the Tulgey Woods, did she fully understand why creatures come to this place- because *this* was the place that would break you down until there was nothing left... and then- you just completely disappear. *There will be no more fighting, no more caring, and no more me.*

The darkness was coming in; she could feel it in her heart. Its powerful shade overpowering the brightness of the trees and all the creatures below, casting upon them the heaviest of burdening sorrow until they faded away into the darkness.

Wendy nodded and sat upon a large rock in the center of the last bit of neon glow. Sobbing tears fell, shining down upon her face. "If I die here, will I be forgotten?" She asked the darkness that surrounded her. She wiped her tears as if wanting to face her end with dignity. "Right. Right. I know you cannot answer me," she said to the darkness approaching. "Oh, well. I suppose it is of little matter now; for if I was being honest with myself, then I would have realized that the world already forgot about me a long time ago. And now, here in the world of Wonderland, I too have forgotten who I am. I am nothing," she whispered, closing her eyes, waiting for the darkness to consume her entirely and bring her the end.

Then suddenly, a familiar voice echoed through the darkness and a glowing smile that could shame the brightest moon, appeared in the trees. "And the mallrats... out grabe."

Wendy opened her eyes in a bit of shock, "Oh, Cheshire Cat, it's you!" She said in excited relief.

The magenta colored cat looked around her, seeing how close the girl had come to her end. He chuckled to himself; for while he was still under the control of the Mad Fairy's magic, he couldn't help but enjoy the delicious irony of the situation. For if the fairy had not cast him to forcefully interfere, then the lost girl would have died a mere moment later. Another chuckle tickled him as he spoke again. "Whatever are you doing out here? You won't find the White Rabbit in this place."

"Oh, no. That's not why I'm am--- erm I mean... I'm through with rabbits," she cried.

"But one does not come into Tulgey Woods because they are through with rabbits; they come through because they are through with everything. Are you?"

"Am I what?" She asked.

"Through with everything?"

Wendy thought on it for a moment, but no sooner had the words been said out loud, did she realize her answer. "No, I am not. I just wanted to find my way home but... I can't," she said, bursting into tears again.

But the Cheshire Cat just simply laughed again, "Well, of course, you can't find *your way* home. Everything in this world is always the *queen's way*," he said in a deep intimidating voice that frightened her to her very core.

"But I have never met any queen here." She said timidly.

"Oh, but there is... there is." The Cheshire said in a snarling tone. Little did Wendy know how forced his words had now become.

"Well, now that I think about it, I *did* hear the White Rabbit say he works for the queen. Maybe... I mean... If I could speak to her, then maybe she could help me get home."

The Cheshire Cat's wide smile glowed brightly with such anticipation. "What a marvelous word... *maybe*."

"Do you think the queen would help me? I mean, do you think she will like me?" Wendy asked, not noticing his menacing tone.

"Oh, yes!" He chuckled. "The queen will be absolutely *mad* about you!"

Wendy felt her nerves crawl under her skin as she asked her next question, "Which way is she? I don't think I can handle getting lost in this place again. Everything here is all just so uttering confusing."

The Cheshire Cat stood up excitedly, ready to point her in the right direction; for once he got rid of the girl, he would be one step closer to getting rid of the spell that the Mad Fairy had wrongfully cast upon him. "Well... I suppose that some go this way," he said, pointing his finger to the left. "And some go that way," he said, pointing his finger to the right. "But I, however, happen to know a *short* cut," he said arrogantly pulling on what appeared to be a lever that had only been a mere tree branch a moment ago.

Then a large opening within the thick bark of the tree suddenly appeared before her. The sunlight from the other side was so warm and inviting that it made her realize how cold the Tulgey Wood had been.

The green grass was trimmed to perfection. It smelt ever so fresh and danced with the wind so beautifully, that one could almost forget to look any further. But once your eyes did so dare look beyond, one could then only stare, for what surrounded the Crimson Palace was the most exquisite garden one could ever imagine. Roses the size of two human hands appeared both bold and beautiful upon the bushes that edged the enchanting castle above. Somehow as she was lost in her admiring state, she failed to notice that she had stepped beyond the opening tree and was now far away from the dreaded woods of disappearing creatures behind her.

Suddenly, she heard a man's voice, coming from the woods. He was shouting out a name, but before she had a moment to think or make out what the man was saying, the tree quickly closed back up. She looked down to the ground, wondering if she should try to open it up again, but then she shook her head, for she knew what to do. No longer would she be distracted by silly curiosities.

A smile appeared on her face as she gazed back up at the magnificent castle before her. She was nearly there. And maybe; just maybe... the Queen of this Wonderland would help get her back home.

CHAPTER NINETEEN

WHAT HAPPENED TO ALICE

Hook swung his arms, using all his force to try to break through the wooden barrier between them, but it was no use. Even with the slashes of his sharp blade, the secret portal to the Crimson Palace that Wendy had just crossed seemed to be closed to him. Having gotten so close to her, and failing, brought Hook's boiling anger even closer to the surface.

But even through his rage, Hook was quick to notice the chilling laughter that echoed through the trees. Like a bright crescent moon, the Cheshire Cat's smile emerged from the darkness above him. Catcher barked, howling in immediate aggression. Hook looked down to see that Catcher too, was showing all of *his* teeth... but it was not that of a smile at all.

Hook tried to calm his companion down, for he never seen him so violently out of control, but nothing worked. It was as if Catcher just simply couldn't hear or see anything beyond the black tunnel with the magenta cat laying arrogantly calm on the other end. Catcher charged at the tree, scratching and biting- taking only a second in between to bark again viciously. Suddenly the Cat waved his paw, instantly silencing the dog.

"What did you do?! What did you do to my dog?!" Hook shouted. But the Cheshire cat giggled at his anger. "Calm yourself, human. He is merely muted for the time being. Serves him right, you know. Honestly, if you could've heard the things, he was saying to me. Tisk... Tisk." Hook drew back his sword, ready to plunge it into the vanishing creature, but what the Cat said next- stopped him. "How interesting that girl is... It is no wonder how many admirers she has in this land. If you should want to find her in time... I would seek the others like you."

Hook was confused, "What others like me?"

"Like who?" The Cat said.

"Like me! You said to seek the others like me... Who are the others?"

"What others?" The Cat replied sheepishly.

Hook raised his sword to the animal in a temper, "I have no time for riddles, cat."

"Aw, that is indeed a great shame, for there are *others* that always make time for riddles." The Cheshire replied, chuckling as he gazed up through the trees behind him.

Hook followed his gaze back towards the division of seven roads, and it then as he remembered what the Mad Hatter had screamed out to her, that he suddenly understood what the Cheshire Cat was talking about. "Ahh, the *others*... You are speaking of the Mad Hatter and the March Hare from that insane tea party..." he said out loud, but as he turned to face the mischievous Cat again, he discovered that the mischievous creature had already begun to disappear back into the darkness of the Tulgey Woods. The last of the creature to fade was his bellowing laughter as Hook and Catcher made their way back... *back* to the dreaded Unbirthday celebration.

Hook may have failed to stop Wendy before the secret portal within the tree closed, but at least now he knew where she was going. The path back to the March Hare's house was easy enough to find... oddly easy. For unlike the rest of their strenuous journey, there was not a single thing to distract Catcher. There weren't odd noises or a twist of direction. There weren't funny looking creatures scurrying about, nor was there any strange odors to fill the air.

It was as if someone or something had made the rest of the odd little world beyond the path disappear. There was however one magical sensation that Hook recognized all too well, and it wasn't a welcome one at that... They were being watched.

And though Hook was no fool, the sudden waves of menacing laughter that guided them didn't leave a shadow of a doubt as to who this mysterious little helper was.

Hook didn't know why the Cheshire Cat was helping him, nor did he trust his help, but right now, in this second... his main concern was the madness that lay ahead.

As he approached the house, the steam that hovered over the garden gate made it increasingly difficult to breathe. Hook turned his head to take in one last clear breath before opening the latch. As he entered, he ordered that Catcher stay at his side for he had already seen the March Hare's homicidal games. The two insane figures were still singing their absurd song when he approached their table.

"Excuse me, gentlemen, could I have a word with you, please?" Hook said sternly.

The March Hare was the first to look up, curiously eyeing the uninvited stranger that was now standing at his table. It was then that Hook noticed how incredibly sad the Mad Hatter appeared. Sure, he was singing the words to their song, but his spirit seemed absent.

"I am here for Wen... I mean, for *Alice*," Hook said, quickly correcting himself for the sake of the Hatter.

The sad Hatter looked up pitifully, "Alice is... gone."

Hook nodded, "Yes, sir, I know, but I'm afraid she might be in trouble.

The Mad Hatter quickly stood up from the table. "What do you mean? What kind of trouble? I told her which way to go! I told her, right? I was so sure that I told her the right way... Where is she? Where is my Alice?" The Hatter pleaded.

Hook could see the man's tortured soul through his eyes. It was a sad sight to behold, but before he could say anything in reply, the March Hare jumped in.

"How rude you are
To interrupt our tea
Now go away
And let us be!"

His strange little song was made odder by the twirling dance he did along with it; kicking random objects off the long purple table high into the steamy air. Both the Hatter and Hook ducked as teapots, plates, and flatware flew towards them at high speed. This madness was infuriating to Hook. He didn't have the time for such crazy nonsense. After all, there was no guarantee that the Hatter was even going to really be able to help him. Maybe this was just a trick played on him by the Cheshire Cat.

He is probably getting a good laugh right about now. These two fools cannot help me. They cannot even help themselves. "Sorry to have bothered you, fine gentlemen. I will just find a way to the palace myself. Please forgive my intrusion."

But before he could take a single step away from the table, the Hatter rushed towards him, "Why do you ask for Alice and then speak of the palace? My Alice would never go there. No- No!... I told her the right way to go; to our hideout until I could come to collect her, and we could go home. Alice wants so badly to go home."

Hook smiled in compassion, "That's right; that is exactly what Alice wants. But I'm afraid if I cannot find her, then she will never be able to go home. Do you think that you can you help?"

"Help Alice? Of course, I will..." The Hatter replied rapidly.

"Do you know how to get to the palace then?"

"I dooooooo," said the excited Mad Hatter. "Come, I can show you the way."

Hook quickly took a step back, "Oh, I don't think that is such a good idea. I just thought if you could get me on the right path, then I could take it from there."

His words struck the Hatter with sudden anger and distrust. "Who are you to tell me that I cannot help finding my own daughter? I've lost her once, and I cannot... I mean, I *will not* go through that again! Now, I am going to the palace, and you, whoever you are... can come with me!"

Hook could see that there would be no changing his mind, but as it would seem, Hook wasn't the only one who didn't want the Hatter to go. The March Hare now appeared on the brink of a full-blown frenzy. His eyes went red, and his ears perked tightly. He crawled slowly towards them, frothing at the mouth. It suddenly became clear that the moment had brought him one step closer to becoming a wild animal.

"You wouldn't dare go anywhere without me!" He shouted to the Hatter. "You swore! After what I've done for you... You can never leave me!"

The Hatter quickly tried to calm the manic creature, but he was beyond words, and beyond all reason. "Jam! He needs the jam!" The Hatter shouted as he raced towards their table, but before he could get his hands on a single jar, the Hare tackled him on top the table.

The scuffle was short lived, however, for in that moment, a pistol fired in the air. Both the Hatter and Hare were instantly struck with fear as Hook brought the gun down and pointed it at the shaking rabbit. "Enough of this! I need to find the girl, and I need to find her now!"

Hook was ready to shoot the Hare. He was, after all, a serious threat to all those around him, and he had already witnessed the near murder of Wendy in one of the creature's earlier manic episodes.

"Please don't hurt him!" The Mad Hatter screamed in urgent haste! "Have mercy! He doesn't know what he is doing."

Hook wasn't amused, "Oh, doesn't he?!"

"No, no, you don't understand," the Hatter insisted.

"What is there to understand? He is a lunatic!"

"No, believe me, he was such a kind soul before we came to this land. He would have never hurt anyone. He was a gentleman; the kindest man I'd ever known. And I'm sad to say that it was his kind heart that got him stuck in this world with me. All of this is my fault!"

"How is all of this your fault?"

"Because he only came to this place to help me find Alice. We knew that she was in another world, but we didn't know which one and we both ended up here."

The Mad Hatter's words had stopped the March Hare. It was only for a second, but it was enough time for the Hatter to reach out a spoonful of jam. The Hare hesitated, but against all that raced through his chaotic mind, something in the Hatter's desperate eyes told him to open his mouth.

Once the Hare had swallowed the jam, he slumped, falling instantly sedated into one of the wing-back chairs that surrounded the long table.

The Hatter turned back to Hook with a tear in his eye, "Please, you can't hurt him... he's the only family I have left."

"Wait... family?"

The Hatter nodded, "He may be mad, but he's my brother. And he's right... I made him a promise. I cannot leave him behind. But we have to hurry, for I'm not sure how long the jam will last on a mind as far gone as his."

Hook nodded, but there was one burning question that still needed an answer. "I realize this may be a sensitive subject, but if you came here together, then *why* is he so much more..."

"-crazy! -I have wondered about that many times myself. I suppose it is because my sanity had more to fight for."

"And what was that?"

"...Alice." The Hatter's eyes looked off in the distance as if sorting through his clouded memory. Hook could see how hard it was for him; how hard it had always been.

"If you don't mind me asking... what exactly did happen to her? What happened to Alice?" Hook asked, putting his hand on the Mad Hatter's shoulder. "Do you remember?"

The Hatter chuckled at such a question. "It is the *only* thing I remember. I used to think it was out of love that I couldn't let it go; that remembering what happened that terrible day was..." The Hatter stopped, shaking his head as if suddenly lost in his train of thought.

"What?" Hook asked kindly.

"I was wrong. It's not out of love that the memory of my loss has replayed in my mind every agonizing minute of every day... but rather that it is what this world used to break me. Even so, it was the very thing that has kept me going," he chuckled lightly. "Not to say I'm not a *little* mad... I am a Hatter, after all."

159

"What happened to her?"

The Hatter let out a sad sigh as he began to answer: "My grandmother's house. I spent a great deal of time there growing up. It was very big, you see; perfect for running around as a child, but there was this *room*."

"What kind of room?"

"My grandmother always said that it was forbidden. She even tried to put locks on the door, but they never worked. All one had to do was put their hand on the door handle, and the door would open. I dared to enter the room once... and only once."

"What was in there?" Hook asked, overwhelmed with intrigue.

The Hatter's eyes twitched in pain as he tried to remember his terrible past. "There was a *wardrobe*. It was covered with a large sheet, as were each of the windows within the room. I remember the moment I heard something come from inside the wardrobe. I remember that there was something about the strange noise that scared me. Still, I couldn't help myself. I pulled off the sheet and uncovered the dark secret of my grandmother's home."

"What did it look like?"

"It was massive. I do not remember exactly how old I was back then, but I do remember that it towered over me.

"What happened then?"

"I could feel the chill of frost coming from inside of it. The smell of winter instantly filled the air. There was a large oval mirror on the front, big enough to reflect a grown man. I must admit that it looked incredibly ancient and beautiful. Still, there was an ominous aura that it radiated throughout the room. I should have run out of the room right away, but I couldn't resist looking at my reflection. When I say that I couldn't resist, I mean that I literally couldn't take my eyes off of the mirror. The odd thing was that I wasn't looking at myself at all. It was someone... I mean *something* else. Beyond any measure of self-control, I reached for the brass knob of the wooden door. I had almost pulled it open when my grandmother suddenly rushed in and grabbed me. I wasn't allowed back into her house after that, but years after she died, and my brother and I were the only ones in our family left... I went back."

"Why?"

A tear of guilt fell down his cheek as he answered, "Because it was Alice's birthday. She begged me to have a tea party with all her friends, but we were poor and had such a small home. I could see how

161

ashamed she was of it. Not that I blamed her really, I wasn't much of a skilled hatter, to tell the truth. But Alice, she was always so fond of the hats I made. She was very sweet that way, my daughter. She deserved so much more; she deserved better." It was in this moment of the Hatter's despair that he dropped his head.

Hook wasn't sure if he could continue with his dreadful tale. He patted the sobbing man's shoulder, urging him to continue: "Go on, Hatter. Tell me what happened."

The Hatter lifted his head and wiped his red eyes. "It was a week before her birthday when I got the deed to my grandmother's house. Alice had come home crying that very same day. The other children picked on her a lot, you see, because of me and the poor conditions we had to suffer. I couldn't afford to buy her pretty dresses or ribbons. She had only what I could afford, which wasn't very much at all, I'm afraid. When I went to hug her; to console her that day, she ran away from me. It was something that she had never done before. I decided right then and there what I was going to do. I told her that we were moving; that we would be going to a big house with *nice and fancy* things. I told her that she would never have to see those awful children again and that where we were going, she could invite every child in town to come to our house for her birthday. I promised to give her the best birthday party in the world. I sold my small home and used the money to buy all I could for the occasion. I bought her a pretty blue dress that made her eyes sparkle. I dusted off every trinket and treasure of my grandmother's as decoration for the party. Alice fell in love with all the teacups. She insisted that we lay them all out on the table," the Hatter chuckled for a mere moment before his smile fell again. "I guess... I guess I was just so caught up in it all... I loved seeing her so *happy*. I forgot to warn her about the wardrobe. When the kids arrived, they were all so different from the ones that we had lived around before. They were not only kind to Alice; they *envied* her. Watching them fawn over my daughter that day was one of the best moments of my life. Her smile. Her glow. She looked so beautiful. After the tea party was over, I brought out the most exquisite four-tiered birthday cake anyone has ever seen. Not to say that I made it myself, for in case you haven't notice... nothing I make could ever be considered as anything more than disastrous. But I did use the money I got from the house to hire the best baker in five towns. The girls loved it."

Hook smiled, "Sounds like a marvelous party."

"It was. I had never seen her look so happy in her whole life. She smiled at me before she blew her candles out. After they all ate their cake and drank their tea, they each ran off to play hide and seek in the house, but before she left, she hugged me. She said, "Thank you, Daddy." He sobbed in anger. "Do you believe that! She thanked me!"

"Oh my god," Hook whispered, reaching his hand over his mouth in affinity as the Hatter ended his sad tale.

"After that, she ran inside that big horrible house... and that was the last time I saw her." A sense of defeat hung in his tearful eyes then. It had suddenly become clear why the magic of Wonderland had given Wendy her new appearance. It wasn't just for the sake of Wendy losing herself; it was also for the sake of another occupant of this twisted world. It knew that the sight of her would confuse him, give him false hope, and ultimately, he would be forced to witness as the madness took over what he believed was his daughter's mind or worse... watch her die. The real suffering would be to have to endure not only that she doesn't remember who she truly is, but that she had no memory of him at all. And then, at the end of it all, he would have to lose her all over again, causing him to finally lose himself to the madness and wither away into the chaos like his brother before him.

Hook imagined what it must have been like for him. To see what fate awaited him through his brother. To see Alice and her not remember who he was. Hook couldn't imagine a worse torture, and he knew there was no greater harm than to try to convince him that his daughter is still missing; that *this girl* wasn't really her. But if Hook allowed the Hatter to believe that he saved her- from this land and this terrible fate, then maybe, he himself, could also be saved."

"My poor Alice. How could I have failed her again? I promised after her mother died that I would always protect her, but I just keep failing her. I really am the worst father," he sobbed, lifting a tiny teacup to his lips.

At that moment, Hook thought of Blackbeard. "You're not a bad father, Hatter," he said, putting down the man's teacup. "Sure, you lost her, but you have gone above and beyond to find her. You have breached the veils of other worlds and endured more magic than I can imagine. You have never given up hope, and now you are ready to risk your life to save her... Look at me, Hatter! You *are* a good father, and we are going to get Alice back."

CHAPTER TWENTY

A TALE OF TWO SISTERS

W endy had dreamt of fairy tales all her life, but never in her wildest dreams could she have imagined a more beautiful sight than the one that lay before her. A true smile appeared on her face as the cool spring breeze, caressed her skin, and lifted her long blonde hair behind her shoulders. At the center of a surrounding glade of evergreen trees and a hedge maze designed in the shape of a swirling heart, was what looked an enchanting cathedral, a mesmerizing castle of crimson stone and glittering glass.

As she set her eyes upon such a vision, she knew deep in her heart that she need never again seek the magic of love at first sight, for she had found it hidden beyond the darkness of Wonderland. With no fear left in her mind, she stepped in the labyrinth of red roses. The scent of the gorgeous flowers seemed to consume her with warmth and comfort. There was a reverent feeling about the garden of walled shrubbery.

The sound of trickling water nearby led her to a small pond. Unlike the rest of the maze, the pond was edged with all sorts of lovely flowers. As she looked down into its shallow brilliance, she could see bright, lively fish playing within the clear spring water. It was then that she suddenly heard a familiar voice behind her.

"They do look like they are having fun, don't they?" The voice said.

Wendy turned around, but she didn't see anyone. "Who said that?" She asked.

"Who? Whooooo are you?"

She quickly looked up, following the sound of the creature's voice, to find that it was a fluttering blue butterfly. She smiled happily, "Oh, Mr. Caterpillar... or should I say, Mr. Butterfly, I am so happy to see you here. It is such a lovely place, isn't it?"

"Well of course it is. It should be no wonder, child, that I am here; for do butterflies not love gardens?"

Wendy giggled at his words, "I suppose you are right."

"I do find myself wondering however what *you* are doing here," the Blue Butterfly said.

She looked around at her beautiful surroundings, "Oh, I had almost forgotten why I came here. I had hoped that the Queen would help me get back home."

The Butterfly said nothing to such a notion but merely fluttered his wings slowly in the air. His silence made her uneasy.

"What is she like, this Queen? Have you met her?" Wendy asked, nervously.

"I have not," he replied sternly. She looked down glumly just before he spoke again. "But... I have heard of her."

This time, she looked up at him with curiosity sparkling in her eyes, "Heard of her how?"

"I do not remember how or when, but through my many travels, my knowledge of the other worlds and who rules them became utterly vast. The tale of the Snow Queen and the Queen of Hearts is known to many across the ancient lands."

"Will you tell it to me, Mr. Caterpillar?... Oh, sorry. I meant to say butterf-"

"It is alright, child, for I still sometimes see myself that way. I was a caterpillar for such a long time; it is hard to truly feel different, despite my new form. But to answer your question, yes, I *will* tell you. Sit there upon the stone and listen to my cautionary tale. Wendy did as he said and sat herself down upon the largest stone next to the pond.

A moment of realization suddenly made her giggle. She was in a magical world, sitting next to the most enchanting of castles, ready to listen to a fairytale told by a Blue Butterfly. No one would ever believe such a story- but now at this moment, she also realized that she didn't care.

It *was* real. All of this had been.

She didn't need anyone to believe where she had been or what she had seen, because now she understood that she had become everything she had learned and more; that maybe it *was* okay that she didn't remember her true name, because she simply isn't that girl anymore. She wasn't sad, scared, or angry. She was just a young girl that was ready to hear a good story. Once she was entirely comfortable, the Blue Butterfly began:

"The tale of two sisters began in a tiny cottage in the faraway woods. The oldest of the two was Snow White and the youngest, Rose Red.

With pale skin, lavender eyes, and glittering silver hair, it was known to all that Snow White was more fair. Rose Red, unlike her sister, was dark haired. With amber eyes and sun-kissed skin, she did not appear as beautiful as her sister, but what she lacked in psychical beauty, she more than made up for in heart. Rose Red's kindness knew no bounds. Different as they were on the outside, the two girls were sisters, a tie shared by blood. The reason for their fame is simple... and one that would be remembered for all time."

"And what reason was that?"

The Blue Butterfly looked down at her with a grave expression. "Do not interrupt me, child. It is rude!"

"Oh," Wendy said, quickly putting her hand over her mouth.

The Butterfly grunted, turning his nose back up into his theatrical pose. "As I was saying... One night, a cursed bear came to their cottage, asking for some food and shelter. The girls agreed, and the bear came back for many nights. As time went on, they had all become quite good friends. Then when the bear suddenly quit coming back, the girls grew worried and went to go look for him. But to do so in the winter would have been impossible, so Snow White ordered her younger sister to use her powers to change the seasons early.

Though Rose Red knew it was wrong to disrupt the natural order of things, she too was concerned about their missing friend... so she did the unthinkable and changed the season. Many of the animals and magical creatures were shocked with such an abrupt change; Rose Red knew they had to hurry, since the change would soon affect the source of many creature's food and shelter. Crying with worry, Rose Red pleaded with her sister to change the forest back to its frosty state as soon as the bear was safely retrieved. Snow White agreed coldly, and the two sisters began their quick search through the woods.

After a couple days, the girls made their way into the center of the woods, they heard a horrific scream. When they rushed to see what it was, they discovered a dwarf hanging off a tree by his long beard.

He was screaming in anger, "Finally! Something sinister has happened out here! This tree sprouted up and snatched me up in its blasted grasp! I have been up here for two days! You must get me down! Get me down... now!"

But the fully blossomed tree limbs were too tight. Rose Red felt so guilty to have done this to him. "I am so sorry, Mr. I had no idea that when I did this, that..."

"Wait! *You* did this?!"

"Yes, but..."

"Stupid fairy! Stupid fairy! Get me down! Get me down from here now!" He bellowed in fury.

But against all their better efforts, the girls could only release him by cutting his long beard. Rose Red felt so badly for having caused him such dismay. When he got to the ground and felt his short beard, his eyes turned red, and his blood began to boil. His breath huffed strongly, as he reached into his boot to grab a small jagged blade.

"Wait! What are you doing?!" Asked Snow White in utter shock. But it was too late... the angry dwarf charged at Rose Red with his knife and proceeded to cut her hair and face."

"Oh, my goodness!" Wendy shouted in a loud gasp suffused with both shock and fear. Only this time, the Blue Butterfly did not feel the need to scold her for the interruption. Instead, a tiny crooked smile rose up upon his left cheek, pleased with his own dramatic performance. But he wasn't the only one enjoying himself, for Wendy too was on the edge of her seat excited to hear his next words. *How thrilling it all was to be the one listening to a good story for a change.*

To heart's delight and relief, the Blue Butterfly cleared his throat to speak again: "Yes, tragically, Rose Red's screams could be heard throughout the entire forest on that day. The cuts came quicker and slashed ever deeper with each blow that struck. The dwarf's rage was such that even he himself had been cut during the frenzy he had unleashed upon her.

Amongst the chaos, Rose Red cried out for Snow White to help her, but through the agony, and the blood that poured down her face, she could suddenly see her sister's face through her crimson covered eyes.

She had expected to find her sister fighting the dwarf; to be urgently racing to her aid, but as she gazed up at her sister, she found that she was still standing in the exact same place she was before the attack. But the worst was yet to come. There was no expression on her face; no fear, no worry, no urgency... nothing. She was merely watching the dwarf trying to kill her. "Sister! Help me! Please."

But when Snow White said nothing in return to her sister's desperate pleas, Rose Red had one remaining request left for her sister; that she honors her promise to return the forest back to its natural state. She knew that if the dwarf carried on for much longer, she would surely slip into the darkness of death. But just when the ground began to flood with the warmth of her blood, the dwarf suddenly turned around and began to make his way toward Snow White. It was in that moment, as the wintery sister screamed, that their friend, the massive bear, came racing through the bush of trees to her rescue.

The bear ripped the dwarf away from Snow White and threw him at a nearby tree with deadly force. The dwarf instantly became overwhelmed with fear, apologizing, and begging for the bear to spare his life. Rose Red too, pleaded mercy for the dwarf, insisting that forgiveness was the answer to all their problems. "Please do not kill him!" She screamed weakly.

But her words only made the giant bear grow more agitated. He growled and shouted at her in reply, "Rose Red, you do not know all that this evil creature has done. He is the one who stole all my treasures and riches. He is the one who used his magic to turn me into a bear, and then he captured me and locked me away in his cave, hidden deep within the forest. There I was, sleeping for days by ways of his dark magic. But after two days without any of his spells, I finally awoke. I escaped and found him here just in time. He would have killed Snow White, and I am going to make him pay!"

Rose Red had heard the terrible deeds of the dwarf, but the idea of death still seemed to be too horrifying for Rose Red to imagine, "No, please don't do this. Snow White, please... tell him not to do this.

It was then that Rose Red saw something in her sister's eyes. It was ominous and sinister. The bear turned to the frosty sister, waiting for her decision. "Snow White, give me your answer, and I will do whatever you say," the bear said.

Snow White looked at her troubled sister; at the desperation in her sobbing eyes. A thrilling calm came over her as she observed the blood that poured down from every gashed wound that the dwarf had carved into her sister's face. The crimson color of warm blood that shined like rubies drew a smile across Snow White's face. It was then in her second of everlasting pause, and transformation that she heard the final plea of the dwarf. Too bad that his interruption of her precious moment was a crime that she just couldn't forgive.

"Do it," Snow White said plainly.

The bear didn't hesitate. He did as she said and killed the dwarf right then and there. And as the diabolical creature drew his last breath, the bear realized that the curse that had been placed upon him could never be undone. His loyalty had cost him his true self, but something about those final moments had brought out the Winter Fairy's true self.

Though most would have imagined that the bear felt regretful, the truth was that his actions had brought out the savage animal within him. He had acted on his fierce protective impulses for her, and that is how he remains to this very day."

"But what about Rose Red?" Wendy asked.

"She cried and ran to the dwarf's aid, but by the time her weak body reached him, the life had already gone from his eyes. Even in her feeble state, she dug a grave for him and offered her forgiveness and blessings. Afterwards, however, when she and her sister got back to the cottage, Rose Red finally unleashed her own anger. "How could you do that? He died! He died at your will! It was all your decision and you killed him."

Suddenly, the smile on Snow White's face made it so clear. She not only had no remorse for what she had done; she was relishing in it. "Sister, you have no idea what that felt like; to have someone love you that much; to kill for you... That kind of devotion- it's just... it is absolutely incredible."

Rose Red was sickened by her every word. "You're a monster."

Snow White's face contorted with anger, shouting: "How dare you speak to me in that way. I will be your Queen one day."

"You will never be *my* Queen." Rose Red said.

Snow White's sinister laugh sent chills down Rose Red's spine. "Oh, my dear sister, one day you will learn... you should never challenge me, for it might be a lesson you do not survive."

From that day on, everything changed. It is said the girl's magic affected their hearts. Snow White's cold blood and hard heart made her cruel and unyielding. Rose Red, on the other hand, had a warm, comforting heart, much like the power that she held inside her. As the girls grew older, they both fell in love with the Prince, but despite Rose Red's kind soul, The Bear Prince could not resist Snow White's seducing charms; no one could. It was a fact that she seemed to find the most exhilarating. But it didn't end there. Snow White was not content just having won the only heart Rose Red had so desperately wanted, she also ordered his sister to marry the Prince's only brother, a tiny, little man named Basil. Their wedding was the laughing stock of many kingdoms near or far.

It was no mystery how unhappy the Rose Red was in her marriage. She tried on many occasions to escape the place of such ridicule, but every attempt ended in yet another betrayal; one including her own mother. Finally, Rose Red met a man name Draven, a commoner that agreed to help her leave the lands of her sister, and in their travels, they fell in love. They built a house on a hill, surrounded by gardens and animals, and for a while, they lived happily in peace. But then... when word of Rose Red's happiness got to Snow White, now known as the Snow Queen of her realm, she took it upon herself to find her long lost little sister.

The legendary day that everything turned to ice was the day that the Queen and her guards found that little house on the hill of theirs and destroyed everything Rose Red loved... everything except Draven, himself.

Snow White stood proudly amongst her destruction and demanded loudly: "You must bow to me, Sister. Bow to me and give up your power and you may live a long and happy life in my Citadel with your true love at your side. I will denounce your marriage, and you may marry whom you choose. All you have to do is accept me as your Queen."

But Rose Red knew the cost of her happiness, and what it would mean to give up her power. It would mean ending the lives of many animals and fish. It would disrupt the balance of nature for the sake of one Queen's power. All that was green, alive, and soulful would have to die for her to keep the one man she loved. In the end, Rose Red turned down her sister again, but she would have to pay the ultimate price.

After Rose Red denied Snow White her power, the Queen then used her strongest magic to make Draven break Rose Red's heart and leave with her instead as his new love and only heart's desire."

"Oh, my goodness! How dreadfully sad!" Wendy whispered, barely able to contain the tears in her watery eyes.

"Ah, but it wasn't over yet. Before Snow White left, she made one final offer to her dearly beloved sister."

"Fine, Sister, you may have kept your powers, but that is all you will have now. Because where I will send you is a world that will take away your very sanity. It will be a realm all your own. Do with it as you will. Alas, you won't be alone, for you shall take the husband you chose, Basil. He with you to be at your side. You will be adored by all who know you, but you will never have your happiness again... for I have that in *my* keeping."

The broken-hearted Rose Red was then sent to the mad world known as Wonderland to be the Red Queen. And that is the tale of the two sisters."

Wendy wiped the tears from her face. "That was such a sad story. Whatever happened to Rose Red's true love? Draven?"

"It is said the Snow Queen made him her slave, never to leave her side. Many have spotted him nearest to her throne as her most precious trophy."

"Oh my gosh, that's so awful."

"Yes, it is awful, but I tell you this very important tale for one very important reason."

"What is that?" She asked curiously.

"We all love our Queen, truly we do. But this place has a way of... well, let us just say it makes things a little more intense. The Queen expects certain things. Just do as she says! Exactly! Okay?"

Wendy wasn't sure what he meant by that, but she nodded. "Alright, Mr. Caterpillar, thank you."

"Y-O-U-? Whooooo are you?"

Wendy giggled lightly, "I'm afraid I still do not know who I once was, but I am starting to understand who I am now."

The Blue Butterfly smiled at her with a gentle nod. "Don't forget your mushrooms," he said before flying away into the crisp, clean air.

CHAPTER TWENTY-ONE

THE QUEEN OF HEARTS

As Wendy made her way through the labyrinth of roses, Hook and Catcher were following the mad brothers to the crossroads of the seven roads.

"Are you sure you know where you are going?" Hook asked, unable to shake his reluctance.

The Hatter turned to him with a crafty smile, "Of course, we do. We have been in Wonderland for a long time."

Hook nodded, "So... everyone in Wonderland has been to the palace?"

The Hatter and Hare looked at each other, "Well, the ones that last have," the Hare said.

"Oh, I see. But you two... you have-?"

"-met the queen? Yes, we have!" The Hatter and Hare said in unison.

"What of the king?" Hook asked.

The Hare laughed wildly, "What of the king!? He is nothing but a tiny little weasel! But our queen... she is the true ruler of this land! We love our queen!"

The Hatter nodded rapidly.

Hook was a little stunned to see such devotion. "I'm sorry. I am a little confused. You love your queen, yet you fear her meeting your young Alice... why?"

The Hatter's happy expression fell as he answered, "Because Alice wants to leave Wonderland and because our beloved queen demands unyielding devotion from all her subjects."

Hook squinted his eyes in confusion, "I don't understand. You behaved as if she were in danger."

The March Hare snickered at the pirate, but the Mad Hatter nodded, "You see, when Alice tells Her Majesty that she wants to leave this land and return home, our queen will see it as an act of betrayal."

"What will happen then?" Hook asked.

The Hatter and Hare looked to Hook, but didn't dare answer, for to think of such a fate was far too horrifying to say out loud.

Wendy had gone far, moving ever closer to the Crimson Palace that was covered in the most vibrant of green ivy. It seemed that with every step she made, the more enchantingly beautiful the castle was. It was as if she were looking at the very art of mother nature herself. For the closer she came to the queen's castle, everything became more alive; more pure; happier. Suddenly, there were all of these elegant creatures, both animal and floral, appearing in front of her. There was one creature, however, that struck her eye; one that set its glowing yellow eyes upon her. It was a magnificent red fox.

Wendy couldn't help but feel infatuated under its bewitching charm. Its golden, amber coat surrounded its underbelly of soft white fur, and the black edges of its nose, eyes, and pointed ears seemed to be the very outline of its magical appearance. When the creature fled through the maze, Wendy knew it meant for her to follow it. And so, she did. She raced through the labyrinth, behind every turn and hedge, until something else caught her eye. There were three men in the form of playing cards standing before her, urgently working on a certain hedge within the garden.

Wendy could see the panic in their every expression, but as she stepped closer to see what was the matter with them, she was stunned to find that the cards were painting the hedge's roses- *red.*

"Oh, my," she said, surprising the group. Unsure of who stood behind them, they all froze and wept.

"We are so sorry! It was a dreadful mistake!

You have to believe us three!
We didn't mean to plant white roses
upon this rose bush tree."

Wendy shook her head and hands, "Oh, no! You need not fear me! I just stopped to see what was wrong."

"If it is true, we need not fear you
That you just stopped to see
Then please, young girl, pick up the paint
And help us dreaded three."

"But they are just roses, why do you all fret in such a way?"

"Don't you know who rules this land?
The beloved Queen of Hearts
If she should see white upon this tree
She'll rip our heads apart."

Wendy gasped with her hands on her neck and said, "You mean that she will..."

They all nodded in unison.

"She will shout her demand
To cut off our heads
And by the end of the day

We all three will be dead."

Wendy's eyes went wide as the dreaded three continued.

"Please, young child
We need all the help we can get
And if we should succeed
We will all be in your debt."

She felt unsure, but something about the desperation in their eyes told her to pick up the paint. And before she knew it, she was helping the group of cards paint the white roses *red*. Though the dreaded three raced urgently, there was for her, a spirit of fun in it somehow. That is until they heard the sound of a marching army coming towards them.

Wendy peeked over the hedges to discover a vast army of red playing cards coming through the massive maze of roses. As they came closer, she couldn't help but notice that the cards that were coming from all directions wore but one suit... the red hearts. This was especially odd because the dreaded three that were franticly painting next to her were wearing *black* suits of diamond, spade, and club. And now they were all racing around her, trying to get rid of the evidence. Yet, it was no use.

185

Yep, they were caught red handed.

The paint was all over them, and yet they had failed to cover the last remaining white rose on the hedge. The cards fell to the ground weeping. Suddenly, Wendy noticed she was the only one left with a paint brush in her hand as the queen's army came in through the clearing. One by one, the formation divided until there was, but one figure left. Wendy quickly dropped with the others, pleading for mercy as the figure emerged out of the shadows into the light of day.

Suffused with unbearable curiosity, Wendy opened her eyes and poked her head up... and it was in that very moment that two rows of red cards raised their horns and announced the arrival of none other than Her Majesty herself, the Queen of Hearts.

It was a moment that Wendy would never forget; the very first time she saw the queen. She was absolutely striking. There was no other word for it. But it was not her natural features that made it so, but rather everything else. Her hair was long and exceptionally dark. Each strand appeared like black silk, was decorated in wild fashion with golden flowers placed ever so perfectly within her twirling curls. Upon her head lay a radiant crown of rubies and gold. She kept her face painted brightly; with white for her skin, pink for her cheeks, tiny red jewels glittered on her lips, and possessed the longest eye lashes that Wendy had ever seen. There were two tiny red hearts that were painted on either side of her amber eyes. Her dress was glamorous, with four different shades of red, and black and white lace, designed like the trees of a swirling forest going up to her corset of red jeweled beads; each stitched into a pattern of roses that covered her all over. But what Wendy liked about her most of all was her wings. They didn't look like a fairy's, though she understood that's exactly what she was. They were down and tightly wrapped up, and yet one couldn't help but notice their magnificence. Wendy could see their animal likeness. Being brown and white, they appeared like a hawk's wings. They were absolutely incredible, just as everything else about her was.

Finally, the queen turned the corner, and as she did, she found the cards and Wendy laying on the ground. She immediately seemed to understand that Wendy was not responsible for this heinous act against her. Nevertheless, she slowly made her way to the dripping rose bush. No sooner had her eyes set upon the white roses, did her blood began to boil. With massive power and extraordinary strength, she ripped the tree from its very roots and waved the bush in a scolding manner.

"Who has been painting my roses red?!" She screamed, frightening everyone around her. Immediately, the dreaded three began pinning the blame on each other; each ready to put their friend's head on the chopping block. The queen listened to their lies with amusement, barely able to contain her laughter.

"Enough!" She demanded, silencing all around her. "That is quite enough. You three, stand up!"

"Us three, Your Majesty?" The black cards wept.

"Don't act like knaves! Of course, I mean *you three!* Stand up, this instant!" She shouted.

It was then that the three sobbing cards pulled themselves up to their feet. A rush of empathy came over Wendy as she heard each of their knees knocking in fear, trying not to buckle.

"Now, you all know the laws in this realm... And I ask for so very little. All I ask is for your loyalty, your honesty. So, when I find that there are those in my midst that have betrayed me..."

"But please, my queen
We did not mean
To upset you thus."

"I say again, you traitors, you have broken my most absolute law! And there will be no mercy for you... none at *all!*"

"But we dreaded three meant well
Though you may not now see

188

We tried to fix our grave mistake
That is planted on that tree."

"Silence, you- *spies*! I know who you truly are and what you meant to do! You have been sneaking about my kingdom, thinking that I would never discover; that I, the Queen of Hearts, would never know. But when you planted that tree, my roses revealed where your hearts truly lie. It is written on you as plain as a card, wearing the black and white color like the very evil you serve. For if you were truly mine, *red* would be your only suit. Alas, you serve my most hated enemy! You came into my kingdom and tried to deceive me! But where you have failed, others will learn..." Then the angered queen turned to her men and announced loud and clear, "Off with their heads!"

The red cards did as they were told and dragged the treacherous three off to their fate. Wendy laid frozen in fear, not knowing what she should say or do.

But the queen bent down and gave her a smile, "You need not fear me, little child. My darling fox already spoke to me of your arrival. I know that you had nothing to do with the black suit's betrayal. Though given your participation, I feel I should tell you that I do not tolerate my subjects helping traitors."

Wendy gulped a breath of fear, "I- erm... I am- I did not..."

The queen quickly snapped her fingers and shook her head, "Stop mumbling, child. It is not very becoming of a young lady to speak so poorly. Now I have already told you that you have nothing to fear. So, if you wish to speak to me, you should do so properly. Come now, lift up your chin and look me in the eye. Line up your toes and start with a curtsey. Open your mouth a little wider, speak loud and clear, and remember, you must always address me as, "Your Majesty."

Wendy nodded politely, hearing the faint sound of the Blue Butterflies' words: *Do what she says... exactly and oh so precisely!*"

So, she smiled and bowed as a little girl should, but as she opened her mouth, the Red Queen spoke instead: "Tell me, child. Do you play croquet?"

Wendy was stunned by such a random inquiry. "Well, I... I mean yes, Your Majesty, but I..."

"Wonderful! Then we shall play it now!" The Red Queen shouted in a domineering tone.

Wendy gathered her courage and spoke urgent and clear, "But, Your Majesty, I was hoping that you might help me find my way..."

The Red Queen turned with a face most intimidating, "Your way?! This is *my* land! Always, it's *my way!*" Her powerful voice nearly knocked Wendy off her feet.

"Of course, Your Majesty. Forgive me," Wendy said timidly.

The Red Queen smiled at her sweetness. "No matter, child. Let us forget it and play a quick game. It puts me in great spirits to play in my garden. As to your mysterious request, you may ask it of me when we arrive at my palace... I mean, after the game, of course. Do you agree?"

Wendy did not know what to say, so she just simply nodded and said, "Yes... Thank you, Your Majesty."

CHAPTER TWENTY-TWO

A CHESHIRE GAME

Wendy had not only always been fond of games; she was also quite good at them. Yet, for the life of her, she could not remember playing a single one. As the Queen's men scurried around, setting up the oddest of croquet equipment. For Wendy, her body moved as if there were some sort of understanding within her that she herself could not control, and though the Red Queen had called the game *croquet*, Wendy found her version of the game to be most curious.

The red cards spread out to be the hoops upon the fresh green grass. Instead of two mallets, the queen and Wendy were each given a flamingo. One was purple and the other was yellow; each came along with colored hedgehogs to match.

The Red Queen was, of course, the first to take a turn. She gently scooped up her yellow creatures, and after a small sweet kiss and a pat on the head, she placed the yellow hedgehog on the ground. As the Queen of Hearts assumed the position, Wendy's eyes couldn't escape the gazing awe from all that stood around her. There was no denying their unshakeable love and devotion for Her Majesty.

Suddenly, a tiny little man with a red robe and a golden crown came running into the garden, silencing every creature and card. His face appeared kind and child-like. His voice was small and meek. He wore a long brown wig in the French fashion, and even wore the same extreme make up upon his face that the queen herself wore. It didn't make sense to Wendy. Nothing about their relationship did. The queen was tall and exotically beautiful. The king, however, was exceptionally tiny, and plain. They were different in every way possible, and yet it seemed that the tiny king had found a way to mirror his love for her, even by means of altering his appearance.

Once all was settled for the game, all in the enchanted garden eagerly watched their queen take her first swing. When the yellow flamingo hit the hedgehog, Wendy was stunned to see how far the creature and the hooped cards would go to make their beloved queen happy.

The hedgehog rolled every which way in order to get through the correct series of hoops and hit the peg at a very quick pace. The incredible amount of cheating was enough that it left Wendy's jaw dropped, but as she looked around, she found that there were no other stunned faces, but rather just the sound of the crowd clapping, showering the queen with roaring praise.

"Well, this game is off to a great start." Wendy uttered under her breath. "Great start."

Meanwhile, Hook and the mad brothers were drawing even closer to the magnificent garden themselves. The journey between the three had been going smoothly, that is until the group suddenly came upon the faint sound of whispers. One of the voices, however, Hook knew all too well.

"Your treacherous efforts still fail you, Mad Fairy. For the girl has already softened the queen and is playing a friendly game of croquet at this very moment. It is a game, I find, that puts Her Majesty in the best of moods. I dare say that in the end, the queen may even want to help the child... just as so many others here have."

Hook and the others quietly peeked their heads through the bushes to find two shadowed figured hidden in the shaded darkness of the trees. The pitch-black air that surrounded the two was pierced brightly by the Cheshire's glowing smile.

"Do not celebrate so soon, cat! I still have power over you," the other voice said.

The Cheshire's smile slowly fell, "What will you have me do?"

"You say that Her Majesty is playing a game of croquet with the girl... Let us see what happens when the game is turned up a few notches." Tinker Bell then whipped out the blue wand, and with a zap of its power, she screamed loud and true:

"Hear my words and do my will
Drive her mad and make her kill.
Go to the garden
where they play croquet
make her lose
in a wretched way.
Humiliate the Queen
Make her cut off her head
And come collect me
When the girl is dead."

The Cheshire's full form did then appear. With a subtle laugh, the cat bowed to the Mad Fairy.

"Why do you laugh creature?" Tinker Bell asked in anger.

"I will go to the garden and do as you say, but all will go against you. For much like the girl, we are now not alone. My only regret is that I won't see your fall."

It was at that precise moment that Catcher barked at the sight of his fully emerged form. Tinker

Bell turned in fright, stunned and afraid. "That dog...
No! It can't be! That cannot be his. I would have
known if he were here," she said, turning back to the
Cheshire, but he had already begun to disappear, by the
very power she had unleashed upon him.

"You should not be so deceived by my
appearance, Tinker Bell. For somewhere deep down,
you know who I *truly* am."

Her eyes widened as the whisper fell from her
tiny lips, "Hook." She shook her head, unsure of
herself. "No, that is impossible, we left you for dead."

Hook laughed at her words, "A mistake I fear
nor you or your former master can remedy now, for I
am very much alive and have come to take the girl."

Still reluctant to believe what she saw with her
eyes; she couldn't fathom such an oversight. "This must
be trick, by the cat or this land, but it couldn't be you."

"My form was changed by magic, not uncommon
for this place, though I find you yourself have very
much changed."

She buzzed in anger, glowing bright red, "You
lie! I have not changed! Not at all!" She screamed.

Hook chuckled out loud, amused with her
tantrum. He could see now why the cat had called her

196

the Mad Fairy, and that like every other creature of this land, she was ever so desperately trying to hold on to her true self. "Well, my dear, though you still hold your homicidal charm and beauty, it appears that in this world, you now speak with words instead of those god-awful bells."

Tinker Bell looked as if she had just been shot. *How could she not have noticed such a thing? Was he right, had other parts of her changed?* She wondered.

"I would not fret over such an improvement, for I found your previous ways of communication to be all but excruciating. Not that it matters, for it all ends right here. So, say goodbye and your prayers however you please, but be sure to be quick, for I fear this place has stripped me of what all patience I had. Worry not, fairy, for it will be quick and beyond all your deserving."

As he raised his blade, fear and confusion suffused the green fairy, and she quickly tried to fly, but suddenly she was struck- frozen still in the air. Hook ran towards her with his sharp blade ready to strike her heart, but a sudden voice stopped him with a blast of blue light.

"Stop!"

With his hand shading his eyes, Hook could see it was her... his beloved Ainsel had come to them all. It wasn't in body but in power and magic. Like a glittering ghost, she towered like stars over the colored trees. The Hatter and Hare gazed awestruck at her presence, as did the green fairy.

"No, that is not possible! You could not truly be here!" The Mad Fairy screamed.

All of the sudden, a blue mist of diamonds came in through the darkness, wrapping its power around the Mad Fairy. Though both Hook and Tinker Bell took a second to figure out what was going on, they did know exactly who was responsible.

Ainsel.

The Blue Fairy's sparkling form lit up the dark forest at that moment, pointing to the very wand that the Green Fairy had taken from her.

Hook wondered at her power, "My love, I don't understand. Is this a trick, or are you truly here?"

She turned, smiling at him, "Yes, and no. My body is not in this world, but rather by magic... By my own heart, I am so happy to see you, James."

Tinker Bell chimed in anger, squirming to escape the Blue Fairy's power, but it was no use. She could not move.

"It was my wand that called for me. The power she wielded to cast such magic is what brought me here."

"I must destroy her, Ainsel. For even if we do escape this Wonderland, she will never stop seeking Wendy's end. This madness will only end with the death of one or the other. I can feel the influence of this land inside me, and I will surely starve if I do not leave soon. I have chased after Wendy across this dark place and have endured the most maddening of creatures. And it is all this fairy's doing!"

"No, James," Ainsel said plainly.

Hook shook his head with frustration, "After all she has put us through... she *deserves* to die!"

Ainsel raised her hand to silence him, "I agree with you, James, but not like this. There are rules for my kind, though I find it difficult myself to stay true to them when the fairy in question has spent all her years breaking them and taking no responsibility for the consequences of her bad decisions. Nevertheless, I shall take her before the Grand Elders to await their final judgement of her dark, withered soul. No doubt their sentence for her heinous crimes of treachery will be swift and severe. I promise you; she will never hurt another soul again."

The Mad Fairy chimed in laughter, "You can never destroy me! Not completely! Not you! Not Hook! Not Wendy! And not even the Grand Elders! So, take me to them if that is what you wish. I will be glad to leave this wretched place... but I promise you both this here and now that no matter what you do, or where I go, as long as the Wendy girl lives, she will never truly be rid of me."

"What! What do you mean?" Hook said furiously.

Another chime rang into his ear as she answered, "My body may be destroyed, maybe even my magic, but I *will* live on through another."

"-Wendy..." Hook whispered quietly into the air.

Tinker Bell smiled smugly, "That's right."

"How?" Hook growled.

"I'll be hidden in her mind; in the place where she holds her darkest nightmares. And just as she has made me suffer, so too shall she. And just as I failed to get rid of her, she too will never be rid of me. Let her feel safe in the days of the sun and let her feel the warmth of family and love again. But once she drifts off into the land of dreaded sleep, that's where I will be waiting for her. When she speaks of the malicious creature that haunts her darkest nightmares... just know that it is me. And if she should ever think me real or dare I say... *believe* in me. Then on that day, when she speaks the words, by the power of magic, I will be born again! Mark my words, here and now, this is not the end for me. Wendy will be my beginning, and I will be her end."

Hook stepped towards her, "Well, that's *not* going to happen," he said in a near growling tone.

Tinker Bell chimed in sinister glee. "Oh, fear not, pirate, for it will not be today, may not be tomorrow, but someday, a long time from now... Wendy will meet her fate, and it will be a death beyond even Peter Pan's imagination. I will be her end! You can be sure of that! You cannot save her from me! Not today! Not ever!"

The March Hare and Mad Hatter looked at each other, curiously, "I seriously do not have the faintest idea of what she is talking about," said the Hare.

"Neither do I, but I am sure glad they are not talking about Alice." Said the Hatter.

Before Tinker Bell could chide them, the stolen wand that she had stolen, suddenly floated away to its true master, the Blue Fairy. Ainsel flicked her wand, causing an invisible twine to tightly wrap around the Mad Fairy, making her completely unable to move as

Ainsel sent her through the portal, where she would be sent before the Grand Elders to meet her true death.

Once Tinker Bell was gone, Ainsel started to fade away.

"No, Ainsel, wait! There is so much..." Hook desperately called out to her.

Again, Ainsel rose her hand to silence him, "You have done wonderfully, darling, and I know you will succeed. I shall see you again soon, my love. *Very soon.*"

Back at the garden where the Queen of Hearts and Wendy played, all was going well, leaving laughter and joy to the day. Though it was easy to see that the creatures were in favor of their beloved queen, Wendy too found herself eager to make her happy.

For when the Red Queen was happy, her smile was enchanting. She glided like an angel across the fresh green grass with the long train of her dress behind her. Her royal stature could be seen by the very way she carried herself so. To be around, her grace and charm were to feel truly honored to be in her presence.

Wendy was truly having a wonderful time... so wonderful in fact, that the idea of leaving Her Majesty, just to go home to a place of rejection and ridicule- seemed absolutely ludicrous.

The Red Queen was winning, to everyone's joy and excitement, and Wendy loved listening to the queen talking. It was strange, somehow. She felt drawn to the Queen, but not just for the same reason as everyone else. It was something more than that-something familiar. It was as if someone had taken the kind heart and compassion from her mother and the unyielding temper from her father and put it inside one person... that person would be the Queen of Hearts. For much like her father, even in his worst moments, he still knew compassion and fairness.

Yes, there was something about the queen that made one never want to be without her, or worse... never want to displease her.

It was the queen's turn again, and as she stood in form; a sudden figure started to emerge from on top of her back. Wendy gasped in shock when his form took color. The bright magenta fur shined beneath the sun.

Seeing him again reminded her of the Tulgey Wood. He reminded her of the feelings she had prior to seeing the palace. He reminded her of what it felt like to be completely and utterly hopeless. His visage made her blood boil in anger, as if he was the very symbol of all the dark things in Wonderland, when in fact, that is exactly what he was.

"So how are you getting along?" The Cheshire asked.

Wendy turned away from him, crossing her arms in temper.

"You are not getting along then? Is the game not fun?" He spoke from on top the queen's back, yet the words could only magically be heard by her ears. "You know what would make this game more fun? If we got her really angry!... Should we try?"

Now Wendy faced him in fright, "No! No!"

The Red Queen turned around quickly, "No what, child?"

Wendy curtsied again before speaking, "I apologize, Your Majesty; for I was not yelling at you, but rather at the cat on your back!"

"A cat?" The queen screamed before quickly looking behind her... But there was *nothing* there. The sneaky creature had rapidly disappeared. The crowds laughed. Her blushing face heated, feeling very foolish. As the queen looked to Wendy for blame, the Cheshire suddenly appeared again.

"Oh, look! There he is now! He is sitting upon your head!" Wendy shouted.

The Red Queen urgently reached up, but again... there was no cat there. She started to squirm, racing around trying to find this elusive creature, but there was simply nothing there. The crowd laughed harder, falling to the ground holding their bellies. Shame and embarrassment completely suffused the queen at that moment. Such public ridicule reminded her of being in her sister's kingdom.

Such horrible humiliation had brought the Queen of Hearts to her boiling point. It was then that she charged at Wendy, holding up her yellow flamingo in a scolding manner. "Now I warn you, child. If I lose my temper... you lose your head. Do not make a mockery of my kingdom, my subjects, and above all, don't you dare attempt to make a fool out of me! Do you understand?" She asked sternly, with her amber eyes glowing with fury.

Wendy bowed all the way down to her knees, begging, "But, Your Majesty, I didn't..."

"Stop! If there is one thing I cannot abide or forgive, it is a direct lie to my face. For it not only implies that you think me a fool, but that you do not respect me enough to be honest and truthful. So, I say again... Do you understand me?"

Wendy nodded with a single tear falling from her big blue eyes, "Yes, of course, Your Majesty, I understand.

The queen scoffed, turning back towards the game, making the entire garden silent. Each subject was eager to watch the queen's next turn that had been so rudely interrupted before. But as the queen bent down once more, the Cheshire Cat appeared again with a smirk.

"You know we *could* make her really, really angry. What good fun it shall be," he chuckled as the queen drew back her flamingo to take her next shot. The Cheshire then quickly appeared on the ground, moving the curved beak of the bird under the queen's extravagant dress. "This ought to do it. Don't you think?" The Cheshire's voice echoed in her ears.

This time Wendy screamed, rushing to the queen's aid, but it was too late. When she pulled up the giant bird to swing, she tripped on her dress and fell face

first on the ground, leaving only her undergarments for all to see.

There was no denying it; the entire palace had seen the great fall. Wendy froze in fear, holding her hands over her eyes, hoping maybe if she couldn't see the catastrophe in front of her, then maybe she could pretend that it didn't really happen. It proved to be the typical hopeless wish of a child as all of the queen's guards, the White Rabbit, and even the Tiny King came rushing in to protect her dignity.

But there was something about all of their faces that disturbed her greatly. They appeared as if they were surrounding a volcano, knowing full well that it was about to erupt and could quickly kill all of them.

And it was from that very volcano, that a bellowing voice did roar... saying: "Somebody's head is going to roll for this!"

Then *boom!* The queen's power of fury exploded, spreading her large falcon wings, throwing everyone and everything around her far into the air. Wendy fearfully lowered her hands from her eyes and took a deep breath, but when she opened them, she found herself face to face with the raging Queen of Hearts.

The queen rose her bejeweled hand and pointed her finger... "Yours!"

CHAPTER TWENTY-THREE

THE DUCHESS

The Red Queen's rage terrified every inch of Wendy's being. Tears welled up in her eyes as the queen demanded her death. "Your Majesty, please. I would never seek your displeasure or disgrace. It was the Cheshire cat that shamed you so, not I! Please I beg of you... believe me!" Wendy cried, but the Red Queen sneered at her plea.

"Foolish girl, you lie again! The Cheshire Cat may be a mischievous being, and a naughty creature beyond even my control, but he would never dare to cross me in such a dishonorable way as this. If I were not already having you beheaded for the crimes you have bestowed upon me and my palace, I would have you poisoned for spreading such a wretched accusation!"

Wendy trembled like a child caught in a blizzard of crushing fear. Sharp burning tears fell freely down her dainty face. With her very last breath of bravery, she spoke in the whisper of her known truth, "You're wrong, Your Majesty. My words are not lies. It was the Cheshire Cat that wronged you, not I. So, you see, my *Queen*... it is *your* accusations that are false."

The Red Queen bent down towards her closely. Her makeup of white paint dripped down her face of sweating anger, revealing the legendary scars from the dwarf's jagged blade that carved into her beautiful skin. The past marks of what her unfaltering mercy had brought her all those years ago, appeared before Wendy's very eyes. "How... how dare you speak to me like that! Off with you! Off with your head!" The queen bellowed loudly for all to hear.

The cards quickly rushed upon Wendy, grabbing her by both her arms, when suddenly a tiny arm reached from behind the queen, pulling on her rubied gown.

"My dear! My dear!" Said the Tiny King.

"What?!" She asked harshly, annoyed at his sudden interference.

"My dear, I say, something is not right. I fear there may be more to this that you think..."

"What are you talking about?" She asked, rolling her eyes.

"What I am saying, my beloved, is that there has been another crime afoot!"

"Another crime? What? Where?" She asked feeling overwhelmed.

The Tiny King timidly cleared his throat to answer: "Well, my dear, your *tarts* have been stolen!"

The Red Queen's arms shook in fury, now glaring at Wendy with a murderous rage. "This is all *your* doing!"

But the Tiny King yelped in interruption, pulling on her gown once again, "But, my dear, the girl has been here in our sight all this time."

"Well then, tell me, *husband*, who else could have done this?!"

"Well, actually... the guards say the culprit is..."

"Is who... you say? Speak up!"

"Uh, they say that it was the Cheshire Cat, my dear. Many say they saw him with their own eyes. I dare to say that I even saw him myself. And you know, my love, that I would never lie to you; not for anyone or anything in all the worlds."

What he said, she knew was true. He had never betrayed her. And though she did not truly love him, he had remained ever loyal at her side. She took a deep breath, calming her heart, "But you cannot deny that this child's actions have been more than suspicious from the start. I cannot shake this feeling that she is tied to this somehow. She may not be guilty, but I doubt her innocence as well…"

"That let us have a trial, my dear. That would be the proper thing to do."

She huffed in surrender; for she knew that he was right. "Very well then. Have the Duchess escort her to the Mock Turtle until all is prepared."

The Tiny King looked up at her confused, "The Mock Turtle? Why?"

"Because I still do not trust her, and I will not risk another mishap, not for me or my land. He will keep his eyes on her, however tearful they may be, and I will come collect her once the trial is ready to commence. Have my cards gather a jury, witnesses and everything else I will need to judge her case. I will sentence her myself; may the gods have mercy on her soul."

"But, Your Majesty, the Duchess herself is still imprisoned on your orders."

The Red Queen scoffed in reply, "Yes, but surely the pepper has worn off by now. She should be just fine. Now, do as I say! I am in no mood for any more arguments!"

At that, the Tiny King rushed off to do as Her Majesty commanded. For he had learned many years ago that when his wife was in one of her foul moods, no head was safe... not even the king's.

Just as the Red Queen had believed, the Duchess was indeed in whatever normal state she could manage after the pepper. Once the cards informed the Duchess of her new charge, the reluctant lady approached, ready to escort the young girl suspected of treachery. She took Wendy to a hidden path behind the Crimson Palace that appeared to be leading to a distant cliff overlooking an endless ocean. With each step they took towards its rocky edge, something about the splashing sounds of the sea on the other side made fearful tears well in Wendy's eyes. When the Duchess saw her crying, she stopped to console her. "Little girl, do not weep for the sea... For it has plenty of water already."

Wendy couldn't help but smile at her silly words. "I am not weeping for the sea, but rather for the sea of emotions that swell inside of me. I swear to you, though I fear it does not matter now, that I did not mean to offend Her Majesty. In fact, it was only in her presence that I was able to escape the many horrors of this land."

The Duchess chuckled, "This land is not so bad. Much like everything in life, once you accept something for what it is... it tends not to bother you as much."

Wendy stopped and looked at her with complete disagreement, "I have been to Tulgey Wood, and I must say... that is *not* what I saw," she sobbed, remembering their faces as they disappeared into the nothingness. "I just do not understand. The queen is so lovely, and though it may sound strange coming from someone on trial, I believe that all her subjects truly love her. And even now as I am likely to die at her will, I too still feel love for her. The Blue Butterfly told me of Her Majesty's tragic past. Rose Red, whoever she once was... if she is still inside of Her Majesty somewhere, I do not understand how such a kind soul could deliver such a horrible fate upon all of those in her realm. Those who hold nothing if not complete love and devotion for Her Majesty. And even now, though I am innocent, she wills my death."

The Duchess placed her hand upon the girl's shoulder. "My dear, the power of Wonderland has been here long before our beloved Queen of Hearts came to rule this land. True, the many forms in which the creatures of this realm change, have much to do with Her Majesty's own design."

"But why?" Wendy asked sadly.

"Well, my child, while most of magical beings hate humans, Her Majesty can hardly bare the sight of one. For even her most generous Majesty can see that it is only animals... nature- that is honest and true in heart. Nature does not deceive or act out of malicious or evil intent. People by name, think themselves better: individuals. When in fact at the root of their soul; they are all the same: ambitious, devious, self-serving, and despite being given any sort of kindness, one could expect something of untoward cruelty to fall upon them in return. With nature it simply is not so. For if you speak kind words to water, does it not crystalize with enchanting beauty. If you speak lovely compliments to the grass or even a flower, does it not grow and bloom with more vibrant joy. Trees, flowers, creatures and more have no individual name, for they are what they are. Without an individual name, nothing is then set above others. The water here is clean and clear. Some have even spoken about its healing powers. Nature has a lot to offer, but... *mortals* know nothing but destruction. The Red Queen knows of the lands magic; if one should choose to let go of their previous devious heart, like *that of a human*, then they can live as happily as this strange world will allow and *she* will help you make it so.

But those who fight it... those who cannot let go of the person they once were will continue to change until there is nothing left to change into. But it is not so with everyone here. Surely, you have met those who carry with them a certain amount of acceptance or maybe even joy?"

Wendy thought back to the garden choir, the odd twins, the sailor dodo, and even the mad tea party, though it was hard to imagine that was a happy occasion, she realized nevertheless that the Duchess was right; there *were* indeed some in this land that were quite content as they were.

"I know that to ask every person to shed every ounce of their humanity upon their very arrival is wishful thinking indeed, but if one should let who they once were completely go away, then it is then up to nature- magical or not to decide their fate. The power that maddens the living here, is not caused by Her Majesty. In fact, it is a power so strong, that she finds herself fighting its influence every day. We should all be so grateful to have a queen with such a kind soul, for I dare not think what might have happened if someone else held the crown. Wonderland may be dark- *scary* even, but imagine what it would be like without the heart of Rose Red. Believe me, she does not mean to be so cruel, it is not in her nature, but the fact is..."

"-What?" Wendy asked curiously.

"Well the fact is... you are *human* and therefor against all the kindness the queen herself possesses; she cannot see beyond what you are. She believes you to be treacherous, evil, and a danger to her and her kingdom.

She can see into many hearts, but when she looks inside a human- all she sees is a black heart, brought on by their sins against others, goodness, nature, and even themselves. If you know the old tale of the two sisters as well as you say, then you know what was done to her and all that she has lost. She has suffered in a most wretched way and has done so much for all of those that need her. For without her, there would be no spring or summer... and let us never forget that it was a sacrifice that will torture her eternally. So, for every creature or mortal that admires the sight of a freshly blossomed flower or feels the warmth from the great sun upon their skin... remember that it is *all* because of her! The Red Queen's heart broke so that others could live. She has never sought praise, worship, or any token of appreciation. She did not even seek her throne, but if one should dare to cross her and burden her tortured heart again... then that one shall die, but those that transform into flowers, animals, and so fourth- are not unhappy. For to her, they have had their wickedness stripped away from them and given an entire new life under the rule of the most beloved queen in all the realms. So, as I said before, if you have become an enemy of Her Majesty, then I am afraid there is little you can do to prove it... After all, she would never believe a human over a creature of Wonderland."

The sound of the sea crashing against the craggy cliffs were getting louder now. They were getting close. *I wonder how many worry when they are being taken to a cliff- that they are going to be pushed off.* Wendy

216

wondered to herself. *I know it is a morbid curiosity, but certainly a reasonable one. After all, it would be just the two of us and after how many times my life was in peril in... Neverland.* Suddenly all the attempts on her life came rushing back into her mind: the murderous mermaids, the soulless lost boys, and of course, the murderous pixie- Tinker Bell. They had all wanted her dead and had nearly succeeded if it had not been for- Captain Hook.

Somehow, in that moment, her entire adventure in Wonderland felt no more than a silly place. Sure, there were parts that were scary, but as the clarity of all she had endured in this world and the next, she suddenly realized how truly awful Neverland was, and how lucky she and her brothers were to have escaped the lost island... for something inside her told her that they were the only ones that ever had. She dared not think about where Peter Pan was now, or if Captain Hook and the Blue Fairy survived that horrible day. Another heavy tear fell as she remembered hearing the crunching and screaming of Hook under the jaws of the massive crocodile. To think him alive was maybe just another impossible wish from the mind of a silly little girl, but... she wished for it anyways. She gazed up at the sunlit sky. There were no stars in sight, but she nevertheless prayed and whispered from her the very depth of her soul that Captain Hook, his nice doctor, Smee, the sweet dog that had licked her face once, and the Blue Fairy who had so desperately tried to save them- were all alive and well. She wished harder than she ever had before and hoped that maybe- just *maybe...* someone out there could hear her desperate plea.

As they drew nearer to the rocky cliffs, Wendy could feel the inevitable farewell between her and the Duchess. A sudden urgency suffused her, making her tiny feet stop abruptly.

"What is it, child? Why have you stopped?" The Duchess asked.

Pleading hope sparkled in Wendy's eyes in that moment, "Wait! Duchess, there must be hope for me, for while I may be human- so *too* are you. Please excuse me for saying so, but I have not seen any signs of you transforming into an animal like the rest of this realm. You are no flower, no animal, nor a card. You are human! Yet you say you have survived the powers of Wonderland a long time. How?"

The Duchess nodded, "It is true, I am human. I was brought here out of kindness of the Red Queen's heart. For in her generosity, she permitted the Tiny King's request to have me brought here with them. Out of her graciousness towards him, she granted his request to bring me, the king's own cousin, to her court. The Tiny King and I grew up together. All throughout the many kingdoms, many teased him. It was always something and it was always awful, as I am sure you yourself remember from the legendary tale, though that shines only a flicker of light upon what Basil went through his whole life. So, cruel they all were... but not me. I was never so. I stood up for him, even when doing so often got myself punished. I was his friend; his only in the entire world, and I suppose that is why he asked Her Majesty if I might come into this world with them. The queen has used her powers with great effort to keep me in proper stability, both in body and mind. Even so, the power of the realm itself has compromised my life. Why, even my own baby turned into in a pig during a screaming tantrum. In this world, the madness *will* find you... It always does."

"I have thought myself mad before, but now that I am free from the ones that drove me to it, I would do anything not to return to such a living nightmare. What can I do? You must know a way to help me! You must!" Wendy cried, hugging the Duchess tightly.

The Duchess smiled and patted her on the back. "Just focus on what you can remember... anything at all. Believe me, it helps! And I find that keeping yourself busy, distracts the mind. If your mind is too busy doing other things, I find there is not much room for things like madness. I myself prefer to cook!

"I cook until my kitchen
has dishes from the floor to the ceiling.
Then I throw them all away and
start again from the beginning.
Many have said

that the pepper makes me mad,
so much like today,
the Red Queen put me away
but when I get home
To keep my mind at bay
I'll get busy cooking
To keep the madness far away."

The Duchess looked up and took a deep whiff of the salty sea air. "It is just a few more steps now. If I were to embark a last few words of advice, it would be this. If this world senses your fear, it will make you its prey. If you wish to keep your head clear from your crippling panic, then I suggest you listen to the Mock Turtle's history. It is quite a lot to take in, believe me. I doubt you will have room to think of much else, but if you should still have such space in that feverish mind of yours, then you should then speak with the Gryphon. He will dance and sing... you need just to follow along. Do you understand me, child?" The Duchess asked sweetly with her hands caressing Wendy's cheeks.

Wendy nodded with a gentle smile. "Alright. I shall try."

"Good, girl. Now, go. They will be just at the top of the cliff there. You are on your own now but worry not... for the Queen of Hearts is a fair and just ruler, and I have faith that even with her damaged mind, she will not put you to death. The Red Queen will come collect you whenever the court is ready for your trial to begin. Good luck, dearest child. I truly wish you all the very best."

Wendy hugged her again, before taking the last few steps up to the steep cliffs, where she would meet the Mock Turtle and the dancing Gryphon.

CHAPTER TWENTY-FIVE
AN AUDIENCE WITH HER MAJESTY

As the Hatter and Hare approached the only other clearing to the Crimson Palace, the twitching Hare showed all signs of having returned to his unnatural state of hysteria. For the journey had taken some time, and in that time... the jam that had calmed the manic rabbit down back at the house had all but vanished. The Hatter and Hook quickened their pace, but the mere sight of the beautiful palace covered in ivy and flowers made it almost impossible to keep the March Hare's mind at bay.

Even the Hatter, without even a sip of tea, found himself in a fit of glee as they stepped towards the magnificent gardens. The Labyrinth of roses, however, struck Hook with another feeling entirely. Such a tedious maze was beyond what patience the pirate now possessed. He could see the beauty and even felt the enchantment of the kingdom's lovely surroundings, yet through all the majestic radiance that laid before his eyes, he could not see the one thing he had so desperately sought- Wendy.

"Something is wrong," the Hatter said.

"What do you mean?" Hook replied.

But before the Hatter could answer, they were suddenly rushed upon by a large group of cards. Hook drew his sword ready to battle, but the cards held out their post and announced that by order of the queen, all witnesses to the crimes against Her Majesty must be escorted to the palace," the leading card said.

Hook squinted in question, "Back away, cards! We know nothing of the crimes against Her Majesty, but if you would be so kind as to escort us to the palace, we would like an audience with the Red Queen."

The cards whispered amongst each other for a moment before surrounding the three. "Her Majesty is preoccupied with the young girl at this time. You may wait in the rose gardens until the court proceedings are at an end."

The Hatter jumped in fright before Hook could even speak another word, "The girl? My Alice! She is to appear in the court?! No! Alice would never do anything against her most beloved Majesty! Please... take us to her!"

The cards gasped in unison, "You dare to grant the treacherous child your favor! Above your own queen!"

The March Hare laughed hysterically, "That's what he said! Are you all deaf?"

The cards rushed upon the rabbit with their sharp posts pointed at his very neck. Hook quickly stepped in, interjecting on his behalf. "Gentlemen... gentlemen. Please, let us speak freely. We are as you say- *witnesses* and should, therefore, be taken inside the Crimson Palace to appear in court. We only ask to be taken in peace."

The leading red card scoffed at his words. "You speak of peace... even as your sword remains aimed high."

Hook lowered his blade, "You are right. I had forgotten it was so," he said calmly placing the sword in the belt around his waist. "Now please... take us to the palace, where we can properly be of service in this most delicate matter."

The cards whispered again, nodding amongst each other before aligning themselves in a perfect line, marching into the labyrinth of roses- towards the Crimson Palace where the Queen of Hearts anxiously waited for the trial to commence.

As the three followed the cards, Catcher's pace was that of joy. Though many creatures throughout the kingdom were also heading towards the beautiful castle, Catcher appeared the most untouched by the land's enchantments — his coat, still light and young. His legs and tail moved gleefully upon the fresh green grass. He had neither wings nor a beak upon his face. And it seemed that every eye of every creature glared at him with most vigorous envy. In such a joyous place, full of nothing but love and beauty- their jealous hatred was noticed quickly by the escorted three.

"You must watch over your pet with great care; for I can feel how greatly they detest him and may act out of madness should they lose control."

Hook sneered at the surrounding crowd of unusual creatures of Wonderland. "Let them try. I will kill anyone that dares try to harm him."

The March Hare chuckled, nearly choking on his own breath. "Now that would be great fun indeed, but it would never come to that! For if any one of them should lose their head... the queen will make sure of that! No cruelty is allowed in here! Not beyond the clearing there," the Hare said, pointing the place where they had entered.

"But not all who are here have much sense left in their minds," the Mad Hatter stated in reply.

The March Hare snickered loudly and said in rhyme, "Well, I sure hope not! For what fun would there be if everyone acted so sensibly."

Hook grabbed his face in annoyance, "If the gods will have mercy on me... any at all! I pray I will never have to hear another spoken rhyme for the rest of my days!"

The Hare laughed harder, as did the Hatter too. "It is but merely just another symptom of Wonderland, you will find yourself speaking in such a way if you do not leave soon," the Hatter said, forcing himself not to rhyme as well. It was an effort that seemed to strain him terribly, though Hook was immeasurably grateful.

"I apologize for speaking in temper. I admit this place has worn my patience thin- a virtue I had greatly lacked before."

The Hatter and Hare looked at each other, but spoke not another word, for they both knew that patience was but the very first of many concerns in this place. Even the Hare dared not speak of what awaited him if he should not escape. Though it was a hope that he, in all honesty, could not fathom, for no one ever had. For the Hare, their mission was simply to retrieve Alice, for if they succeeded, then the journey he had taken for his brother all those years ago would no longer be lost in vain. He himself had accepted his fate in this land a long time past, but the Mad Hatter had not. But now, once the Hatter had his Alice, then maybe he too could finally be at peace, and they could all live happily in their house, drinking tea at their never- ending parties within the magical world of wonder. The Hatter, on the other hand, wanted no such fate for his beloved daughter. For if she could escape with the man next to him, then maybe she could still have the life he had always wished for her- and relieve himself from the guilt of robbing her of that chance. It was a hope he held high after seeing the magic of the Blue Fairy. If she believed that the man would succeed, then so too did he.

After following the marching cards to the Crimson Palace of ivy and jewels, the three entered a tall set of beautifully carved wooden doors, slowly opening before them. The inside of the castle looked like a majestic cathedral, with the art of all seasons carved into the wood and walls of crimson colored stone. Each twine of ivy and roses that covered the walls and ground were jeweled with crystals and glittering stones. There were windows throughout, though without a single shard of glass within them. The spring air from outside was free to come in, as was the sweet sound of a bird's song and a butterflies' kiss. Swirling trees reached high as the pillars of the castle, each leading to a staircase that reached to Her Majesty's throne.

There she sat with her gown's train spilling down the stairs like scarlet water. With her head held high, the golden crown with the most beautiful of rubies laid upon her long dark hair that curled in wild waves across her sun-kissed shoulders. Her repainted face was stern with lingering anger, yet one still could not deny her stunning features. Her amber eyes glowed fiercely beneath her very long eyelashes. The red upon her lips-painted in the shape of a heart to match those jeweled beside her eyes, and the blush of her cheeks seemed to define the high cheekbones of her face. Laying upon the lap of her gown was her red fox, staring down as she petted him gently. Just like her sister, there was a tall staff at her side. Made of exquisite cherry wood and swirling golden ivy reaching to the top, where there was a jeweled heart shining in the rays of the sunlight that gleamed through the windows.

Much like the Snow Queen was covered in white, there was no mistaking the defining color of the Queen of hearts. Rose Red was in all manner the Red Queen, and it suited her well. For while Snow White had her charms of dark seduction, the very nature that surrounded this queen, was most kind- both in nature and of course, heart. Her presence demanded respect, where her sister's demanded fear. And it was known to all that knew her, even the Hatter and Hare. The brothers bowed nice and slow, and Hook followed their cue. The queen's fox then looked up at her, as if communicating a dark secret. Then the Red Queen stood from her throne, staring at Hook in confusion and fear.

"Who are you? And why are you here?" She said both loud and clear.

"Your Majesty, we are here as witnesses to..." The Hatter spoke softly.

"Not you, Hatter; for I know very well who you are. I am speaking to you!" She said, raising her hand covered in red lace and pointed her ringed finger towards Hook. "I can see past your guise given by this land, and I can see what is in your heart. I can feel my sister's magic, though it failed to pierce through your shield. Why have you come here to my palace?"

"I assure Your Majesty that I am no friend to your sister. It is true I have been to her realm, and I killed many within it. No doubt I am her most hated enemy," Hook stated.

The Queen of Hearts chuckled in reply, "No, my kind sir, for that I am! But if you are indeed her great enemy as you say, why then did you leave her alive?"

"She was not the one I was there to destroy, but in killing the one, she so dearly loved... the suffering she was left to endure was a fate far worse than death. I left with her vow to seek the destruction of my life and devour my very soul."

"Who did you kill?" The Queen of Hearts asked, intensely.

"Her daughter," Hook replied. "She was evil, and I take great pleasure that she died by my hand."

The Red Queen's face flinched, unable to feel anything but remorse. "Though I hate my sister, I hate it more that I find her great loss- pleasing. Her mind then went to Draven, and a moment of crashing fear overwhelmed her. "You say you killed many in her realm. Did you... I mean- those closest to the crown...?"

"Those that stood by her side were left untouched by my wrath. There was a man and a..."

"-Bear," she finished.

"Yes, they were left alive. Along with some in her court."

The Red Queen sat back down, humming in thought, "Then you should take proper care, for destroying lives is an art that my sister has truly mastered. If you have come for my protection, I fear I cannot offer much."

"Though that is not why I am here, I think Your Majesty underestimates your own kingdom. For like I said, I destroyed a great deal of her realm and killed nearly all of the Unseelie court, and you yourself have quite a vast army that would gladly die for you. I find that you are indeed the Queen of Hearts... your entire kingdom loves you."

"I know that! I do not doubt their love, loyalty, and devotion, but unlike my sister- I do not take pleasure in those that will kill for me. I will not now- nor ever sacrifice my kingdom, my powers, or the lives of all in this realm... I may be the Queen of Heart's, but it was my own heart that I sacrificed to be free from my sister's rule of cruelty."

Hook stepped up the staircase, "Your Majesty, I am sorry for all that you have lost. I could not imagine losing my love. I found mine through the very thing I hated above everything else."

The Queen of Hearts smiled, "Fairies... As I said, I can see what is in your heart: vengeance, rage, hatred... Yet somehow, you fell in love with one of my own kind," she giggled lightly. "How funny life can be." Then suddenly her smile fell, regretful and stern, "I am sorry to be the one to tell you, but you should never have come to this land- and I'm afraid you are never going to see your true love again!" She said in a harsh plain tone as if it was simply a fact.

Hook was stunned, "Why do you say this?"

"I have done what I can to make this world- my world... a better place. Unlike the other realms and those of my kind, I do not send out the guardian for just any souls. I wish nothing more than not to have to steal any at all, but that is how magical realms survive. But if I am forced to take from the mortal world, I take those that are consumed with loneliness, sadness, and those that have begun to lose their minds- whatever the cause... and thus have lost the love from all of those around them. I offer them a place of acceptance, foolishness, nonsense... a place ever-changing- where the person they once were can disappear. I give them a chance to be loved again!" She said, picking up her beautiful fox. "All I ask is for absolute loyalty in return. I can see you believe in your heart that you came here to rescue someone from this land, but I say to you now that if they are here... they must truly belong here. There are those like you who are here because they sought someone else- including the very company you kept on your way to see me."

Hook looked down at the Mad Hatter and March Hare.

"And just as they have stayed, so too will you. It is my most absolute law, and it will be broken by no one- not even by me. I am sorry, but it simply just cannot and will not be done. So, go... find the one you came for, and build a life here as the Hatter and Hare have done. Accept this realm into your heart, and I promise- all will be well."

Her words had clutched at his chest, shortening his breath, "I have already found the one I seek. I hear that she is here on trial for crimes against you."

"We are here as witnesses for her, Your Majesty," the Hatter said timidly.

The Queen of Hearts then sat upon her throne, lifting her tall wooden staff. "I see," she said, stroking her fox with a sinister twinkle in her glowing fiery eyes. "What a pity... I had so hoped we were to become perfect friends!"

CHAPTER TWENTY-SIX

A WEEPING HISTORY

As Wendy approached the high cliffs, the whipping sound of wings crashed before her as the Red Queen herself came floating down in front of her, with the long-jeweled train of her dress circling around her as she touched the ground.

Wendy gasped and bowed, "Your Majesty."

The Queen of Hearts held her tall wooden staff within her right hand, twisting it ever so slowly, mirroring the contemplating thoughts that stirred in her head. "I am afraid the court is not yet ready for your trial. Some new... evidence has come to my attention," she said in an angry tone, but quickly looked up to the cliffs with a sly smile. "Have you met the Mock Turtle yet?"

Wendy shook her head, not quite understanding what the Red Queen had meant about *such evidence*.

The Queen of Hearts then twirled the staff around her, gathering all the sunlight that shined upon the spring air. The rubies of the staff's heart glittered like scarlet stars stirring in the sky. "You must go then. Go! And hear the Mock Turtle's history," she said walking next to Wendy up to the top of the cliffs. But no sooner had they reached the edge of the rocky domain, did the queen scoff at the sight of a sleeping Gryphon laying upon the surface.

The Red Queen bellowed at him, nearly blowing off his every feather... "Wake up, you- lazy fool!"

The Gryphon woke up as if suddenly slapped awake. His golden-brown eyes were wide and blood shot. "Your Majesty! How lovely it is to see you!" He stated loudly like a soldier.

But the Queen of Hearts was unamused with his laziness. "You forget your place, Gryphon. It is your charge to watch over the Mock Turtle. It is no secret that his wallowing depression makes him a danger to himself. It is up to you, as it has always been, to bring him joy when he is enthralled in his darkest moments. Forgetting your impertinence, I have brought you this child to watch over.

"Take her to the highest rock,
and let her breathe the fresh sea air
Let her stand on the edge of our world.
Where the influence is thinnest here

Let the clarity of her mind
Be unclouded by all
And when she remembers
That's when I will call...

Have the Mock Turtle tell her of his history. I eagerly await the result. Let us all learn the truth of who this young girl is and how she came to my land. Once I can see who resides deep in her heart, then I can decide if she is to keep her head. Farewell now Gryphon, and do not let me find you sleeping again. For if I learn that you have grown lazy and disobedient, I will be most *displeased.*"

The way she said the word... "*displeased,*" and what it truly meant was not lost on Wendy or the Gryphon. The creature nodded its head nervously, bowing repeatedly until the queen's large falcon wings had completely carried her away. Wendy did not like the look of the tall creature standing next to her. She so wanted to turn racing back, hoping to find the Duchess, but something sensible inside of her told her that to do so, would only intensify the Red Queen's anger towards her. So, Wendy followed the Gryphon up the steep rocks until they could hear the faint sound of great sorrow. The closing distance to the sobbing cries of a broken heart grew louder as the two approached what appeared to be- the Mock Turtle.

"Come on, girl! Come on! Come on!" Said the Gryphon, trying to get her to address the Mock Turtle herself. His demanding manner made his words pick at her nerves in a most wretched way. For though she had come from a life of proper class and ways of order, she had never been bossed around so much in all her life. Little did Wendy know, that it was that precise moment that she was starting to remember something... not only something about herself, but something about her true self- the girl she was before she came here. The Gryphon grew annoyed waiting for her to speak and decided to poke at the Mock Turtle himself. "Excuse me, sir, but the Queen of Hearts has brought this girl here."

The sobbing creature looked up with great big swollen eyes, "Why?" He asked, his voice hoarse from his many hours spent crying.

"She has come to hear your history," the Gryphon stated simply.

The Mock turtle whimpered as he stood up from the rocky ground's surface. "If the Queen of Hearts wills it, then I suppose the girl will hear it."

"Come on then! Come on!" The Gryphon shouted, forcefully shoving Wendy down upon a most uncomfortable rock nearby. It seemed no matter how much she squirmed or adjusted herself, she simply just could not get comfortable. Agitated, she looked up at the two creatures, ready to hear whatever it was that she came here to hear.

"You do not have to tell me, sir, if it upsets you so," she said to the sobbing creature. But the Gryphon and the Mock Turtle turned to her with ghastly shocked faces, as if she had just said the rudest thing anyone could possibly say. Quickly noticing this, Wendy hastily spoke again, "But I would so love to hear it!"

This seemed to satisfy both of the creatures that hovered above her. The Gryphon sat next to her, making the seat even more uncomfortable than it was before. The Mock Turtle then posed, as if he were in a grand theatre. "I...." He spoke with what felt like the longest pause in the world afterward. "... came from the sea." He finally finished, though each word was painfully slowly spoken, and had even caused Wendy to feel a little sedated.

History indeed! She thought. *We will all be history by the time he has finished this horribly slow story.*

But as the Mock Turtle went on about his history in the sea, the subject of his schooling had somehow called into question her own. He asked if she had studied this or that, and to Wendy's great surprise... she remembered the answer to each and every question. She remembered the school she had attended, and the many girls that were her friends.

She remembered how the school teachers thought her odd, and how her father had scolded her on such matters on many occasions. She even remembered trying to intercept a letter that was to be delivered to her father's workplace concerning her behavior. She failed of course, and even managed to bring shame to her father when she accidentally ran into a group of men standing around him. She remembered that her father was a respectable bank manager, and that his name and honor was of most importance to him. He wanted the perfect family and expected each and every one of his children to behave as properly as his darling wife, Mary... her mother.

Like the waves that splashed against the cliffs, Wendy's memories came crashing over her. It was both overwhelming and yet such thoughts hazed such pure relief within her. She was so consumed by all that had returned to her, that she had managed to mentally escape the Mock Turtle's sobbing history, in mind, but in body, she remained beneath his tears. Suddenly, her horrific travels now appeared no more than that of the grandest of adventures.

She was now sure of herself in a way that she had never been before. She neither felt loneliness, nor the abandonment that had so often tormented her heart. For now, in her mind, her once clouded mind was clear and the images of all that had helped her had loved her, emerged before her eyes: the Blue Caterpillar, the Mad Hatter, Captain Hook, Mr. Smee, and the Blue Fairy, Ainsel. Though the image of those who caused her sadness such as her family, she knew that what they did, they did so out of fear. Her parents and even her brothers... she had scared them in the way that many mortals fear. They simply do not know what lies beyond the veils of their world. Her stories had frightened them, just as they had frightened her, but now... she was not afraid.

If I die today, I die an adventurer. If I die today, I die a dreamer. And if I die today, I die Wendy Darling.

The magic of the cliffs and the infinite sea had brought her more than just a smile, and though she did not know why the Queen of Hearts had truly sent her here, she was grateful. For to not know who you truly are felt like the cruelest of tortures, but for those that dare not take such a thing for granted, can see that to know who you truly are, is the purest treasure a soul can hold. And now that she was here, with the Mock Turtle and the bossy Gryphon, she decided to enjoy every moment of their company and their utter nonsense that came with the rocky cliffs overseeing the magical waters below.

"Since you have never lived in the sea, as you say... Have you then never been introduced to a lobster?" The Mock Turtle asked.

Wendy nearly mentioned her past times of eating lobsters, purely out of the excitement of remembering them, but hastily corrected her wording so as not to offend or frighten the two creatures. "No, I have never."

The Mock Turtle and Gryphon then jumped in glee, "So then you must not know of the Lobster Quadrille?"

Wendy smiled, for she could say that she indeed had never heard of it. The two creatures then went on to explain the silly dance. By words, it was too confusing, even with the clarity she now possessed. So, they then offered to show her and the three went on below, to play within the splashing waves of the sea. The Mock Turtle of course had a song of silly rhythms to mirror the curious dance so precisely.

The dance called for lobsters, yet the two creatures assured her that they could get along without them. And they were right, for though there were no lobsters to dance with, Wendy got the hang of it. It was the just the sort of foolishness that her father would have disapproved of. A fact that made Wendy giggle a little bit.

There was once a time that she aimed to be the proper young lady, the kind that would make both of her parents proud. For though she dreamed of magic and adventure, there was also a part of her that aspired to be as perfect as her mother. *What little girl does not want to be her mother, and why does it always feel like it is the very thing one can never measure up to? But all of that was over now. It was too late to be the perfect daughter- too late to be a proper lady.*

She no longer cared what people thought. For to judge her properly, and how could anybody from her world truly know anything about her now. She had seen too much. She had seen mermaids, and souls twinkle in the distance. She had sung in the flower's choir, and she had watched creatures disappear into the darkness of Wonderland. She need not pretend to be anything other than what she was- what these otherworlds had turned her into. She was free to be who she truly was; it was a of defining glow that radiated through her as she danced. In fact, she had twirled and sang so loud and freely with the Mock Turtle and Gryphon by the sea, she had nearly forgotten all about her trial.

Hook, the Hatter, and Hare on the other hand couldn't stop thinking about it. The queen had placed them in an unfavorable corner of the until the proceedings commenced. Hook was a man of strategy, but the Hatter and Hare were beyond all reasoning. The Hatter rambled to himself, going over everything he could think of to please Her Majesty, hoping to gain her mercy and forgiveness.

Meanwhile, the queen had sent her cards to search the land for the Cheshire Cat, though it was hopeless. He was absolutely nowhere to be found. And though his mysterious whereabouts should have furthered the Red Queen's feelings towards his guilt,

242

her unwavering certainty about the girl's treason remained.

Hook pleaded with the Mad Hatter to calm himself down... That he had a plan- a way of escape. But it was if the Hatter could not hear him at all- for not a single word stopped his panicked state, and before Hook knew it, the two brothers made a sudden narrow escape through a hidden passage in the brush. Hook thought to chase after them but knew he could not. For such an attempt might risk getting lost in the realm once more.

Still, Hook worried that their flight may very well cause the queen's fury to grow ever deadlier than before. So, there he stayed, waiting in the shadowed corner with the most envied Catcher, until the horns from the Crimson Palace blew, announcing all the queen's present subjects to make their way into her court. Hook could hear the whispers beyond the corner of which he and Catcher stood.

They were not kind or even sane, but rather a group of raving lunatics that were seeking the Red Queen's favor, even if it meant lies and deceit. To Hook, who had seen many kingdoms in his time, the scandalous behavior was not unknown or unusual, but rather the most normal thing he had seen in this world yet. For even when the subjects of the land love their one true ruler, ambition has a way of turning the purest heart ugly and vain. And it seemed that this place was of no exception.

The creatures of Wonderland loved their queen so much and in turn desperately sought her love and praise, even if it meant the most terrible downfall of another. Every once in a while, Blackbeard and his crew had been charged with various offenses that brought them to the highest of courts over the years. Such a thing was not uncommon for a pirate. Yet, whenever any military got their hands-on Blackbeard and brought him to their rulers, be they a king or queen, a chief, or otherwise, it was not long before they discovered that Blackbeard could not be killed.

As for the safety of his crew... well all it took was a few threatening words from Blackbeard that could make anyone panic in worry, not only for your own life, but your friends and family as well. It was a marvelous irony to witness actually. For on many occasions, it was the rumors of Blackbeard that lead kingdoms to seek his capture, for to kill a legend will make you a legend thus, but to kill the unkillable, now that would make you a god. So many princes of this world think themselves so high, that it was Blackbeard's greatest pleasure to reveal the harsh truth upon them... that like the commoners of their lands, they too are not all powerful, but are in fact just as insignificant as any other person.

Each visit always ended with the same result, a ruler of lands, dishonored, and more fame for Blackbeard and his frightening crew that never failed to violate a kingdom, disrespecting every manner and every custom of etiquette form. And it was not that they simply acted like themselves, oh no... they went above and beyond to tear the court apart with their drunken outlandish behavior. It was a shameful sport to Hook, and he never took part of it, but rather managed to impress all in court with his charm and quick wit.

He may have been a pirate, but being dressed in the finest of French fashion, and being so well- read gave Hook a most debonair and mysterious charm. Still, Hook had always hated being in such places. For it seemed that no matter what or who's court he found himself, there was always lies and betrayal.

With pirates, it was not so. For pirates had no flare for scandal. There were those who would betray you, but it was all so much more obvious than that of people of high titles. Pirates cared not for titles, but only dared mutiny for gold and fame. Oddly, Hook had not thought in his life to seek either, yet as fate would have it, he had become one of the most famous pirates in all the mortal world.

Even so, he had found through his many travels what titles are really worth. For no one in this world knew nor cared who he was, but rather only sought to make him forget it.

Then suddenly something happened... the horns from the Crimson Palace sounded the alarm that it was time for everyone to come in. It was a sound that struck everyone's heart across the land. Wendy was immediately thrown back into the dangerous reality that waited for her beyond the rocky cliffs. It was only a matter of moments before the cards came marching in perfect formation along the path leading towards the cliffs where she stood, and though she could not see her, Wendy knew that the Queen of Hearts was right behind them. As the cards drew closer, Wendy's own heart began to thump wildly inside her chest as she gazed into their stern eyes. For inside them held not a glimmer of hope or pity. She was still the traitor to their queen, in their eyes.

Then, as the cards parted into two rows, Wendy was surprised to find that instead of the queen standing at the end, her sight set upon a much smaller figure, the White Rabbit. He blew his horn and opened a long scroll, reading aloud the offenses that are being called into question. After reading them, the White Rabbit looked up at Wendy with a hateful sneer.

She could not quite tell if his distaste for her in this moment was based off the most recent question of her alleged treachery, or if his radiating distain for her rooted from the destruction of his precious pocket watch. For though Wonderland was a place for lost memories, she doubted anyone could not forget such a great loss so easily. Whatever his reason for his snarling glare of hatred, Wendy felt not an inch of blame, for in her eyes, neither were in any way truly her fault, but rather the insane actions of others.

She walked through the two rows of towering cards, making her way towards the White Rabbit, slowly approaching the very creature that brought her here. With each step she took closer to him, an overwhelming anger began to boil inside of her. She raised her hand pointing at him shouting, "How dare you look at me like that! *All* of this is *your* fault!" She screamed as if scolding him. But her entire demeanor changed as she saw something magically appear in the garden behind him. The cold chill of death crawled inside her skin as her teary blue eyes set upon the scaffold. Much like everything else around the Crimson Palace, the wooden platform had been stained with the blood of all those in Wonderland that had displeased the Queen of Hearts.

The massive guillotine's sharp blade was still dripping from the black card's death. A woven carved basket held the dreaded threes' heads below the front. The sight stopped Wendy's breath dead in her lungs, and like most complex humans, panic set off a wave of uncontrollable emotions of hysteria.

Screaming in anger and fear, a black shadow began to tunnel around her vision. "I have had it with this place!... This Wonderland! The Dodo sets *your* little house on fire with me in it... and you blame me!

The Mad Hatter and March Hare completely destroy your pocket watch... and you blame me! The Cheshire cat humiliates the Red Queen in a most wretched unforgivable way... and you all blame me?!" She screamed turning around facing all that stood around her. "Well, you are all wrong! Am I really to be put to death for the crimes of others?"

Then as Wendy hyperventilated in the gripping arms of the red cards escorting her forward, the darkness had finally covered her eyes and the rapid breath that raced against her terrorized heart, made her fall within the black vortex of her mind. Not missing a single step, the red cards carried the fainted child into the Crimson Palace, to be brought before her most gracious Majesty, the Queen of Hearts, and as it turns out... heads.

CHAPTER TWENTY-SEVEN

TRIAL OF HEART, CHAOS, AND MAYHEM

All of those that were making their way through the tall wooden entrance of the palace could also see the frightening sight of the place of execution and the young girl being carried to the front, and though it was their greed and ambition that had brought them here, the image of the poor child was enough to bring out the pity in every single soul that walked behind her. Hook of course was feeling a lot more than pity as his eyes set upon her unconscious body. His anger called him forward, desiring nothing more than to whip out his sword and slash through all the cards to get to her and her take away, but there was too many of them, and he remembered what Ainsel had said to him before he left... that though he himself is immune to all fae magic, Wendy is not, and therefor... until he has his hands on her and a good running start, not to risk the girl's harm by acting rashly. It was something that he had to constantly course through his troubled mind as he slowly made his way inside.

Strangely, the entire interior of the Crimson Palace looked completely different than the last time Hook had seen it. The inside now did in fact look like a large courthouse. The twirling tree pillars that went up to the cathedral ceiling now had a large seating area on either side for the jury. The massive staircase that had previously been in the center of the room leading up to Her Majesty's throne, was now a towering bench. The finely crafted platform was magnificent indeed, but it was not alone. There was oddly a tall stack of hardcover books holding up a smaller bench next to hers. No doubt, it was for His Majesty, the Tiny King. Upon both of the benches was a golden oak gavel balanced perfectly upon a matching sound block, cut from the same tree. The Red Queen's however was much larger and, in all manner, to be ultimately used for the final judgement.

One of the red cards stepped forward, announcing to all that they were to be seated quietly. As the crowd of creatures moved towards the two sides of the court, Hook alone stood in the center of the room. The red card that held Wendy in his arms, stayed silent in formation as the White Rabbit, Wonderland's guardian, and her majesty's most humble servant, came forward blowing his horn.

"All devote rise for her majesty, her excellency, our dearest beloved... the Queen of Hearts!"

Every creature then stood, clapping and cheering in awe as she came walking through a mysterious archway of twining red branches towards the massive bench before them. Now out of her scarlet gown that glittered like rubied stars, the Queen of Hearts now wore a long satin robe, stitched in both red and golden regal design. The golden thread that covered her was only outshined by the brilliance of her crown. With her make-up repainted yet again, and her curly locks of long dark hair spun up in woven braids on the top two corners of her head, giving her the shape of an elaborate heart. The red paint on her lips was now lined with gold, as was the corners of the dark smoky appearance of her amber eyes. Her lashes were long and black, somehow making her blushed face even more beautiful. There was a standing lace collar that wrapped around the back of her neck, and the two dangling earrings of glittering crystal. Her presence was both majestic and all frightening to behold. Both in beauty in great power, the queen stood proudly. Though she had approached the bench with a sternly, the roaring praise that surrounded her brought a smile to her face, and though it was obvious to Hook that her smile was once one of warmth and love, the white of her teeth appeared dark compared to the striking white paint upon her scarred skin made it eerie and unsettling.

Nevertheless, Hook clapped with the others, for he dared not cause her majesty further to cause to lash out in her vigorous anger. As her eyes caught his, the stare of her eyes began to glow.

"Why do you stand, sir? Perhaps you have forgotten how to sit?" She said with a witty tone. The crowd of creatures laughed at her mockery, yet Hook did not so much as flinch.

"I am happy to see your majesty's mood has much improved, yet I ask... humbly of course, as I am not part of your council, nor a member of this jury, where am I to sit? For I fear no one here has told me where I, a witness for the child in question, should sit."

The Red Queen's long eyelashes fluttered as her eyes widened. Though it was not what he had said that had brought the heat of fury to her breath, but that by the proper carefulness of them. For that, she could not in all fairness scorn him in front of the others. Yet there was a certain arrogance in his tone that made her anger grow like a fever. She sternly looked to her deck of cards, standing perfectly like dominos along the four walls of the palace court. Their eyes contained only fear as she slowly glanced about them as if looking for one to pick. Hook could see their terror as their post began to tremble in their hands.

"I say this to Your Majesty, not to cause a rift in your court, for I doubt there has ever been a countering witness before myself, and therefore, Queen of Hearts, the fault lies only with me. I look to you to guide me wherever you see fit to place me, so that these proceedings may began, for surely Your Majesty would like to move on to better things."

The queen huffed yet did not argue further. "Very well," she said plainly before reaching out her hand, calling forth her elegant wooden staff. With a twirling motion of her hand, the witness stand suddenly appeared to the right of the bench, and then with one more of a sharp twist, the place where Wendy would stand as charged. Then as the heart on the top of the staff began to beat, a red mist of enchantment did then emerge, casting a waking spell upon the girl, lifting her into the air and placing her inside a boxed stand that would hold her within by the great power of the Queen of Hearts.

As Wendy woke, she could hear but not yet see, something that made her even more afraid.

"Where am I? Am I dead? Why can I not see?!" Wendy shouted.

"Silence in my court!" The Red Queen shouted, twisting her staff and shooting a blast of magic to the girl's mouth, muting her instantly. Wendy continued to open her mouth, yet not a sound could she now utter, "You are not dead, child! Not yet anyways! On request of the Tiny King, I agreed you may have a trial, and I do not break my word. Though I warn you to heed my one and only warning.

Take care how you act
Take care how you speak
For I am all powerful
And you are the weak."

Though she was once again threatened, the mere fact that she could hear a familiar voice reminding her that she was still alive, was enough to calm Wendy's breath. Hook wanted so much to scream out to her but being a man of strategy and not one to act hastily out of emotion, he remained quiet. Though he had a plan of action, and it the moment to act was nearly upon him, the odd little world of Wonderland had somehow diminished much of his optimism.

Yet it occurred to him as a glistening drop of sweat dripped down the right side of his temple, that such nervousness might be the best appearance in the view of the queen and her excitable jury. For if he were to seem so certain- so calm during the final judgement of a young life, the queen may find him suspicious and rush the delicate matter of Wendy's pending execution.

"Now that all of that is settled, so too am I. If there are no further interruptions, you may now all be seat..."

"Wait! We are here! We are here! More witnesses! More witnesses!" The Mad Hatter and March Hare screamed running through the wooden doors. It was in this moment that Hook felt like his jaw would never stop dropping. The two insane brothers then rushed to the same seating as he, each with a crazed look in their eye that was beyond the depth of insanity that they were before. Hook wasn't sure what exactly had caused it... if it was him, Alice, or the tea, but he couldn't help feeling a little responsible.

The queen on the other was far from amused with yet another interruption, not only of the proceedings, but also her speaking... an offense that had caused many to gasp out loud and raise the fury of Her Majesty even further. The worst part though was that in spite of the fact that Wendy had been muted, blinded, and locked in a tall wooden box, the Red Queen glared at her with immense hatred and blame.

But like most in Wonderland, the new turn of events had excited the tiny King, and with the excessive tapping of his own small gavel against an even smaller sound block, he called out with his weasel-like voice, "First witness... first witness! The March Hare!"

Then four of Her Majesty's red cards collected the Hare, carrying him up to the witness stand on their shoulders. The Queen of Hearts sneered at her husband in surprise, "Have you lost your mind?!" She screamed, snatching his gavel right out of his tiny hand.

Her words made the Hatter chuckle madly. It was a sound that made both Wendy and Hook extremely nervous, yet the worst was yet to come, for the Hatter's contagious laughter had spread to his brother now standing upon the stand closest to Her Majesty, and the raving lunatic, the March Hare.

The rose red blood of the queen was nearly at a full-blown volcanic state. "Why do you laugh at me, sirs?" She asked in an alarmingly calm seething voice. And although it was incredibly frightening to all the members of the jury, the March Hare merely bent back his seat and took another sip of tea, as if ignoring her entirely. Her body began to shake with the fuse that was about to blow from inside her. "Such disrespect! I speak again and I warn you, if you fail to answer me thus, then you shall suffer a fate far worse than that of the one you came to defend... You have come here as a witness! So, tell us... what did you see, March Hare?!"

Within a mere second, the craziest creature there may have ever been in Wonderland was now face to face with the erupting Red Queen. "Nothing! I saw nothing whatsoever!" He screamed so dangerously close to her, that it shocked her far beyond any measure of anger she could ever imagine reaching. Instead, she turned her immediate rage over to the jury.

"He said he saw nothing whatsoever!"

After ducking and dodging what felt like cannon fire, each member of the jury wrote the quote of the insane rabbit upon their boards. The frustration of everything that had already happened was more stress

256

than the Red Queen had endured since she and the Tiny King had first arrived in this land. It was not the strangeness of the realm's creatures that got to her, for that was simply nature in its freest form.

Even chaos could be seen as beautiful in her eyes, and beyond the labyrinth of roses that surrounded her Crimson Palace, mayhem could run more wildly than what was possible in any of the other Nine Realms. But this... something about it all just felt so different- so wrong, and it had dwindled her every nerve-ending, and an escalating anxiety had begun to set in.

"You look stressed, my Queen. You should have a cup of tea. It would calm Your Majesty's mood. Yes! It would calm Your Majesty, indeed," the Hare said.

With her head in her hands, the queen looked up at the witness, "I am not well handled, March Hare."

The insane rabbit smiled, handing a beautiful dainty teacup over towards her, "Feel no shame in that, Your Majesty, for not even the creatures of this world can handle me."

The queen could not help but laugh. She reached out her hand and grabbed the teacup... After all, the creatures of her realm might be crazy, and the Hare might be the craziest, but he and the Mad Hatter had been loyal loving subjects... they would surely never think to betray their beloved Queen of Hearts. *Would they?*

Without another thought, the queen took a sip of the warm tea, holding the teacup and saucer with such care, for she thought it was indeed beautiful. After the second sip, she was already starting to feel its freeing influence. Though her mind had not calmed in the way she had hoped, the tea had managed to care less about what had so previously bothered her to the point of murder. Before she knew it, she was reaching out the cup for another pour. All the while, with the Red Queen's drunk- like demeanor, the insane rabbit began to send her mind to other things- "Does Your Majesty like riddles?" He asked her. And with the sight of her curious smile, the Hatter leaned closer to Hook and whispered quietly, "My poor Alice. Fear not, for I have a great plan, though I am still in need of your assistance, mysterious stranger."

It was then that Hook realized that he and the Mad Hatter had never been properly introduced. "Do you remember your true name, Hatter? The name you had before you came to this land."

The Mad Hatter looked up at him strangely, "As I told you before, stranger, I remember nothing beyond the tragic loss of my daughter."

"But you remembered Alice's name. Why, you even remembered the house and what led you to there that night. Somewhere inside that mind of yours is the memory of your own name, *surely.*"

"Surely," was all the Mad Hatter said, chuckling in reply.

Hook could see he was getting nowhere, and their attention had fallen back to the Queen of Hearts and the March Hare.

"Your Majesty, may I speak to you plainly... or oddly- whichever comes to mind?" The Hare asked the queen.

Feeling much more tolerant and possibly wild, she most eagerly wanted to hear what he had to say. "Do tell, then! Do tell!"

The Hare then leaned in close to her and whispered in her ear, "I think you may learn more from the child if she could see and speak, for to get to the truth you seek, one must go deep to reach the bottom of the pot," he replied, pouring yet another cup of the addictive tea that was opening the chaos in her mind.

The Red Queen looked at the girl, "Well, Hare, I do say... you make quite a skilled argument. A truly fine quality to have in my court. For as you say, we are getting nowhere this way. The queen twirled her staff in a silly-like manner, instantly returning Wendy's sight and voice.

"Well, child, before we call you to the front, I would like my husband to announce our next witness. But when she looked to the Tiny King, he raises his arms in confusion, "But my dear, I cannot announce the next witness without my gavel."

She looked at him as if what he said was ridiculous. "Why do speak to me of such nonsense during proceedings as serious as this? I know you need your gavel to announce the next witness, for what other way could it possibly be done?"

The Tiny King looked up at her nervously shaking as he spoke again, "I meant, my beloved, that you took my gavel after announcing the March Hare. Do you not remember?" He asked genuinely concerned. For it was not like the queen to be so scattered and forgetful. Yet there a part of her- the striking edge that had intimidated him in all their time together, seemed not be softened per say, but rather unfocused instead. He was not sure if it was a good thing or not, but the symptom brought on by tea had already caused to lift the magic from the young girl before lifting any notion of her innocence, nor any doubt of her guilt.

The queen herself looked down on stand before her. The Tiny King was right. His small gavel laid there next to hers, though she dared not show any sign of confusion or remorse. Instead, she laughed as if it had all been in great fun. "Of course, husband. You need not be so serious. I know that I took your gavel. How could I not? Is it not up here right before my eyes?" She said with snorting breaths, laughing with all the others in the court. "Here, take it and kindly call forth the next witness," she said dropping the Tiny King's gavel from her high stand. When the gavel fell through the air to the king below, the gavel knocked him in the head and nearly knocked him off the large tower of books upon which he stood. Nearly falling a great distance to the Palace grounds, the Tiny King caught one of the larger spines of the books that held him. With great urgency, he desperately pulled himself up, all the while, the mocking laughter of the court and the queen did not cease. Finally, as he reached the top of the tower of hardcover books, and collected his breath, he raised his gavel and tapped the sound block three more times.

"When the Red Queen is distracted, and the time is right, take Alice and get her home. I beg of you," the Mad Hatter whispered to Hook as the White Rabbit announced his name in the background.

As four of the cards collected the March Hare and brought him back to the box, The Hatter and Hook looked to each other as if it was the last moment between them. This was it! This was when the plan of two worlds would come into play to save the life of Wendy. The four cards then proceeded to pick up the Hatter, but before he was taken completely beyond reach, he grabbed Hook by the collar, and whispered but one word into his ear before letting go and made his way towards the witness stand, carried on the shoulders of the queen's cards.

Hook and Wendy both took a deep breath, unsure of what might happen next.

CHAPTER TWENTY-EIGHT
AT THE WORLD'S END

When the Mad Hatter reached the stand, he lifted his large ridiculous hat, covered in feathers, buttons, ribbons, and more, to reveal a beautiful yellow teapot. He then poured himself a cup of tea and took a sip of its heated comfort. The queen, however, did not want to take another cup for the moment, fearing she might say the wrong thing again. Once could be easily dismissed, but if she were to make a mistake again, however small, it would be noted by those most important, and if this trial was not enough to prove it, what she hated more than anything else, was feeling humiliated. So, she tried to stern her expression, and speak in a plain harsh tone. "Hatter, you have come here as a witness for the child. Explain yourself!"

The Mad Hatter smugly took another sip of tea before answering, "Forgive me, Your Majesty, for I am not all in my head, what is it exactly that I should explain?"

The Queen of Hearts scoffed, "Well why you believe this girl innocent of the treasonous charges, for you Hatter know very well that all in this realm- my realm... there is not a single soul in Wonderland that would dare torment me in such a wretched way as that."

"Such a way as what, Your Majesty?" The Mad Hatter spoke in circles.

"I speak of course of what happened in the garden!" The Red Queen screamed.

"What was it that happened?" He asked with a curious face.

What is he doing up there? Hook thought. *He is going to get her all worked up again!*

"I speak, Hatter, of the heinous trickery that brought such shame upon my person."

The Mad Hatter nodded, "Ah, you speak of the Cheshire... cat."

Suddenly, blasting out of the yellow teapot he had brought with him, was a mouse in full panic. "Cat! A cat! Where is the cat!? What has it done now?!" cried the scared little mouse.

"Oh, my!" Said the queen as the Mad Hatter rushed back up to the stand with a small white and pink painted jar of purple jam.

"The jam! We must give him the jam! It calms him down, but we must hurry before his heart pops out of his chest," the March Hare and the Mad Hatter said in unison. But the mouse had blasted so high; it would take a moment before they could reach him.

Under great stress, the mouse tried to calm himself and think of happier things.

"Twinkle, Twinkle, Little Bat,
How I wonder what you're at
Up above the world, you fly
Like a tea tray in the sky
Up above the world, you fly
Like a tea tray in the sky."

By the end of the song, the March Hare was the first to reach the poor creature and cover his face with jam. As the Hare put the now sedated mouse back into the teapot, the queen, pitying the tiny creature, wondered what could have possibly caused such a reaction. "I do not understand what happened just now," the Red Queen asked in confusion.

The Hare then leaned in close, as to be as quiet as possible. "It was the word that upset him so, your majesty. For we have seen what terrible wretchedness that elusive Cheshire creature has done, and now... it seems that he is no longer the mischievous creature that was the eyes and this land. For his schemes have since turned dark and malicious in intent."

The Queen of Hearts said not a word to the Hare but rather just turned to the jury. "You heard the witness. Write it down, for that is by far the most important piece of evidence we have heard yet." Then she turned back to the Hare and pointed in the direction of the seating. "Go back where you belong now, Hare! It is the Mad Hatter I will speak with now."

The Hare did as he was told and made his way back towards Hook and Catcher. Wendy, on the other hand, now understood that there was a plan afoot. For the mouse's extreme reaction was indeed caused by the word 'CAT' but it was not the fault of the Cheshire Cat. Something else was going on... though she did not know what.

After that, the Red Queen herself was ready for another cup of tea, and the Mad Hatter was all too eager to oblige. After a subtle giggle, the queen asked the Hatter in her sternest tone. "Now, Hatter, where were you when these treacherous crimes were committed in the garden?" She asked.

The Mad Hatter smiled, stirring his hot tea with a small silver spoon. "I was at home celebrating."

"And just what was it you were celebrating?" The Red Queen asked, displeased that there was anything other than herself being celebrated.

"My Unbirthday," said the Hatter.

Seeing his queen's displeasure, the Tiny King reached up to pull on the queen's satin robes, "Oh, but, my dear! My beloved!"

"What is it, husband?" She asked in annoyance.

"Well, dearest, do you not see... today is your Unbirthday too!" He said sweetly.

"Is it truly?" She asked excitedly. "I must have forgotten."

"Fear not then, my sweet queen, for I never have, nor ever will," said the Tiny King.

His sweetness made her smile. She had never truly loved him, but she had grown to care for him over their many years together. He, however, did love her immeasurably, and with such unconditional devotion, the Red Queen had never felt the true loneliness that her sister had hoped to achieve by sending her to this realm. Like the dreaded three, the black cards were sent like the seasons to poison her realm and thoughts, by order of who truly holds their heart... the Snow Queen. But Rose Red has been quick to remove such poison from the beginning, a fact that had made her a person to both fear and love. The law of the realm was simple... If the queen does not have your heart, she will have your head!

Where the girl's heart truly lied, the queen did not know, but the Cheshire would not stop his devotion to her without reason. *And if he had, where then does his heart truly lie now?* The queen could not help thinking that all of this came back to the little girl standing in her court. The blame had to be hers, for she could think of no other cause for the Cheshire's heinous acts against her. *Yes, the blame has to be the girl's...* she thought.

Suddenly, her thoughts were interrupted by the Hare rushing back up to the bench with what appeared to be an unraveling table top cover of the mad tea party, and just like at the March Hare's house, the teapots and teacups came alive and began to play their little tune. The entire court began to sing along with the brothers as they very excitedly sang their vivacious Unbirthday song. Wendy could not help but roll her eyes at the utter nonsense of it all, but as all of the queen's cards flew upward above her, the steam from the various sets of teapots and teacups had already begun to fill the air. Soon, the entire courthouse had turned into a full-blown madhouse. Every creature of the jury and every card in the Red Queen's service was quickly getting drunk with madness. There was no longer order, but rather an explosion of chaos and mayhem.

This is it. This is the moment. Hook thought, seeing that with everyone surrounding the celebrated Queen of Hearts, Wendy was no longer in Her Majesty's sight. Getting to Wendy, however, proved to be a whole other matter entirely. For it seemed that the tea had created an all-out frenzy of magical creatures, beyond even the queen's control. Careful to not let anyone trample on Catcher, Hook pressed his way through the crazed crowd looking for Wendy. But with the towering height of the Red Queen's cards, and the various animals in the air and on the ground, it seemed that Wendy had already disappeared, and Hook's heart was beating faster by the minute.

Catcher wasn't the only one in danger of being trampled on. Wendy was still magically bound to the box, and now that she could see, she was completely terrified. With every bump, hit, and shove, her panting breath of fear intensified as she struggled to break free from the wooden prison that held her. Then suddenly, a bright orange creature with turquoise feathers and a red beak crashed down upon her. She tried to break free, but the creature didn't move. Feeling as though she was about to suffocate, Wendy squirmed. Then she felt them... *the mushrooms.*

She could not reach the one in the left pocket of her pretty blue dress, but when she tried to reach the one in her right pocket, she found that she could only scrape the top with her fingernails. Nevertheless, with one last effort, Wendy then used all her strength to reach the scrapings to her mouth. She didn't know if such a small portion would work, but even if by some miracle it did, she had no idea if she would grow high, towering over all in the palace, or if she would shrink below to be crushed like a bug under a foot. So soon as the bits from her nails touched her lips and tongue, did her body shoot up into the air, causing her to duck her head, for fear of hitting the high palace ceiling. The sudden magic had shocked all throughout the courtroom, shocking even the Red Queen in her changed state. Hook, the Mad Hatter, and the March Hare then looked at each with great fear, for once again the court was struck silent, and all eyes were on Wendy. It was then that the Hatter's eyes filled with tears, while the Hare's filled with wild madness. Before Hook could act, the palace echoed with the Tiny King's voice. Fearing for the queen's safety, he spoke with more command in his tone than ever before in his life. "Rule 42! All those in the court that is more than a mile high must leave the court immediately."

Like with all food and drinks in Wonderland, the mushroom had made Wendy intemperate. "I am not a mile high!" She screamed in return. Having been scared for such a time, she could not help the arrogance that came from towering over all those who wanted her dead.

Hiding behind one of the cards that guarded her, the queen poked her head up, reiterating her husband's brave words. "So sorry, but if it is a court rule, then you must leave!"

Wendy then realized she had completely broken apart the box that had previously bound her.

Nevertheless, the queen's actions as of late had proved to be most unjust, and she felt compelled to defend her case, for if she was going to leave the court, she wanted to leave it innocently and without any followers. "I will leave, most gladly," she said gazing around the room, unaware that the one that was so desperately trying to reach her was not her enemy, but Captain Hook. As it were, Wendy's anger would not permit her to see anything or anyone beyond Her Majesty, the Queen of Hearts. "And as for you... *Your Majesty*. I must tell you then when we first met; I thought you beautiful and loving. Having heard of your tragic past, and that of your wicked sister, the Snow Queen, I pitied you. But now, I see that all her efforts were not in vain... for I see now why she chose to send you to this world. It is not just your precious creatures that lose themselves to their madness... but also you!" Wendy shouted.

The Red Queen shoved the card before her and shouted in reply, "What is this? What do you say?"

Wendy bent down towards her so that her warm breath could be felt on the queen's face, "I am saying, Your Majesty, that in your tyranny and bloodshed, you have lost who you once were... you may be the Queen of Hearts, but you are not Rose Red."

Though the words of the child had burned the queen greatly, it was in that moment that Wendy began to shrink back down to her original height. All in the court gasp, though Hook was nearly within reach of her.

271

The Red Queen looked down at the child. Rubbing her hands together, her bloodthirsty thoughts consuming all of her being. Wendy looked up at her, terrified, knowing she was likely to die at any moment. "What was that you were saying, little one?" The queen asked mockingly, seeing if the child had any bravery left. But to everyone's great surprise, the next voice that was to be heard by all was none other than the Cheshire Cat himself.

"Well, I believe she called you a heartless bloodthirsty tyrant!" The Cheshire said, sitting upon the Red Queen's crown. It was in that moment that the queen's fiery rage suffused her completely.

"Off with her head!"

Suddenly, the March Hare rushed up behind her, stealing her wooden staff and ran away, jumping through one of the windows, catching the attention of the entire courtroom. "Stop him! Guards! Stop the March Hare! He has stolen my staff!"

It was then that the cards flew into the air from every angle, trying to find the insane rabbit. Feeling the Red Queen's wrathful anger trapped within the four walls of the Crimson Palace, every creature tried desperately to flee. With the castle again in chaos, Hook rushed to grab Wendy by the arm. The girl turned to him with a frightened gasp, but as she set her eyes upon him, with the help of Ainsel's magic, she could see his true form. Not quite believing her eyes, she hesitated.

"Come with me now, Wendy Darling! We must hurry!" Hook shouted.

His words stole her breath, for it had been some time since she had heard her true name. Without another thought, she nodded, allowing the pirate to scoop her up and carry her through the palace doors and into the labyrinth of red roses. With Catcher following quickly behind, it seemed that the queen's enchanting fury had spread into the land. The thick branches above them whipped with such wild fury that not a single leaf still stood on its whims. There were no roses, only thorns as Her Majesty's wonderous garden turned into a beautifully wicked nightmare. As the magical realm reached out to rip tear them apart.

Racing into the darkness once again, the raging sound of the queen's voice echoed around them. "I will not be undone by a mortal girl's words! For I am queen of this world, ordained by the gods and mother nature, not the temper of my sister! I am not unjust. I am the Queen of Hearts! You hear me, traitors? I am the Queen of all Hearts!"

Her voice was drawing closer, and it seemed her power had stirred up all the madness in Wonderland. The ground was now turning into water, the sky was black, and out from the darkness came every dangerous illusion. Though Hook was immune to the fae charm now flooding the realm, Wendy was not.

Crying in fear, she lost all hope. "How are we to get out of here?" She wept, closing her eyes to escape the terrifying view that clouded her sight and mind. The dodo, the caterpillar, the twins, and even the Mad Hatter and the March Hare appeared on the rising water before her. Each approached her with crazed eyes and anger. That is... all except the Hatter who appeared to be crying with the sadness of such wretched devastation. It was then that Wendy realized that the flooding water below was made of the Mad Hatter's tears. The sad whisper of her name then echoed from the water, "Alice... Alice... Alice."

"I'm so sorry, Hatter. I'm so sorry," Wendy cried out.

"Calm your heart, child. We are nearly there," Hook said stepping out of the water, and up onto higher ground in the black forest. It was then that Wendy saw the sign that would make her weak in the knees.

"Tulgey Wood. Do you mean to take us to our end? Our death?" Wendy spoke faintly.

Hook put her down and placed his face in front of hers. "No, Wendy Darling. We have not come here to die, have you forgotten the tales of my many adventures?"

Wendy's tears stopped for a moment as she thought. "No, I have not."

Hook smiled, "Then, my dear, when have you ever known me to surrender?"

Wendy smiled, weakly at his bravery. "But..."

"But what?"

Wendy gulped, gathering some bravery of her own, "But... you have promised me your protection before, and you did not succeed."

With a huff, Hook nodded. "You are half correct. This is the place where those of this realm come to meet their end, but what you do not know is that these woods are at the end of this world, and I have the key to get us out... or rather the door." It was then that Hook reached into his pocket for the very thing he had taken from the room of which he had entered Wonderland. Wendy looked down into his hand to find a tiny looking glass.

"I do not understand," Wendy said.

Suddenly, the distant voice of the raging queen drew closer, making Wendy's heart race with fear again. Catcher rubbed up against her with comfort. Then out of Hook's other coat pocket, he took out a little bag of fairy dust. Hook then placed the enchanted mirror on the ground and sprinkled the blue fairy dust upon it.

The tiny looking glass then grew tall, standing against a purple tree. Hook then reached out his one hand and spoke in great haste, "Come now, Wendy, let us leave this place. Catcher was first, running happily through the portal. With the Queen's wrath approaching, Wendy turned to see Her Majesty, the cards, and her creatures charging towards them. Hook rapidly took her hand and raced through the mirror to the mortal world on the other side, just in the nick of time.

CHAPTER TWENTY-NINE

THE DEATH OF WENDY DARLING

With a deep inhale, Hook and Wendy looked up. "Where are we?" Wendy asked.

"Hook looked around and scoffed, "The woods... I hate the woods."

Wendy laughed, her eye catching his furry companion, "Looks like Catcher loves it."

Hook shook his head, "Yes... he always does."

It was then that Wendy took her first breath of relief. "It is sort of beautiful here," she said looking up at the sun shining through the forest of vast trees. The air seemed to glitter within the beams of light between them. The sound of little critters scurried around, bringing Catcher great joy. The sense of danger had left them.

They were safe. They were home.

"Where are we? How did we get here?" Wendy asked.

Hook looked behind him, setting his gaze upon the doorway, the looking glass. Then with great rage and most sincere pleasure, Hook smashed the mirror. Wendy gasped as all the enchanted pieces fell to the ground.

Sensing his temper had frightened her, Hook turned and spoke playfully, "Guess I have bad luck now... but small price to pay, eh?"

Wendy chuckled lightly. That is... until she looked down at the broken shards of glass and saw her reflection. "I look the same! Why do I look the same? Why do I not look like me?" She asked suddenly feeling panicked all over again. "How am I to return home now?" She said with a quivering lip and fresh tears falling from her eyes.

Hook froze, not knowing what to say. After all, what could he say... *she was right.* Wendy dropped to her knees, weeping. Catcher was quick to come to her, rubbing his face against her wet cheeks. Hook slowly lowered to the ground, raising her chin to face him. "I am so sorry, Wendy. I didn't know." The sadness that flooded over her blue eyes mirrored the ocean of misery he had carried in his own, and it broke his heart. "I know my words are of little comfort to you. Though I swear to you I will do everything I can to atone failing you once again."

"How?" She asked weakly.

Then he wiped her tears away and stood back up upon the ground. The sun was setting, gracing its orange beauty upon the forest. Hook looked up at the crescent white moon already appearing in the sky.

"I call for the stars
to paint the night above,
I call for the fae
that holds my love
Take us from the woods
And carry us to the sea
Come to me
My Blue Fairy."

Wendy looked up to find she was suddenly surrounded by water, and there was wood beneath her. The motion of movement sent chills down her spine as she realized that she was in fact now on a moving ship. It was something she had hoped to never feel again. For since the magic of the cliffs, she had regained all her memories, and those of her sailing through the sky with Peter Pan.

The visions of the brutal death he had wrought upon the lost boys, and the smile upon his face then crashed over her mind. Seeing Wendy suddenly suffused with fear and distress, Hook rushed to her. But before he could say a single word, the calming magic of blue dust fell upon her. Hook looked up to see his beautiful Ainsel hovering above them, with her wings carrying her slowly down towards them. With Wendy now calmed by her soothing magic, she stood in awe at the lovely fairy with azure hair.

"James, my love, how happy I am to see you," she said embracing him. Within his arms, she let her wings fall, so as to be only held up by him. It was her most cherished feeling, to feel his touch. She kissed him softly, before turning her eyes to Wendy.

"I am happy to see you too, Ainsel. To see you again was my greatest wish. But I fear I did not succeed... we did escape, but the magic of Wonderland has not left the poor child."

Ainsel bent down to look at her. "I can see her true form, but I'm afraid the magic that hides her is power much stronger than my own. I cannot change you back to your true appearance, Wendy Darling, I am sorry."

"There must be something you can do to help her get home to her family," Hook said. It was then that Wendy saw a look of pause between them. The answer was in Ainsel's eyes... there was something else wrong. "What is it, Ainsel?" Hook asked seeing her dread.

After some hesitation, Ainsel let out the very breath one breathes before giving bad news. "Well I fear that even if I could change her appearance back to its true form, her family would only think her a phantom."

"What? Why?" Wendy asked.

"I'm afraid the Darlings have thought their daughter dead for a long time. They have mourned her. If they were to see her now, they would never believe it was truly her. Mortals have a hard time believing in things beyond their measure of logic and possibility... even when something is right before their eyes. Seeing their daughter as she was all those years ago would only bring them further pain."

"You said all those years ago... How long have I been gone?" Wendy asked looking up at the both of them. "It couldn't be that long. A week... a month... I don't care how I look! I can make them believe! I want to go home! Please!"

Ainsel shook her head, caressing Wendy's cheek. "Shhhhh... Wendy, you have been gone from this world for over fifteen years."

Wendy gasped, shaking her head, "No. No that is impossible," she said looking over at Hook. "That is impossible, right?"

But Hook himself was stunned, unable to look at her, for what good would his sorrow and pity be to her now. Instead, he looked to Ainsel in confusion, "Is it true? - Fifteen years?"

Ainsel nodded slowly. "Yes."

Hook closed his eyes, huffing in such strong frustration that it made him shake. "So, it was all for not! Why did you warn me? Why did you let me think I could save her and bring her home? Why did you not tell me, Ainsel! Why!?" He shouted, giving Ainsel and Wendy a trembling chill.

"You shall not shout at me, James!" Ainsel said feeling a great frustration of her own. "I will not be spoken to that way! For if you would kindly calm yourself, you may remember the words we have shared in our moments together... and remember that I did in fact tell you that the worlds of the Nine Realms do not share the same concept of time as the mortal world. Though I admit I did not know how severe the change would be in the case of Wonderland, but how could I? For she is first that has ever come back..." she said looking down at the broken glass. "... and the last,"

Wendy sobbed under the weight of reality that now faced her. "No!"

"I am so sorry, child. I truly am. For time designed for mortals is most cruel and unfair. It waits for no human; however special they may be. There is nothing I can do to change time for you, but I say to you now that you, my dear, have changed history. You have not only survived one of the Nine Realms, but two. You are the bravest child I have ever encountered, and I hate that magic has wrought you such wretched pain as this. But though you may not see it now, you have been given a second chance. You are not lost, nor dead. It is time, Wendy Darling to stop trying to be who you were before, but rather embrace who you are now! The past is gone, and there is nothing we can do to change that, but you must not squander your second chance. Take control of your future, for it lies in your hands alone. And I pray you never forget that you are not alone. We both are here for you and will help you in any way we can. You need only wish on a star, and I will come to wherever you are. You have survived what no one has. You must not waste your life feeling sorry for yourself, my dear, but discover what brings you joy," she said kindly wiping away her tears. "It took many to save you, Wendy. Do not let their efforts be in vain. Grieve the loss of your past but know this as well. The past is never gone as long as it is remembered."

Wendy thought on the Blue Fairy's words... remembering not only the nightmares of late, but of all those who had helped her in the magical worlds. The caterpillar, the Mad Hatter, Captain Hook, Mr. Smee and Catcher, even the Cheshire Cat in his own way had assisted her great escape. Wendy chuckled, lightly nodding. "You are right. My life has been quite the grand adventure."

Ainsel smiled at her, "And I cannot wait to see what you do with the rest of it."

Hook smiled too, wrapping his arm around Ainsel's small waist, looking down at the child with pride. "I only wish your family knew of your legendary tale."

It was then that an idea struck Wendy's imaginative mind. "Sometimes one must make their own wishes come true," she said turning to look at the blue fairy. "You are right. I will not waste my future, nor will I forget my past. I know what brings me joy- what has always brought me joy... telling stories."

Hook nodded, seeing the sparkle in her eye.

"My family *will* hear of my story, as will the world, because I am going to write it," Wendy said with fierce passion in her tone.

"I thought myself finished with reading magical tales, but I will most happily read the published works of Wendy Darling," Hook said.

But Wendy shook her head, "No, not Wendy Darling. For in this world, she is dead. I must go by another name."

"But..." Hook started.

"No. She is right," Ainsel said.

"Do not worry, Captain. I know who I really am and will never forget it again," Wendy said plainly.

Hook sighed, "What name will you take then?"

Wendy looked down thinking. Then as she glanced at her reflection from a piece of glass that lay broken on her left shoe, it came to her, "Alice... Alice Woods." Then she turned to Ainsel and asked sweetly, "I will not squander my second chance, I promise, but I do need your help with something."

"Anything. You need only ask." Ainsel replied.

"While I understand everything you have said, there is still the matter of..." she stopped.

"Of what, child." Ainsel asked encouraging her to continue.

"... where am I to go? Where am I to live? I am after all still a child in this world, am I not?" Wendy said.

"You can stay on my ship, with my crew at your command, and more money than you could ever hope to spend. You can write on the sea and will be given all you desire."

Wendy smiled, but shook her head. "Captain Hook, you are most generous... in everything, but I have been your burden long enough. I respectfully ask for a home of my own. A place where I can tell my tale, in hopes that in doing so, that I may be among those who try to bravely warn those in this world of the danger of magic and of the worlds beyond this one. I want you to tell me all you know about the Nine Realms, so that I might help or even save someone from the nightmares I have suffered. I don't want to be the victim anymore... the damsel in distress. I want to be brave, a protector of this world, a strong hero like you."

Her words had managed to soften the heart of a pirate, and with his eyes beaming brightly with pride, he bent down towards her face and spoke with the tone of a father to a daughter. "You will be, and I think I know just the way."

CHAPTER THIRTY

A NEW GUARDIAN

Though Wendy was eager to hear what came next, Ainsel suggested they sit and dine together. The very mention of food was enough to make Wendy's mouth water and her stomach grumble. But it was not the food that excited Hook, but rather the first view of his new ship. As they walked along the main deck towards the back, the full sky of bright twinkling stars shined their brilliance upon the sails, and the water beneath them glittered with their reflection.

It was a sight Hook had significantly missed, though its beauty was nothing compared to that of Ainsel's radiance. Having been gone for more than fifteen years, it seemed Blackbeard had spent his time creating the grandest ship he could for Hook to sail. Not sparing a coin or a man to work, the ship's magnificence was edged into every inch. With the finest of gold lanterns, wood, and red sails, Hook could see that his father had seen to each and every detail. It was a magnificent vessel, one that would shame even the Jolly Roger, and it now stood below its new captain's feet. There was no crew yet at his command, but on this

287

night, it was Ainsel's magic at the wheel of the ship, carrying it across the sea. The archway of every door had the carvings of warding symbols, each with a handle of the purest iron. Hook shook his head, smiling as they made their way through the ship covered in meticulous protection. Hook gazed at the vessel's every wonder.

When they arrived in the dining quarters, there was already a magical feast waiting upon the long wooden table. Five shiny golden candelabras stood lit upon its surface, their amber glow flickering upon the glorious feast. The great wall at the head was covered in windows, with the most amazing view Hook could ever have hoped to dine with. For Wendy, it was the sight of the food that brought her rushing her to the table. But as she reached out her hand for a small loaf of warm buttery bread, she hesitated.

"Do not fear the food, sweet Alice," Ainsel said kindly. "It is mortal food, I assure you. You will not grow or shrink after it has touched your lips, but merely warm and fill your belly afterward."

Wendy then excitedly sat in the nearest chair and consumed all the delicious sweet and savory treats she could reach. Hook and Ainsel sat on either side of her and joined in on the feast before them. At the right corner of the room, there was a rather large place setting for Catcher. With pillows and silver bowls of meat and fresh water, Catcher was quick to dive in and was sound asleep in no time. After a few bites of the delicious feast, Wendy looked up at Hook with her pressing question still unanswered. When the Captain caught her gaze, he knew it was time to tell her. "I apologize for making you wait, but I thought we could all use a little luxury before diving right into the business of magic again," Hook said.

"You said you knew a way for me to a hero like you... how?" Wendy asked.

Ainsel smiled at him besotted, sitting back in her chair, eagerly ready to hear it as well.

"Before the Mad Hatter made his way up to the stand within the Red Queen's court, he whispered something to me."

"What was it?" Wendy asked most curiously.

"I had asked him his real name, the name he had before Wonderland. He said he did not know it, but just before the cards took him away, he pulled me in close and whispered it in my ear- Geoffrey," Hook paused at the faces of Wendy and his fairy. Both looking even more confused than before. "You see, Wendy... I mean- Alice, when I was looking for you, I found myself in need of help. As I am sure you well know, the Hatter was most desperate to help find his long-lost daughter. When I asked to her his sad tale of his loss, I was surprised to find I learned a great deal from it. I now know of a hidden veil within this world. It sits in an abandoned manor on a hilltop far away. The Hatter said the house now belongs to you. For you, Alice, are now the last remaining in his family. But the house is not so much a gift as it is a curse. For inside its grand walls, is a wardrobe."

"A wardrobe?" Wendy said, surprised.

"Indeed, a wardrobe... but not just any wardrobe. This one is magical. It leads into another world beyond ours, the third in the Nine Realms. So, my idea is this, you my dear take the house as your own. I will give more than enough gold for anything you may need or require. You will have people to wait on you and cook for you. You can write your stories if that is your wish, and I will be sure you enjoy every luxury this world has to offer. It is a fate that the Hatter would have wanted for Alice, and in a way, I feel as though we are doing this for him as well."

Wendy smiled, "I like that idea, and it pleases me that you would think of the Hatters happiness, and not just my own. But what about the wardrobe? What of its danger?"

"The Magical Wardrobe has been locked away for a long time. Not even the fae know exactly where it is, making it a secret doorway in this world. Sadly, the magic of those on the other side still have the power to call them to it," Hook said.

"Them?" Wendy asked.

"The children," Ainsel said.

"Is that what happened to the Hatter's daughter? Did Alice go into the wardrobe?" Wendy asked.

"It is true; there is the danger of magic. There will be whispers, both ominous and inviting. They will call on you, urging you to open the door, but you must never listen. I believe that by your vast experiences, you will not be so easily influenced by their charms. The whispers are not the real danger, for they cannot do anything if you do not open the door... the real danger is what awaits any child that dares to turn the knob," Hook said most sternly at Wendy, "You, my dear, are a survivor if I've seen one, but the sad fact remains that many others have not had the same luck as you or I. Many lives and souls have been stolen and devoured from this world. You say you want to protect others from the same wretched nightmares that tormented you so... Well then, I say, we get a guardian of our own... I say- we make you the guardian of the wardrobe, a protector of this world. Keep others from the room, try to avoid it yourself if you can. It is not a life without fear, but also with an important purpose. Write your stories, tell such tales that will be whispered in every ear across the lands and sea. Tell this world what happened to Wendy Darling. And if you should like it, I will tell you many other tales too. There is much to learn of the

Nine Realms and the magical creatures that live inside them."

Wendy rose up, fiercely, "I want to know everything."

Ainsel stood up as well, placing her hands on each of Wendy's shoulders, "So you wish to live in the Hatter's house, as a guardian?"

"I do," Wendy said plainly.

Again, the child had struck Hook with pride. "Very well, then."

"But how do we find it? Did the Hatter give you its location?" Wendy asked.

"Leave that matter to me," Ainsel said playfully. "After all, all we fairy need to find something... is a *name*."

CHAPTER THIRTY-ONE

A PRISON OF FEAR

The words spoken by Ainsel, though not pleasing to Hook's ears, were but a sweet relief to Wendy. But the blue fairy's arrogance proved to be rather rushed, for the house of the Hatter seemed to be as lost as he was. Luckily, Hook himself was a master of the compass, able to find anything and anyone without a single spark of magic. But such efforts would take time, and it seemed that time had become as much Wendy's enemy as it was Hook's. Nevertheless, the Captain and Blue Fairy did all they could to keep Wendy distracted from the clock's ticking cruelty.

For Wendy, the best of these distractions came from the many tales told by the famous Captain of this world, and those from the Blue Fairy who came from the others beyond. Throughout the day, Wendy would listen to their stories of the Nine Realms, and of the magical creatures that dwell within them. Wendy looked up at the beautiful sky of painted colors of orange, yellow, and red.

It was on a day as beautiful as this that Wendy craved a good story. Coming up onto the main deck, Hook turned to find Wendy looking out to the sunset. With a smile, he approached her, "It is a glorious sight, isn't it, my dear?" He asked.

Wendy turned to him as he came to stand beside her. "Yes, I have always thought so, but today's sunset reminds me of a painting I admired as a young child," Wendy replied. Hook chuckled at her words. Confused and feeling a tad offended, she sneered. "What? Why are you laughing at me?" She asked.

"Forgive me; I meant no offense. I was just thinking about what anyone else would have said to you just now. Most people would have said that you still are a young child. What a silly thing to say. But I know more than anyone that age means nothing in this world, nor any other. Who I was as a young child was changed dramatically by a series of horrors. They changed me so much so, that in a matter of a month, weeks, or even a day I was a completely different person- a wiser person. So, when I heard you say the words that so many would fail to understand, I remembered the first time I said them, and how uncomfortable it made all those around me. It is rather odd though isn't it?" Hook said, looking out towards the horizon.

"What is?"

"When you realize that age is not truly defined by the amount of time you have spent in this world, but rather by the experiences you have endured. Some make you strong... some make you weak, but either way- they age you."

Wendy thought on his words, knowing the true telling of each of them. "I am the oldest of my siblings. Yet as it is now, they have been in this world much longer than me. They appear older and grown, while I appear young still. True, I have been through a great deal and survived much, but I have not felt the time pass the same way they have. Years have gone by here, while I have endured terrible horrors for no more than mere days. Honestly, I do not know who is the oldest of the three of us now. I thought once I left Wonderland, things would be less confusing, but they haven't at all. My appearance, my name, my age..." After a short breath, Wendy turned to Hook in need of a distraction from her thoughts of time, for though she hated it greatly, she knew she could never do anything to change it. "I survived the fae, and I swore I would not squander my second chance, but I fear I will never feel happiness again."

Hook smiled at her, nodding with empathy and compassion. "I know the pain that comes from being a survivor, maybe more than anybody. My strength and shielded protection did not come without a terrible cost. You know a great many of my adventures, but you do not know all of them." Wendy's eyes grew with interest. "Once, many years ago- my father and I were called upon by a man in France. He was a nobleman in the King's court."

"What did he want?" Wendy asked.

"He had written asking for our help."

"Help with what?"

"The man said that he had made a deal by magic for a great fortune and highborn name, not wanting to live in squalor like his father before him, but he had broken his end of the deal in arrogance. Fearing what evil the fairy would inflict upon him if he were to ever be found, he asked my father for protection."

"And did he?"

Hook smiled a small smirk as he slowly shook his head. "I'm afraid the only sure way one is protected from magic is by magic. There was really nothing we could do, besides giving him one piece of advice... *hide.*"

"What happened to him after that?"

"Last I heard, he had locked himself away in a prison cell far away, hiding his face behind an iron mask. He is well guarded and treated very well, but he is secluded in an isolation most wretched. Afraid of any charms or enchantments, he allowed no one to speak or even visit with him, leaving him only one man to attend to him, bring him food, and empty his chamber pot, he has become quite a mysterious prisoner. It seems his efforts to disappear and remain hidden from the fae have worked, but if you ask me... the fate he has chosen for himself is far worse than anything a fairy could ever do. I cannot imagine a more terrible existence in this world than that of *the man in the iron mask*. He is alone- and he will die alone... in the very prison that he made for himself. When he dies, no one will mourn him or even remember him as anything other than a prisoner."

"If no one knows who he is... how do you know?" Wendy asked.

"The man that attends to him- the *only* man... was given the charge by my father, Blackbeard," Hook chuckled. "And believe me, loyalty to my father is not just bought by gold but leashed by fear. There is no man alive that would dare betray him."

"Yes, I have heard many stories about him... many frightening stories I mean. Why would your father help him?" Wendy asked carefully, hoping her words would not offend him.

"It is quite a story of an interesting turn of events actually. You see, in order to receive such secrecy and protection, the man had to pay my father with the very fortune he had been given by magic. Though I'd like to think that it is also a matter of compassion. My father is also a survivor, but he too hides behind his red curtains and immortal power. Blackbeard is no coward. He is strong, daring, and yes... very frightening, but make no mistake- he is also afraid of the fae. My point is, it is okay to be afraid. You would be a fool not to be. But take it from me- a man with once a bitter soul and vengeful heart... if I can find happiness and love, so too can you, Wendy Darling. Don't let your fear of magic consume you. Keep fighting, have faith, for if you put up a wall of false protection, you may find that you have blocked anything good from entering your life as well. And I don't want that for you, because you, my dear, are a hero. And though heroes must endure tragedy and obstacles, I believe that they always get a happy ending. But you have to believe this as well... for belief is possibly the strongest form of magic that there is. It can bend the laws of logic and reason, and manifest in ways you couldn't possibly imagine. Never underestimate it, nor lean into it blindly. Do you understand everything I have said to you?"

Wendy nodded, "Yes... I understand."

"Good. The sun has set, let us forget the heavy matters for now and go dine with my lovely fairy, and find out when we can expect to see your new home."

298

CHAPTER THIRTY-TWO

THE FIRST KING

With the skills of a magical fairy and that of a pirate, the search for the Hatter's manor was finally over. With little more than a day left on the ship, Wendy was itching to board land and get off the sea. Hook had promised her motion sickness would improve after having time to adapt, but it seemed her stomach proved otherwise.

Nevertheless, Wendy never showed how miserable she really was in front of them. She knew she could probably ask Ainsel to magically aid her nausea, but she knew if she said anything, Hook would feel guilty for having kept her on the ship. It was no secret how protective Hook had become over her. It was nice really... almost like having a father again- one that understood her. But nothing would ever come close enough to make Wendy stop missing her mother. She thought about her all the time, and her brothers as well. She wondered how they were doing, how their life turned out, if they were happy, but mostly she wondered if they ever missed her.

"I can help with that."

Wendy gasped startled to find Ainsel had suddenly appeared in her room. "Goodness, you scared me."

Ainsel giggled, "I'm sorry."

"What did you mean? Help with what?" Wendy asked.

Ainsel came and sat down on the bed next to her. "You may be able to hide your sorrows from James, but let's not forget, my dear, that *I* am a fairy. I can hear your thoughts and I can see what is in your dreams."

Wendy instantly recoiled feeling as though she had been violated in some way. "What?"

Ainsel quickly backed up, "Oh I am sorry, it is just a power I have. I forget sometimes how intruding it must be for a mortal. It is not my favorite quality about myself, and believe me, I am happy that such magic does not work on James. Anyways, I just thought I could help you. I know how unhappy you have been on this ship, and I just thought maybe I could help."

Wendy's eyes squinted in suspicious uncertainty, "Help me with what exactly?"

"Your parents, your brothers, wouldn't you like to see them?"

Wendy's eyes widened in shock, "What are you talking about, you know I cannot go see them. I look like an entirely different person, you said yourself."

"True, but I meant seeing them in a different way... *my way.* With an orb and some dust, I can show you what you wish to see." Wendy still looked a little uncertain. "Come on, tell me who you want to see, and I will show it to you... come on. Trust me."

Wendy sat up straight and took a deep breath before allowing the first words to fall from her lips... "My mother. I want to see my mother."

Ainsel smiled, and with a swish of her magic wand, her glittering blue dust slowly spread on an orb that appeared suddenly floating before them. At first Wendy saw nothing in it, but as she stepped closer, the image of someone began to emerge inside. It was her mother. She looked different, not just older, but changed. She no longer had that spark that Wendy had always loved so dearly. She was sitting in her chair by the fire, gazing into the dancing warm flames. Seeing her this way brought tears to Wendy's eyes... but then her mother turned, almost like she could see her. Wendy stood up frozen.

Can she see me?" Wendy asked.

No, but she is looking at a piece of you... look." Ainsel said pointing back at the orb. Wendy did as she was asked, curious to see what she meant by a piece of her. But as she looked closer, she saw that something small was now approaching her mother's chair. Her mother picked it up, placing it on her lap. Wendy squinted her eyes, straining to see what this small figure was. Then she saw them, the beautiful jade eyes of her beloved Dinah, her sweet baby kitten. She was older, bigger, and still beautiful as ever. It was then that Wendy saw her mother smile."

"Incredible isn't it?" Ainsel asked.

"What?"

"That the cat your mother bought for you for comfort, is now her only comfort when she is sad. In a way, Dinah gives her a way to still love you. You wondered if your family misses you... I can promise you that they do- all of them. Your father is alright, your brothers are alright, and your mother is too. She has some bad days, but that's what Dinah is there for. It's time to move on now."

"I know," Wendy said trying not to cry. "It is hard to not think about them- to not miss them every minute of every day. It is a constant battle against my heart, and it hurts. But something else has caught my attention as well."

"What is that?" Ainsel asked.

"I've already begun to lose my memories of Wonderland. Before, I thought I would write my tales once I had arrived in my new home, but I don't think it can last another second. I have taken little notes here and there, but now they all seem so scattered. I need to start writing now... tonight!"

Ainsel smiled. "I think that is a wonderful idea. What story do you think you will start with?"

Wendy thought on it, "Well since it was my latest adventure that was so confusing and difficult to remember, I suppose I should start with that one. Don't you?"

"Getting things written while they are fresh in your mind is a good start, yes! So, the realm of Wonderland... What an odd little world. But how much do you really know about it?" Ainsel asked.

Wendy was a little surprised by her question. "Well I would like to say I know a great deal about it."

"Really... So, then you know its ruler?" Ainsel asked as if testing her.

"Well, the Queen of Hearts of course," Wendy answered.

"Tis, tis, tis," Ainsel said shaking her head. "No, my dear, I speak of the land's one true ruler... or at least the first. The Fairy that created the realm and made it what it is. The very Fairy whose influential magic still drives its inhabitants mad."

Now it was Wendy shaking her head, completely unaware that such a fairy had existed. "If there was another ruler there, then how did Rose Red come to rule the realm?"

"It is an ancient tale... even for us. One that has changed many times depending on who is telling it. Though it is uncertain how the Queen of Hearts managed to defeat the former King, what is certain is who he once was and *what* he is now." Ainsel then waved her hand in the air, changing the image within the floating orb.

Wendy stood from the bed to gaze into the vision before her. It was then that she was able to see a story unravel from the past, with as much vivid clarity that it was as if she were seeing it from the other side of a hidden window. At first, there was only the familiar lively forest of brightly colored trees, but then through the fluffy bushes below, a crowd of tiny creatures suddenly burst through, scattering in fear from something behind them.

By the looks of their frantic faces, Wendy instantly feared what or who was coming next. Then a wicked laugh came echoing through the woods. Safe as she was, even Wendy's skin crawled with fear from the sound of its chilling malice.

"I never thought I would hear a more sinister laugh than Pan's. I don't think I want to see what could make such an evil sound as that." But no sooner had the last word fell from her lips, did the benevolent creature emerge from the trees. "It's... a monster," Wendy said wide eyed, watching in horror as it stomped through the tormented forest. At first, it appeared like a ferocious dragon, but it was much... much worse. With red wings, green scales, and eyes that glowed with fire, it was a most terrifying sight indeed.

But once every creature had fled away in terror, the monster's form began to slowly change. Wendy gasped as she set her eyes upon a charming looking man. He had long orange hair, each strand falling perfectly in place. The appearance of his pale and fair skin, one might have thought there was no blood running through his veins, but the warmth of his rosy lips and the fire in his eyes, proved that he was most definitely alive. He wore a fancy red coat with matching pointed boots. Underneath his coat, he wore a green scaly vest with golden buttons, and his pants were in a checkered design, colored in black and white and tight to his long thin legs. When he saw that he had scared off all the creatures in his forest, he laughed again. Wendy could see his bright wicked smile. Never had she seen anything so symmetrically odd and beautiful.

"He was called the Amadan Dubh, once the high jester of the Elder court. He is a shapeshifter, a trickster, and one of the most powerful fairies there ever was. No one knows what he did to be sent away from court, though it is speculated that his tricks had become too cruel and his behavior beyond all reason or control. All that is known to be certain about the Amadan Dubh is that he was stark raving mad. One touch by the fairy would send your mind into a depth of insanity that you could never get out of. Pleading for the Amadan's mercy would never save you, for he delighted in the pain and ridicule he had the power to inflict. It is said that his victims are so stained by his magic that they are driven towards the dark woods of Ireland by the whispering sound of his manic laughter echoing in their heads. Unable to resist his magic, they were lured to his shadow dancing on top the loneliest of hilltops. He reveled in his victim's misery. To this day, there are still parts of the mortal world, where whenever a person goes suddenly mad, they call it the touch of the Amadan. Sadly, a cure has never been found to fix the warped and troubled mind touched by him. There was no way to hide or even identify the Amadon Dubh, because he was always constantly changing. But now..." Ainsel paused.

"Now what?" Wendy asked.

"When Rose Red entered the world and saw how he terrorized all the creatures within the realm, she used her own magic to bind him in his monstrous form, leashed to serve her forever. He is now called the Jabberwocky, the once powerful fairy of the Emerald Isle, now known as the Red Queen's greatest weapon." Ainsel said with an odd hesitant tone of empathy for the slaved creature.

"I never saw such a beast while I was there. I say this with great certainty. True, I have already begun to forget a great many things from Wonderland, yet I feel most positive that I would have remembered a creature such as that."

"I have no doubt you are right about that. For the Queen keeps her creature locked securely away until..."

"Until what?" Wendy asked.

"Until the war of Wonderland finally commences." Ainsel replied.

"War? With who?" Wendy asked, desperate to hear the answer.

"The Snow Queen. The time will come when the White Queen gains all the power she will need to leave her citadel of ice and will be back on her trail of conquering all the Nine Realms. But the Red Queen has spent a great amount of time making Wonderland a place of her very own. She won't be giving it up that easily. There is a prophecy about such a war, though who wins the battle in the end remains unclear. I am glad that you are gone from that place, and out of such danger." Ainsel said sweetly. "Come, child, lay down on your bed and get some good sleep. Tonight, I have placed a charm upon you so that your memories remain intact and that you will never again be plagued with nightmares. Allow your mind to be free while you sleep, and you will find that you can do anything. You can play with your brothers as you did before. You can embrace your mother's hug and smell her lovely perfume. You can fly like a bird or swim like a fish, but no matter what your mind decides to imagine, I promise none of it will ever scare you. Beyond that, the charm I have bestowed upon you will allow you to keep your dreams as memories. Do you understand what this means, child?"

"I think so," Wendy answered hesitantly.

"It means, dearest, that you will get to experience two realities, one of them has rules, logic, impossibilities, corruption, and those with the power to hurt you. The other reality though, will be entirely yours, with no rules or obligations other than those that you choose for yourself. You can see who you wish, do as you wish, eat as you wish, and when you wake the following morning, you will remember it all. It is quite a gift... one that many wished they had."

"Thank you, Ainsel. I am incredibly grateful to you for such a generous gift."

"Your welcome, my dear. Now go get some rest, and by the time you wake up... we will be at the place of your new home- the Hatter's Manor.

CHAPTER THIRTY-THREE

SWEET DREAMS

Having not written a thing, Wendy excitedly closed her eyes: ready to dream something wonderful. As her troubled mind slipped into the darkness, she waited for the bliss of another reality to wash over her. At first, there was nothing; just a deep black space. But then she felt something on her, something soft. It was then that a pair of bright jade eyes pierced through the darkness.

"Dinah! Is that you?" The moment the words left her lips, a stream of lights hanging from magnificent chandeliers of crystal appeared before them. Wendy quickly gazed about the room. There were levels of soft, luxurious chairs in rows circling the entire space. Velvet curtains hiding secret exits could be found but not reached. Finally, the last piece of the room appeared: it was a glorious wooden platform.

It's a stage. It was then that Wendy realized that she was in a grand theatre room, and she and Dinah were sitting in the audience chairs. Wendy and her brothers had always fantasized what it would be like to see a show in the theatre, but their father had only ever taken their mother. John and Michael always sulked whenever they were left behind, and it was usually up to Wendy to lift their spirits.

She would create a performance of her own: coming up with the most incredible skits and stories. In truth, she had never truly learned what kind of acts were performed at the Grand Theatre; she could only imagine.

I cannot believe I am finally going to see a show. If only my brothers were here with me. It doesn't seem right that they aren't going to see it too. No sooner had the thought struck her mind, did it occur to her that her brothers probably *had* seen a show in the theatre since she saw them last. After all, they were both grown men now. Her father had always said the theatre was no place for children, but John and Michael were not children anymore- only her. Then suddenly her tinge of sadness disappeared as her two brothers all of the sudden appeared on either side of her. John was to her left, and Michael was to her right. They looked exactly like they had before she left them. They seemed happy, eager, and excited. The sight of them made her heart soar.

"Hi-ya, Wendy," little Michael said. His voice was always so precious, yet she hadn't realized how much she had missed it until this very moment.

"Hello, sweet Michael."

"I say, what a glorious vision: The Grand Theatre. Why I cannot wait for them to raise the curtain," said John in his usual deep tone that was always too proper for his age. He was wearing the same top hat he always wore in public, along with a suit and a cane that matched their father's. Wendy smiled at her younger brother. She had never told him how pretentious he behaved, or how ridiculous he looked in a top hat too big for his head. *After all, why would she? It was rather charming.*

"Wendy?"

She turned to her right, "Yes, Michael?"

"Where are mother and father?" He asked. His longing eyes looked concerned: the way that any toddler does when they can't see their mommy.

"I don't know..." She started to say, but then an idea hit her. This was her dream. Ainsel said she could create anything she wanted. With an excited smile, she closed her eyes and envisioned her parents. After she took a deep breath, she opened her eyes... and there they were. Her beautiful mother sat in a lovely rose-pink gown next to Michael. Her golden-brown hair was tied up in her usual fashion. There was a golden locket that hung around her neck that Wendy had given her for Mother's Day. From the day Wendy had given it to her, her mother had never taken it off.

She smiled at her: with the lively sparkle still in her eyes. "Oh, Mother. You look so lovely."

"Thank you, dear," she replied.

"Shhh," John whispered before looking up to their father: hoping his manner would impress him.

"Yes, children. Be quiet. The curtain is beginning to rise." Father said.

The children clapped quietly, eager to see what awaited them beyond the velvet curtain. At a slow riveting pace, the curtain rose, revealing a line of beautiful young women. They were each dressed in short sparkling dresses in the color of ice blue. Their make-up was bright and dramatic. Their hair was tightly bound in braided buns atop their heads, and each held a tall, glittering feather that matched the sets of high heels upon their feet. With big smiles and rosy cheeks, they began to sing and dance in perfect pitch and unison.

Mary Darling was the first to react in awe at their astounding beauty. Clapping and smiling, she praised their every move. "Oh, look, George, don't they look radiant?" She asked.

"Indeed," he replied coldly. In truth, this kind of response from him regarding such matters was always so. Their father would never allow himself to gaze at a beautiful woman in any way that he found to be unsuitable of a married gentleman. Instead, his face would remain still, with the sort of stone face expression one would expect to see in a painted portrait. Though many would believe it was merely for the sake of their mother's feelings, this was not the case. For not only was their mother not the envious sort but for George, it went far deeper than that. To him, it simply just was not proper of a man of his standing. But such standards, he did not only hold to himself but for the rest of the family as well.

Everyone needed to be what he thought was perfectly proper. Their mother never failed him in that way. To George, his wife and the mother of his children, has always been practically perfect in all matters, and he loved nothing more than showing her off proudly. To him, image was everything, presentation was paramount, and even the three children were allowed no exception of flaw but one: the nursery. The nursery was not only a place for the children to run and play; it was a place of wonder; a place where they could be anything or anyone they could possibly imagine. And now here they were again in the dream world, with Wendy's wild imagination at the wheel. With time standing still, and a blink of her eyes, she realized she could create anything she desired.

"Wendy, I wish there were animals up there instead," Michael said.

With a slight smile, Wendy blinked her eyes and made his wish come true. They watched hippos dance, a lion sing opera, and even saw a wild trapeze act with dressed monkeys. The entire family seemed to love it all. Even John who constantly sought their father's approval clapped and cheered.

The magic of the evening was so that Wendy never wanted it to end. Then the seasons began to change, what was once bubbles floating within the air, had now changed to snowflakes falling from an invisible sky before the ceiling.

Suddenly, Wendy realized it wasn't only her family that was clapping. She turned behind her to find that there was, in fact, someone else in the theatre with them. She could not see who he was, for his face was shaded under the dark hood of a large cloak. "Who is that?" Wendy whispered to John.

John turned around in his seat to look at whoever it was that Wendy was seeing, but even as he faced the same direction and his eyes fell upon the right chair, he did not see anything. "I do not see anyone, Wendy. Ask Mom and Dad."

But as Wendy and John turned back to confront their parents- they were both gone.

"Mom!? Dad?!" Where are you?! Where did you go?" Wendy cried out, but no one answered. As her eyes rapidly searched for them around the theater, she quickly noticed that the cloaked man had somehow moved closer. There was something about him. He did not strike her as scary, but rather mysterious, and anybody that knows anything about Wendy knows about her overwhelming attraction to curiosity.

Nevertheless, the man's dark appearance did call the question... *who was he? And what was doing here in her dream?* After all, he was the only thing or person within the entire theatre that she didn't create.

"John, you seriously do not see him. He is right there!" She said subtly pointing to the man from behind her tall clothed chair, but when she did not hear an answer back from her brother, she perked her head back up and saw that both John and Michael were gone now.

But that was not all: the theater, the stage, it was suddenly all fading away. There was nothing left. The bright and exciting theatre was now empty. She was all alone now- except for... she turned to face the cloaked man again.

The sound of her gasp echoed throughout the room as she found that once again, the man in the large cloak had moved, and this time, he was right behind her- smiling.

CHAPTER THIRTY-FOUR
THE HATTER'S MANOR

When Ainsel came into Hook's chamber and told him what spell she cast upon Wendy, he was anything but happy. "Why would you do that to her? Do you honestly not see how torturous that will ultimately be?" He screamed.

"James! What you fail to understand is how damaged her mind already is. Have you forgotten the promises the Green Fairy vowed before I took her before the Elders?"

Hook huffed, "Of course, I remember, but I do not see why..."

"After everything you endured to save her from Wonderland, I wanted to protect you both from the truth of her condition."

"What condition?" He asked sternly, not liking such secrecy.

After a sigh of sorrow, she answered: "James, a child's mind is fragile, and Wendy's has been twisted and altered more than any human has endured without succumbing completely to madness. Despite the Green Fairy's crimes, the Elders were reluctant to deliver upon her the Eternal Death. Instead, they sought it fit to punish her by merely destroying her body."

"What does that mean?"

"It *means* that her magic is no longer bound to her vessel."

Hook shook his head with frustrating confusion, rolling his hands in a circular motion, urging her to elaborate: "And?"

"Don't you see... with her magic set free, the source will seek its greatest chance to be reborn. The Green Fairy knew this when I took her. She vowed to come back and will use Wendy's nightmares to do it. When you both first returned through the looking glass, I had no idea how troubled her mind was. You have to believe me when I say that I have spent this entire trip thinking and hoping to do anything else, but I fear I run out of time. We are going to arrive at the Hatter's manor by the morning, and it seems that time away from the magical realm hasn't done much to help her tainted mind. The sadness of missing her family has also left her vulnerable. The Green Fairy's magic will find her eventually if her mind continues on the way it is. I do not have the magic to block her from dreaming at all, for the magic from the Dream Realm is far more powerful than my own. Wendy tried to hide her misery and sadness, but I thought surely you could see how troubled she has been."

Hook thought about it for a second, and his answer angered him greatly, "*No!* I did not, in fact, know that!"

"Well it is not your fault, my love. After all, she was keeping her true feelings locked deep inside."

Hook nodded for a moment, but then something stopped him, and he glared over to her. "If she kept her misery so well hidden, then how did you come to know of these *secret feelings?*"

Ainsel winced, "Well... I can hear her thoughts and have been monitoring the influence that magic still has on her dreams."

"Ainsel!" Hook screamed in a fury.

"I will not allow you to shout at me that way! I know you hate the powers of the fae, but I *am* fae. It is just a part of me. I did not ask for these abilities; I just have them. You need to believe in me and know that what I did was the very best I could have done for her. I used a charm that will block out all the bad things."

"No, *what you did* is cause her further mental turmoil. The human mind is such a fragile thing, and now she will be unable to distinguish between two very real realities."

Letting out a sigh, Ainsel grabbed his hand. "I am sorry, but it was the best I could do."

"Your best... well, I have done my best for her as well- seems like our help does nothing but cause her further suffering," Hook replied plainly before leaving the room and the Blue Fairy behind him.

When Wendy woke the following morning, she was surprised to find they were still on the water. The waves were riotous, splashing against the windows with extreme force. Rubbing her tired eyes, she made her way towards the main deck. Doing her best to avoid the showing mist coming down, she reached the upper floor.

Once she found Hook, she saw that he was calmly gazing out from the wheel. Dawn had barely begun to light up the sky, but its glow was ominous and red. The look on Hook's face as she drew closer made her uneasy. When he turned to look at her, he smiled. It was fake, and she knew it. Something was wrong. "What is it? Where are we?" She asked.

"Iceland," he answered plainly. Wendy waited for him to say something else, but it seemed his short demeanor was purposeful. She could see that he didn't want to say anymore, but she wasn't going to let up.

"What is the matter? I thought we would be at the house by today..." She asked.

But before Hook could say another word, Ainsel appeared on the deck. "We *are* here, little one. I am sure James just wanted to wait until you woke up before heading towards the hill," she said pointing to the highest cliff above the water. Wendy's eyes shot up to the hill so eagerly that she didn't notice the angry glare that Hook gave Ainsel. The Blue Fairy may not have been able to read his mind, but she could certainly feel the fury from his gaze. While Wendy jumped for joy at first sight of the decrepit manor, Ainsel timidly approached her tempered pirate. "It is going to be alright, James. She is going to be alright," she whispered near his ear. Still, Hook couldn't shake the feeling that something was wrong- that there was something he was forgetting.

"I see it! I see it!" Wendy shouted. "Let's go up there!"

Ainsel turned to Wendy, smiling: "Alright, sweet Alice, we're going."

Without being able to say with any real reason not to go, Hook docked his ship, and the three made their way upon the land and into the town below the hill. The little town of Vik was all too familiar with the old manor.

Whispers of hauntings and terrible things happening within its walls had managed to scare off anyone from wanting to take the house as their own. Most of the children were too afraid to approach the gate that separated the town from the famed abandoned tea party on the other side, and those that were brave enough to climb over and make their way inside were never seen or heard from again.

Over the years, many had attempted to destroy the property, but no sooner had they reached the grass at the top of the hill, would their minds suddenly change, forcing them to turn around and return to their homes before realizing what had even happened. Legend of the Hatter and the mysterious disappearance of his beloved daughter wasn't the only one tied to the house; it was merely the first. Yet, it wasn't the haunting tales and heeding words from the townspeople that crawled underneath Hook's skin, it was the clouded thought hidden behind the lingering fog of Wonderland.

Nevertheless, he was out of time- for with every step they took, they were closer to the manor's door. With Ainsel and Hook at her side, Wendy seemed to be immune to fear. She entered the door full of childish wonder and excitement. From the moment they entered the creaky entrance, she started running around imagining what creative changes she could bring to its current eerie appearance. Ainsel and Wendy quickly joined together, giggling as Ainsel used her wand to create Wendy's every wish magically. With every swish, the rooms became more beautiful, with vibrant colored wallpaper, and exquisite furniture. Large rugs appeared upon what now looked like newly polished floors. Long curtains with floral designs now hung from the tall new pane of windows. When they reached the broken staircase, Ainsel snapped her fingers to bring each piece safely back together with a rose gold handrail to edge the top of each step that was now covered in a lovely ruby red rug that poured down from the second floor. Once the entire downstairs was finished, Wendy ran up to see the other rooms.

It was at this moment that Hook's silence finally broke: "Wendy wait!" He shouted, running up behind her and grabbing her shoulder. Wendy gasp startled, but as she looked up into his eyes, she could see how fearful he was.

"What is it, Captain?" She asked.

Hook took a breath, thinking of what to say, but his clouded mind still wasn't clear enough to make sense of his overwhelming concern. "I- I don't know."

Wendy turned to look up at the first room when suddenly she saw something outside one of the windows. Down below was the abandoned tea party. All the beautiful teacups and fancy teapots were still on the old tablecloth. Each were covered in rust and cracked by age and time. Its haunting image reminded her of the Mad Hatter, and the terrible loss he had endured on the day of Alice's birthday. It was then that Wendy realized what she thought was going on in Hook's mind. He had always been so protective of her. *How could she think that this would be so easy on him?* She wondered.

She turned to look at him again: "I know... but you don't have to worry about me. I know the danger of the wardrobe, and I promise that I will be fine. I will be a good guardian. Please tell me you believe in me. I need you to believe in me."

Hook smiled weakly: "Of course I do.

"Well then, be happy for me. It was after all your idea to bring me here. You said I would live a life of luxury and comfort."

"I did and you will. I promise you will have more than enough gold to ever hope to spend in your lifetime. I have sent out orders for people to come and wait on you. I want you to write and tell your story; I truly do."

"Then what has you so upset?

"   I don't know. I just..."

"Is it the wardrobe?" She asked.

Hook shook his head trying to figure it out himself, but he just couldn't put his finger on it. Finally, he sighed: "Maybe that is it. I feel like there was something about the wardrobe that I am forgetting, but my mind is still such a blur, I cannot seem to sort it all out in my head. But whatever it is, I fear leaving you here before I figure it out. I just- I worry about you. I know I am the one that asked you to do this, and it felt right at the time, but now..."

Wendy smiled and hugged him. Hook was stunned at first, but his arms slowly found their way around her. The moment was a sweet one- one that Ainsel felt should be private.

"Well, I am going to go ahead and fix up the rest of your rooms, Alice," Ainsel said in a whisper, hoping not to interrupt the precious moment between them. As the blue fairy went on using her magic to create the perfect dream house for Wendy, she was also using her magic to confine all the negative power and bad feelings that suffused the air, to just one room- the room of the wardrobe. After she finished making a most enchanting desk with all the best things a writer could hope to own on top, she used one final zap to make a purple wingback chair. It seemed she had finished the room just in the nick of time as Wendy and Hook began walking in. Wendy gasped in awe. "I love it, Ainsel! All of it! Thank you so much; both of you!"

Ainsel and Hook both smiled. "There is something truly special about a child that happy," Hook said.

"See my love; she is going to be fine," Ainsel said sweetly.

Maybe it was the beautiful appearance that was now surrounding them, perhaps it was the fact that Ainsel had confined all the dark magic to only one room, or maybe he was merely caught up in all their happiness, but suddenly he felt very ashamed. He had told Wendy that she could feel true happiness again, but here he was ruining it for her.

"Captain, come see my room!" Screamed Wendy.

Hook nodded, realizing what he needed to do. "Alright, I'm coming!" He shouted back with enthusiasm. When he reached her doorway, he was stunned by what he saw. There were beautifully crafted bookshelves covering all four walls.

"Are they not wonderful, Captain? Ainsel knew how scared I am of windows, and how much I love books. It looks absolutely amazing. She even made sure to fill each shelf will all the books she thought I would love." Wendy jumped up on her new canopy bed with glittering curtains hanging from every corner. "Is this bed not the best bed you have ever seen?" She asked falling into the mountain of feathered pillows.

"It is, my dear, "Hook said smiling. "It is indeed."

After many hours of decorating her new home, Wendy's excitement had finally worn her out. Hook and Ainsel were happy to tuck her into her new bed. "Sweet Alice, you are happy, aren't you?" Ainsel asked.

Wendy smiled wide: "Yes! I am very happy- happier than I ever thought I could be. But as lovely as my home has become, I cannot wait to enter my dreams again and tell my family."

"Well I have one more gift to bestow upon you in your new home. For though we cannot be here every day, it would make our hearts ache if we thought you were lonely. So..." Ainsel whipped out her wand again. "Now close your eyes."

Wendy did as she was told, though shaking with overwhelming excitement. One could have spotted her two little feet hopping around under the covers. "I am ready."

"Alright." Ainsel whipped her wand and with a final zap, a blue sparkling dust appeared to come down into the shape of a tiny cat. Once every sparkle was in place, Ainsel told Wendy to open her eyes. Wendy looked both elated and a bit confused. "Blow, Alice, blow." Ainsel instructed.

Wendy nodded excitedly and blew each of the sparkles away as hard as she could with the deepest of breaths. It took so much of her energy, she had not realized her eyes were closed, until she heard a faint meow. Wendy opened her eyes to find a little orange kitten looking up at her. Wendy's eyes filled in absolute awe and wonder. Falling forward to scoop up her new furry companion, she gushed and kissed with all the love in the world.

"I know there are things in the Dream World that you will find wonderful, and I just thought that maybe you would want a little something wonderful here too. Do you like her?"

Wendy gleefully nodded, "Oh of course I do, who would not love such an adorable little sweet?"

"What are you going to name her?" Ainsel asked. Hook thought about interjecting in hopes of explaining his take on names, but he did not want a single thing to ruin the smile on Wendy's precious face.

"Marmalade," Wendy giggled. "Her name will be *Marmalade*."

"Well I think that is just adorable, don't you think so, James?" Ainsel asked.

Hook nodded, "It is! In fact, I would go as far as saying Marmalade is perfect."

Wendy hugged her precious kitten before cuddling up beside her on the pillow. "Everything is perfect. Thank you."

Ainsel smiled, looking to Hook in hopes that he too could see how beautiful everything was. Despite his true feelings, Hook nodded.

"I am going to start writing tomorrow. Will you still be here when I wake up?" Wendy asked in a sleepy tone.

Ainsel could see that Hook couldn't bear to answer, so she spoke in his place: "This house is yours, my darling, not ours. You are a guardian of the veil now. Do not worry, we will visit you often, but you need to write and dream up a world all your own. The ship cannot stay this close to the cliffs for long. It will get damaged under such terrible weather conditions. It needs a crew, it needs to be out on the open sea, but above all- it needs its captain." Her last words were said looking at Hook with a gentle gaze.

The idea of leaving Wendy so soon was hard to swallow, but he knew she was right. "Remember, we are never too far away. If you ever need us, you need only wish it, and we will be here quicker than that." Ainsel said snapping her fingers.

"Really? You promise?" Wendy asked.

"By the blood in the water, and the magic of the fae, you have our word," Hook replied.

Hearing Hook's words with the fatherly tone of protection was all it took to wisp Wendy away into the dream world.

CHAPTER THIRTY-FIVE

ALWAYS TRUST A BAD FEELING

While Wendy slept in her new gorgeous bed, Ainsel and Hook continued to do all they could to ward off any dark magic. Despite Ainsel's pleading, Hook opened the door to the one room that even Ainsel couldn't control. From the second he put his hand on the ancient doorknob, he could feel the negative energy coming from the other side.

The forbidden door creaked like a wailing cry as it opened. The stale air on the inside smelled like it had been locked away from another time. With boarded windows, Hook carefully lit a candle so he could see. A quiet whispering breath blew, turning the once sunset flame into a flickering violet. There was so much dust in the room; it made it incredibly difficult to breathe. The haunting energy within the room was enough to make one feel the lingering sorrow to all of those who were taken.

How odd it feels to be alone in a room yet feel the presence of a crowd. Wall to wall, there was furniture covered in old sheets, but there was no mistaking which of them was the wardrobe. At the center, it stood tall and intimidating. Hook removed the large grey sheet that covered its towering wooden beauty. The cloud of dust that followed made Hook choke harshly within the musty air.

With burning red eyes, he peered up into the notorious wardrobe. The carvings and designs upon the ancient wood were nothing short of a masterpiece. One that no other could ever hope to measure up. The mirror that stood on the front of its door was long and oval in shape, with what appeared to be orange rusted along its edge. The center of the mirror, however, cracked and aged, seemed to look more like a window than a mirror. It wasn't just that it distorted one's reflection, but rather how it drew you in closer as if looking for something else.

After a deep breath, Hook brought his hand to the tarnished knob, and with a squeaky turn, he pulled the door open. Not knowing what he should have expected to find once he was inside, Hook stepped into the deep wardrobe. But as he reached past all the dresses and coats, all he found was a wooden panel: no door, no portal, just the backing of any ordinary armoire.

But before Hook completely turned around to walk back out, he heard something. It wasn't a voice, but more like a whistle. After a second of looking, he found that it was coming from a tiny crack within the wood. When he put his hand down in front of it, he could feel the brisk chill of winter. With a frustrated huff, he hit the back panel with great force, but to no avail.

Nothing happened. He was not a child and would therefore never have access to the hidden veil. After walking out of the room, he found Ainsel waiting for him down the hall.

"Well, what happened?" She asked.

"You and I both knew that nothing was going to happen," Hook replied.

"Then what were you hoping for?" Ainsel asked.

Hook shook his head, "I still do not know. I guess I was hoping for some clarity. I thought that maybe being so close to the wardrobe; I could somehow unblock whatever it is that is bothering me before..."

"-Before we leave?" Ainsel finished.

Hook nodded. "It does not matter anyway, though; it did not work. I still don't know what I am forgetting. Maybe we should not leave. I don't think I can."

Ainsel approached him then, seeing what a desperate state he was in. "James, we have to go. You know we do. Catcher is waiting for us safely on the ship. We must find Mr. Smee and a crew."

Feeling torn between his ship being thrashed upon the riotous cliffs and his gut feeling telling him not to leave her, Hook reached to the depths of his mind for a solution- any solution. With a heavy sigh, he asked: "What about her future, can't you use your magic to look ahead?"

"No, James, I cannot."

The speed of her harsh reply surprised him, "What? Why not?"

"It is impossible," Ainsel said hesitantly.

Hook shook his head, not understanding, "What do you mean?"

"I mean what I said, James. It cannot be done. Believe me, I tried."

"You have tried?" How?"

Ainsel sighed, hating having to disappoint him. "I told you that I had combed through every possible way to ensure her safety. But when I tried to look into her future, it was blocked by the overshadowing power of the wardrobe. Such magic surpassed my own in a way that makes such a possibility impossible. Nevertheless, we must believe that she will be okay. This is her home now. She asked for our faith, and we must not disappoint her. For if she feels our doubt, it will surely tarnish her own hope and belief that she can be happy again. If we go on treating her like a victim, then so will she. Or, we can get back on the ship, and sail away, trusting that the girl that survived two magical realms can handle a lifeguarding one of the hidden veils."

After a few minutes of silence, Hook nodded. "Alright, Ainsel, alright. I know you are right."

Ainsel smiled, "You mean you are going to be okay going back to the ship?"

Hook gulped, "Yes. We can go."

After they went through the front door and down the hill towards town, they could already see the waves crashing upon the wharf. The sails from the ship whipped wildly through the air, the waving image of the skull and crossbones seemed to be calling its captain back to the wheel. But before their feet left the land, Hook took one last glance at the Hatter's manor.

From the corner of Ainsel's eye, she could see his lingering concern. It was then that a drop from a splashing wave gave her a brilliant idea to cheer him up. With a subtle snap of her fingers, a crash of majestic blue lightning spread across the dark sky. With a slightly crooked smile, Hook stepped forward onto the main deck just as a magical storm showered upon them.

Ainsel giggled, reaching for his hand, and after an unspoken endearment, they shared a kiss filled with a passion beyond magic and went into the captain's quarters together.

The following morning, Hook woke before the sun. With Ainsel still sleeping in their bed, he and Catcher went out to the main deck to set the sails. The silence of the early morning was always a little unnerving for a man of action, but one couldn't deny the sweet smell of the air in the morning.

There was something so inviting about it. With the chill on the skin of his face, he turned the wheel toward the open sea. Slowly but surely, the ship made its way away from town just in time to see the sun pierce its way into the sky, giving it an eerie greyish hue. It seemed a night alone with Ainsel in his arms was enough to help clear his head a bit. Even with the fog that rose above the water, he could see all that appeared around him.

After a while, everything felt calm and serene as he sailed across the open water, but as the tip of the ship pierced its way through the thinning fog, Hook gazed at his surroundings as if seeing them clearly for the first time. The ocean was as blue as the brightest of sapphires, and the landscape of craggy cliffs was peppered with the image of trolls- frozen forever-solidified into stone.

Tales of such calcified creatures that had dared to lumber out of their dark caves into the bright sunlight could be seen from the Icelandic waters and land. Trolls. Hook thought back at his own experience with the moronic beings. It was not one of his proudest victories since it was his father that had actually saved him. Had Blackbeard not showed up in the nick of time, his entire body would have been burned alive over the fire, the trolls had built in hopes of cooking him for dinner.

The real haunting thought of it all wasn't that he had somehow escaped such a horrible fate, but that so many before him had not. His only solace was the image of his father smashing the stoned creatures on the other side of their bridge- only to be found by the sad Hudrefolk trolls the following evening, after dusk. Hook smiled, imagining their sad moaning cries echoing throughout the forest by the veil. When I look at it in that light, it was a glorious day. Hook thought, remembering every detail of the carnage he had wrought upon the Third Realm that bloody day in the glittering snow.

But only after a momentary chuckle of reminiscing, did a shocking chill crawl towards his core.

The Snow Queen... The Third Realm!

Somehow within the clarity of such a morning did he remember the dreaded words of Ainsel's vision the night Peter Pan had nearly killed him. He had been so focused on Wendy's disappearance into Wonderland and the deranged mind of the Green Fairy as her predator that he had not heeded the whereabouts of the true villain from the Lost Island within the second star to the right- Peter Pan. Ainsel said that the Snow Queen sent Tinker Bell to the realm of her mad sister but kept the one tool that could bring her the vengeance she so desperately wished for after the death of her daughter- the death he had caused.

Could I really have saved Wendy from two realms, just to deliver her to a house holding a veil to a third? How could I have been so blind? With vigorous panic, Hook rapidly spun the wheel with all his strength. With his vessel turning around to speed back to the Hatter's manor, when a sudden thickness came within the fog, hiding all pathways upon the water. Gasping in frantic thoughts, he screamed out for Ainsel's help.

The Blue Fairy rushed to the deck, unaware of what was happening. "What is it?" She asked in alarm.

"Wendy! She is in danger! We have to head back right now!"

Ainsel let out a breath, "James, I told you she is fine. You are still not thinking clearly. The effects of Wonderland are just making you paranoid. Come back to bed with me."

No! I am thinking clearly for the first time since I left for that wretched place. The wardrobe! It leads to the Third Realm!"

"Yes, I know that. You already knew that. Now really..."

"No! There is something I forgot! Something we both forgot!"

"And what is that?" Ainsel asked.

"That the Third Realm is where *he* is! -Peter Pan."

The name sent a chill down her spine, sending a crashing wave of guilt to suffuse her. "Oh my... how could I have?" She started, when Hook snapped.

"Ainsel, we do not have time for that! We need to get back, now grab your wand and zap us back to that house!" His booming voice shook her. She snapped her fingers to make her wand appear, but when she whipped it: not a single sparkle appeared. Feeling stunned, she tried again- but still, nothing happened. "What is wrong?" Hook asked, seeing her nervous appearance.

She shrugged, "I do not know. My magic... it's not working. I cannot zap us back to the house."

"Why is it not working?" Hook asked in great frustration.

"Ainsel gulped before answering: "I- don't know. Maybe it's just because I am tired or stressed or something..."

Hook shook his head, "Well, do you think you can get rid of the fog. I cannot sail in this; the ship will crash against the surrounding cliffs."

Ainsel nodded nervously, whipping her wand again. The two anxiously stared at her wand, but still, no magic came. Something else was wrong.

"Do you still think it's your nerves?" Hook asked.

Ainsel looked up into his blue eyes and shook her head, helplessly, "No. There is something blocking my magic- something very, very strong."

Suddenly the sound of pipes playing in the distance brought the thickening fog higher, making it impossible to see a thing- or even each other. The music seemed to carry upon the Icelandic air, even reaching into the very halls of the Hatter's manor.

While Wendy was sleeping next to little Marmalade, she was doing her best to control the details of her dreams; it seemed the cloaked stalker was never beyond the corner of her eye. Whether it was the sound of the ominous music or the winter chill that woke Wendy from her traveling slumber, one will never know, but as her glazed eyes opened, she followed the music down the hall unripped from her dreamy state of mind- into the room with the magical wardrobe.

Once she had entered the darkened room that held the veil, it wasn't the music that finally whipped her back to the reality around her; it was the haunted beings that dwelled within the room. The faces of the children from the village came before her, pulling her arms and tugging her dress.

With a gasp of fear, Wendy gazed into their desperate faces. There was something terrible about the sight of them. With their bodies and the core of their souls devoured, what was left of such a miserable being was all that floated before her very eyes. They tried to speak words, but with nothing left but the essence of what they once were, they could not say a thing. They all just circled around her moaning in misery and despair.

The vision of them overwhelmed her, forcing her to flail her arms and scream for them to go away. After a few moments, the air was clear, and the moaning was gone, leaving the black room completely silent.

Suddenly, the one lantern in the room lit a flickering violet flame, lightening up the room. With a gasp, Wendy quickly gazed about the room expecting someone else to be there with her. A loud scream filled the room as her eyes set upon the sight of someone in front of her, but as she stepped closer, she realized that what she was seeing was her own reflection in the tall oval mirror.

But it was not the reflection of Alice that stared back at her; it was her true reflection. *How curious it is to find yourself standing before you as a stranger?* Not only was it her former appearance, but it was also how she looked before magic had ever entered her life. After a gentle smile upon the reflection's face, the image of Wendy Darling started to fade away into a swallowing darkness. It was then as she stepped closer that she realized what the wardrobe wanted her to do. She smiled as a wave of bravery came over her. She was a Guardian of the Veil now; she wasn't going to fall for such a trick. The mirror may have been able to show her what she wanted, but she knew that it could never give her what she lost. Feeling pleased with herself, she smiled and turned to walk away, blowing out the lantern in her hand.

But just as her hand touched the door handle, and the room filled with the darkness once more, she heard a voice came from behind her- the only voice that stole her breath from her throat.

"Wendy Darling... how lovely it is to see you again."

CHAPTER THIRTY-SIX

WISH UPON A STAR

Though Hook himself had explained the danger of fear and loss of hope, he had never quite embraced the power of faith. His inspiring words to Wendy, however, were taken into the depths of a susceptible child's mind. He had convinced her that her survival was no mistake, but rather a means of a grand destiny. And that kind of faith- the kind that not only keeps your will going but also evolves you into something more powerful than your former self was what was radiating through Wendy as she confronted the one that had brought her so much turmoil. Meanwhile, Hook and Ainsel were consumed with a terror as impenetrable as the fog around them. Little did they know, they were already too late; within a reflection from another world- into the Hatter's Manor, Wendy stood face to face with the mysterious cloaked figure that had stalked her dreams. No longer was he the little boy of Neverland, but now an enchantingly beautiful man called the Gancanagh. Peter Pan had become even more powerful, and well beyond even the Snow Queen's command or control.

344

Before his arrival to Her Majesty's realm, those that were closest to the crown were the Prince Bear and the former love of the Queen of Hearts, but now it was Pan that stood at her side. Though he brought more souls to her feet than any other left alive in her court, his wild soul and devious shadow would have been cause enough for her to remove him from her kingdom if it were not for one thing- he was the only means to bring her the revenge she ached for every minute of every day. For the last fifteen years they have scoured the human world looking for Captain Hook, never knowing that all that time, he had been in the realm of the Snow Queen's very own sister. But the second that Hook, and Wendy Darling had come back through the veil of the looking glass, Pan felt their presence. His connection with Wendy was born the day he used magic to enter her soul and alter her mind. And though he had previously not held any hatred towards her, he had since heard the details of the Elder's final judgement resulting in the Green Fairy's death. The loss of his beloved Tiger Lily had changed him, but the loss of his only true friend had changed everything. This was no longer a matter of fun and games; *this was war.*

"Peter Pan, it's you!" Wendy said in complete surprise. "You look so- different."

"As do you, Wendy, but the eyes... they never deceive, do they? You may have a different face, a different body, blonde hair, but in the end, your eyes tell you who you really are," he said in his usual smug tone.

She nodded, eyeing his new appearance up and down. "I guess the fact that you said you were the boy that would never grow up was also nothing more than a lie." Her words and tone shocked him. Wendy had never been any more than a pathetic little pawn he used in his games, a pawn he was hoping to use again. But something about the new aura she carried told him he wasn't the only one that had truly changed.

Well if he wasn't going to be able to manipulate her by charm, then he was going to go straight for the point: "I need something from you, Wendy."

"What? You need something from me?"

"Yes, and to be perfectly honest, I would say you more than owe me."

Wendy widened her eyes in shock, "If you actually believe that I owe you than you are even madder than I am," she said before turning her back to the mirror and whispering a quiet wish for Ainsel and Hook to return.

Suddenly, Pan's malevolent laughter echoed off the walls through the glass. "You need not worry, Captain Hook and Ainsel are trying to return to you this very moment, and I will allow them to once you and I come to some sort of arrangement."

Wendy's eyes squinted in suspicion, "What arrangement?"

"I want you to walk through this wardrobe and deliver me your soul so that I can raise Tinker Bell from the ashes. I will deal with James and his wretched fairy afterward."

"I will never do that! You may be more powerful now, but if you could force me through the wardrobe, you would have already. I do not know where Hook and Ainsel are, but I don't need them here to tell you- No!"

"You know what, Wendy, I tried to play nice. You asked that I take you and your brothers from the window, and I did it. You asked for a grand adventure, so I graciously gave you what you so desperately wished for. I gave you pixie dust so that you could fly, and I took you to Neverland even though I hadn't taken your souls. And after all my kindness, you ran away and conspired with my enemy. Then! After you sent me a note with a bomb and tried to have me killed in my own home, I still took you and your little brothers back to your home safely! I have been nothing but generous to you!"

"You really believe all that! You think yourself generous! You tortured my mind, soul, and nightmares. My family gave up on me and sent me away because they could no longer deal with the mess of broken pieces you left behind. Then after being experimented on inside an asylum, your little green friend sent the White Rabbit to lure me into Wonderland in hopes of driving me into madness. I've lost my family, my little brothers, my identity, my appearance, my name, and the last fifteen years! I don't owe you a single thing, but thank you, because until now, I thought I had already given you everything. But now I know that I not only still have something that is mine, I have the one thing that could prevent you from getting back something that you have lost- that makes me happy!"

"Oh, stop pretending to have the plight of an actual martyr here, please. I have lost things too. I have lost everything! And if you don't come through this door, I promise that I will make every day for you a living breathing nightmare that you can never escape from. You think it's scary to see me in your dreams now... just wait- for I can make things much, much more terrible."

It was in that moment that Wendy realized something... something that made her smile. *My dreams... Ainsel's protection spell. If I saw him in my dreams, then that must mean...*

"What?" Pan asked, confused by her reaction.

She looked up into his golden eyes and giggled.

Her laughter made him shake in murderous anger, "What is it?!"

"Sorry, Peter, but there is just a little tiny problem with that threat of yours."

"Oh, yes! And what is that?"

"There is a reason you were able to enter my dreams... I'm not afraid of you anymore."

He didn't understand her realization, only that it angered him immensely, "Enough of this! I may have grown since we last met, but so has my grisly imagination. Let us see how you feel once I get my hands on your precious captain and his pretty Blue Fairy!"

Wendy laughed at such a threat, "By all means-bring them here. I would love to watch you lose again!"

With a red burning face, Peter disappeared from the mirror just as Wendy walked out of the dark, dusty room. Back at the ship, Hook and Ainsel were working together to carefully move the ship little by little, when suddenly the fog completely disappeared. Peter made his way onto the ship, only to find that it was completely empty. Both Ainsel and Hook were just gone. With bubbling fury, Pan raised his arms, "No!"

Hook and Ainsel looked around in shock as they realized that they were no longer even on the ocean. It was nighttime, and they were outside a tiny home inside what appeared to be a quaint little town. "Where are we? How did we get here?"

Ainsel thought for a moment when suddenly she understood, "A wish brought us here."

Hook was taken aback, "A wish? But then who..."

Suddenly, they heard something coming from inside the house. "It sounds like someone is chiseling wood," Ainsel whispered.

Hook shook his head in confusion. "Come on," he whispered, pulling her towards a small window in the front. At first, they didn't see anyone, just a normal little home with a bed, a goldfish in a bowl on top of a pine wood nightstand, a large oval rug lay upon the floor, and various lanterns were lit all around room. It was almost as if the person inside was afraid of the dark. Suddenly, something small came out from the far end of the house. It was a little, tuxedo cat.

"Look, Figaro. Isn't he amazing?" Said a little man's voice.

Hook's eyes widened in absolute shock... *"Mr. Smee?!"*

† Like a bolt out of the Blue †
Fate steps in and pulls you through,
When you wish upon a Star,
Your dreams... come true.

Made in the USA
San Bernardino, CA
30 November 2019